Jade's Peace

Melissa Stevens

To Maverick
I hope you enjoy

Mel Ste

i

This book is a work of fiction. Names, character, places and incidents ether are the product of the author's imagination or are used fictitiously, and any resemblance to actual persons, living or dead, business establishments, events or locales is entirely coincidental.

ISBN 13: 978-1492396086
ISBN 10: 1492396087

Other books by Melissa Stevens:

Kitsune series:
CHANGE
FIGHT
HUNT

WMC Series:
ESCAPE

Novels:
ROBIN'S NEST

Dedication:

This one is for all those people who helped raise me, you know, the ones who weren't actually my parents.
John and Terri
Madeline
John and Jackie
Frank
Not to forget all the extended family, who are too numerous to name here.
I wouldn't be how I am if not for all of you,
Thanks again.

Special Thanks:
To Kari Trumbo and Editor's Note for the outstanding help with my
editing for all the books, I couldn't do it without you.

To my dad, for answering all my bizarre questions without any questions of
your own, I'm not sure my explanations would make sense anyway.

Chapter 1

JV slowed her pickup as she passed the city limits sign entering the small mountain town of Springerville, Arizona. She took care to stay under the speed limit. She wasn't sure how long she might be in the area and didn't want to get on anyone's bad side, at least not so soon. Over the last two days, she'd come to realize this trip had been a long time in coming and she wasn't going to give anyone a reason to run her off before she was ready.

Her stomach growled.

The sudden sound made her jump. JV glanced at the clock on the dash, 2:17pm. "No wonder, I should have gotten something to eat on the road." JV muttered.

The petite brunette looked around for somewhere to eat. It had been a long drive, several hours and more than three hundred miles since breakfast. She hoped she could find someone from the local Chanat, the cougar shifter clan, and try to get them to direct her to Steve's place.

She scanned the worn buildings on either side of the highway, looking for a restaurant. Most were older than she was, and reminded her of the buildings in a western movie, though there were some newer ones scattered around. The town was obviously aging, but not run down. It was apparent it was well cared for and most of the newer buildings looked like they had been designed to match, or at least not clash, with the older ones. It looked like the town embraced its history.

The aging town took JV's mind back to the last time she'd seen Steve, more than ten years earlier. At the time, he'd been about the same age she is now, but to the teenager she'd been, he'd seemed mature and worldly. He was only home for a couple weeks after he getting out of the Marines, then he'd left town again. She hadn't seen him since.

She remembered watching him with hungry eyes, praying he would notice her, but all too soon he was gone. She'd never forgotten him, or the odd feeling of being pulled toward him she'd felt. She hadn't experienced it since, sometimes she wondered if maybe it was all her imagination.

At first, she'd waited for him to come back, to act on their mutual attraction, or so she thought. But days stretched into years, and eventually JV had given up. She'd tried dating, had gone on with her life, but in all the time since, there hadn't been anyone she'd considered spending her life with. More recently, as the memory of that odd sensation haunted her, she'd come to a conclusion. It was necessary to find out the truth. She had to know if her memory was correct or not, and if the only potential mate she'd ever met wouldn't come to her, she would go to him. She needed to confront him.

It was hard to believe after so long, she was this close, but now that she was in town, more information was key.

***

Walking into the small diner, she let the door swing shut behind her and looked around. The place was decorated like an old log cabin with rounded logs covering the walls and exposed beams. There were maybe twenty tables scattered through the dining room, about half of them were taken. To be so busy, this late in the afternoon meant something, either people around here eat late, or the food was good.

"Have a seat, hon, wherever you like. I'll be right with you." A waitress wearing an old-fashioned pink uniform with a white apron, called as she carried a coffee pot from table to table, filling cups.

JV found an empty table, sat and waited. A moment later, the same woman brought her a menu and a glass of ice water.

"I'm Liz, what can I get you to drink, hon?"

JV looked up; the waitress's auburn hair had been teased into a tall bouffant. The fine lines on either side of her eyes told JV she smiled a lot. JV's enhanced sense of smell told her the woman in front of her was a shifter, a cougar too. "Water's good." She smiled at the older woman.

"All right, I'll give you a few minutes." The waitress smiled back. The expression made her look younger and JV guessed she was somewhere in her forties, though it could be hard to tell with shifters. Sometimes they didn't age the same as humans.

JV placed her order, then watched patrons come and go while finishing her meal. There were only about a half dozen people left in the restaurant when the waitress came back to check on her.

"Is there anything else I can get for you?" Liz asked.

"Actually, there is." JV smiled at Liz, trying to look hopeful. "I'm looking for an old friend; maybe you can help me find him?"

"I'll do what I can, dear. Who are you looking for?"

"His name is Steve Romero. I know he lives around here, but I don't know exactly where. Now that I'm here, I need some help."

A surprised look flashed across Liz's face before she could stop it. "Sure, I know Steve."

"Could you tell me how to get to his place?"

"I can," Liz frowned, "but I can't imagine him not giving you directions himself."

JV's face heated and she looked down at the table, unable to meet Liz's gaze. "He doesn't know I'm here. I'm trying to surprise him." She looked back at the older woman, hoping she would still help.

Liz lowered her voice, "I'll tell you where to find him, but he's our Shaku. He lives too close to our Khan and Karhyn to send you out there without letting them know you're on the way." She smiled for a brief second, "But since I don't know who you are, all I can tell them is there was a young woman looking for him and I gave her directions."

JV understood, Steve was the clan's head of security and lived very close to the clan leader and his wife. While she had to give them a heads up, Liz would do what she could not to ruin JV's surprise. "Thanks," she smiled up at the other woman.

She wrote down the directions and paid her tab, thanking Liz again for the help. She climbed into her truck and headed back in the direction she'd come. It wasn't far, half an hour was nothing compared to the two days she'd spent on the road already.

***

Following the directions Liz had given her, JV turned off the highway and drove along a narrow but well maintained dirt road for about two and a half miles before it opened into a clearing. The road continued along one side of the open space and disappeared into the trees on the other side. In front of the cabin sat a pair of pickups, one several years old and a little beat up, the other newer and still nice looking.

Pulling into the yard, she saw someone sitting on the porch. A tall man stood and headed in her direction as she parked beside the other trucks. She watched him as she killed the engine and slid out. The man coming toward her wasn't Steve. That meant it was probably the clan leader.

"Hello, I'm Nick, Khan of the White Mountain Chanat. What can I do for you?" he asked.

"Hi, I'm JV. I'm looking for Steve Romero?"

"You've found the right place." He looked her up and down before offering her his hand. "He has a cabin around back; he'll be here in just a minute."

Bracing herself against the pain, she shook his hand, and let go as soon as was polite. "All right." She resisted the urge to rub her hand against her jeans to try and ease the sting from her skin, but she was unsure what to do while she waited.

A crease formed on his brow, "I take it Steve didn't know you were coming?"

"No, sir. I thought I'd surprise him."

"What makes me think he may not be so happy about your surprise?" He gave her a lop-sided smile, one side of his mouth lifting while the other stayed put.

JV could only give him a wry smile back. She suspected he was right.

"You wanted to see me, boss?" Steve came around the corner, his voice dying off when he spotted her.

"There's someone here to see you," Nick motioned to JV.

Steve looked stunned. "Jade? What are you doing here?"

"I came to see you."

"I'll leave the two of you to your business." The clan leader turned and went in the house.

Steve waited while his leader went inside. "Why are you here?" he asked, his tone matching the frown on his face.

"I needed to see you." She couldn't put it any plainer.

"Is everything all right?" His displeasure turned to concern when he thought someone might be sick or hurt. "Your parents? Mine? Matt?" He said her brother's name last, dread filling his eyes at the thought of something happening to his friend. "Why didn't someone just call?"

She shook her head, "No, everyone's fine. That's not why I'm here."

"If that's not it then why are you here?" His frown returned. He wasn't happy to see her.

4

JV looked at the ground and slowly started toward him, "When you left, I knew it was because of me. It hurt. It hurt, a lot." She paused, trying to keep her voice even, "At first, I waited for you, and the longer I waited, the more I tried to hate you, because it hurt so bad. Even then, I hoped and prayed that you'd come back. I tried to move on." She looked up at him and paused again, because Steve was shaking his head, then she went on, ignoring him. "It took me a long time to realize that you had no intention of returning, even longer to understand why."

"That doesn't tell me why you're here now, Jade." He put his hands on his hips, still frowning.

"I had to see you again," She knew this wasn't going to be easy. However, it was important to her to find out if what she remembered was real, or if it had merely been the wishful thinking of a starry-eyed teenage girl.

"Now that you're here---?"

The breeze kicked up and blew bits of leaves and needles across the hard-packed ground. The scents of pine, juniper and a subtle musk she instantly recognized as Steve's scent were pushed into her face. His unique fragrance pulled at something low in her body, something she barely remembered and had feared might be a fantasy.

"Now, I see you." She tilted her head to one side. "Without even touching you, I know it wasn't my imagination, it was real."

"What was real?" His scowl deepened.

"What I feel." She knew she was being evasive, but she didn't want to tip her hand just yet. He might stop her if he knew what she was up to.

Steve frowned, "What are you talking about?"

"I'm pretty sure you know. I appreciate that you've tried to forget, I did too. But I can't. So now I'm here."

"I'm not following," his scowl deepened.

She took a deep breath and braced herself, she had to do it. He wasn't going to like it, but she didn't see any other way. She stopped thinking and moved.

She reached out and laid her hand on his arm, waiting for the sharp, burning pain she always felt when touching anyone of the opposite sex. For so long, the touch of any male not related to her had burned her skin. She'd hoped with a potential mate it would be different. When no pain shot through her, she took the next step. She wrapped her arms around his neck. Using his momentary surprise to her advantage, she pulled him down so she

5

could kiss him before he had a chance to stop her.

Placing her mouth against his, she ran her tongue along the seam of his lips until he opened to her, then she pushed inside. She licked and tasted him, drawing him in. She pressed her body against his, letting the instinctive attraction between them speak for her.

His body responded before his brain. His arms wound around her waist and pulled her closer as he lost himself for just a moment.

The second his brain started functioning again, he stiffened and pulled away. She let him withdraw, then stepped back until she stood about a foot in front of him.

"Why did you do that?" His voice had gone thick and husky.

"Now you're following me." JV smirked, spun around and went back to her pickup. "I'm going to go get a room. I'll see you later."

"You're wasting your time, Jade. Go home."

"There's nothing for me there. That's why I'm here." She didn't bother to turn back. Given the chance, he'd talk her into going home, or at least try. She wasn't going to give him that chance.

"There's nothing for you *here*, either." His voice got louder with every exchange.

"I'm not convinced." Her tone was strong and confident, even though she didn't feel it. "If you can kiss me like that, neither are you." She climbed back into her truck and left, enjoying for once having the last word as she left him standing there, watching her drive away.

Chapter 2

She drove the same short stretch of highway for the third time that day, this time with a sense of excitement, missing during the first two trips. Stopping at the first motel she came across, JV rented a room. She carried her bags inside without taking time to unpack, she pulled the holstered pistol from her waistband and set it aside, then she lay back on the bed to decide what to do next.

She'd made the first move. Hopefully he would make the next one but she didn't expect it to be that easy. She'd suspected he was her potential mate, and she was one for him, for a number of years. However, he believed he was too old for her. Why else would he have left and never come back? Admittedly, ten years had been a big age difference.

Seeing him again confirmed it, at least from her point of view. By the way he responded to her kiss, she was almost certain he felt it too. When she considered that she could touch him, actually skin to skin, without pain, it only made her more determined to take the chance. Even so, she had to convince him that a relationship between them wasn't wrong - she wasn't a child anymore. She lay there for a long time, trying to figure out how to convince him to give her, and them, a chance.

The sound of knocking on her door, made JV jump. Her thoughts had been so tangled, she hadn't noticed footsteps approaching or stopping outside her door. Her body flashed hot, then instantly cold as panic flooded her. She fought the urge to hide. Instead, she took a deep breath and pushed it back. She'd been careless. She had to pay more attention. Grabbing her Smith and Wesson .38 Special from the table beside the bed, she pulled it from the holster and went to the door.

Looking through the peep hole, a woman who looked a little younger than herself looked back she had dark hair pulled away from her gentle face. JV took a careful breath, trying to pick up the woman's scent through the

7

door, but got nothing. She opened the door slightly and found the younger woman wasn't alone. There was a man with her. He wasn't much taller than the woman, but he was several years older and stocky. It looked like it might take a truck to knock him over, not someone JV wanted to have to fight.

"Yes?" JV kept her body behind the door, the arm with her pistol held close to her body, out of sight but ready, just in case.

"Hi, I'm Rebecca Hastings. I'd like to talk to you, if I could?" The younger woman was bouncy and perky, something JV hadn't been in a long time.

With the door open she could pick up their scents, both of her visitors were Kitsune, shifters like herself, but the woman carried the scent of the Kahn, not the man with her. She suspected she was meeting the local Karhyn, the head female in the clan and the Khan's mate. She tucked the small revolver into the back of her jeans then stepped back. She kicked the holster she'd dropped in her haste to get to the door, under the bed and out of sight, then opened the door to make room for them. She wasn't particularly comfortable letting a man she didn't know into her room, if it had been him alone she wouldn't even have answered the door, but if this was the Karhyn then he was likely her enforcer, her bodyguard. She knew better than to try to bar him.

Rebecca seemed to sense JV's anxiety, "Bobby, this is the only door, why don't you stay out here and let us have a little girl talk?" She looked at the man for a second, seeming to communicate without words.

He met her look, then nodded silently. He watched her enter the room, and once she was inside, he leaned against the wall between this door and the one next to it. He seemed content to wait there as JV closed the door.

Inside, Rebecca made herself at home. She glanced around the tiny room, then sat on the foot of the bed. "My husband said you were pretty, but he didn't tell me you were beautiful."

JV didn't know what to say. The last thing she wanted to do was to piss of the clan leaders while trying to convince their head enforcer that she wasn't the child he still thought her to be.

Rebecca took a deep breath, "Let me back up. I'm Rebecca."

"You said that already." JV was uncertain as she sat in the only chair at the small table. Her pistol dug into her back as she trapped it between her body and the hard cushion. The slight pain reminded her she wasn't helpless and helped keep her panic at bay.

"You met my husband, Nick, a little while ago." Rebecca watched her as she spoke.

JV nodded, she'd figured that much out for herself.

"He said you came to see Steve?" Rebecca made it a question, as if hoping JV would elaborate. When she didn't, Rebecca continued, "Steve's been a part of this clan longer than I have, he was the Shaku when I got here. He does his best to protect Nick and me, and I'd do a lot to protect him in return."

"You're here to ask my intentions?" JV realized. For some reason the idea amused her.

Rebecca gave a wry smile, "In a way, yes."

JV sighed. She looked away for a moment, staring sightlessly at the mirror across the room as she tried to decide how much to share. She needed someone she could talk to, someone on her side. She needed a friend. But first, she had to come clean, "I'm gonna be honest with you. I've got a weapon. I'm not threatening you, but I need to move it and I need you not to call your enforcer because of it." She watched the other woman, looking for signs she was going to call out to the man outside.

Rebecca's eyes widened, "Okay."

JV reached behind her and pulled the gun from her waistband. Laying the weapon on the table beside her, she leaned forward and rested her elbows on her knees as she dropped her head in her hands.

"How did Bobby not smell that?" Rebecca looked at the weapon, then back to JV.

JV glanced at the gun, then back at the floor, dismissing the weapon she kept nearby, always. "I've masked the scent." It was something she was normally proud of, it had taken a lot of trial and error to get it right, but that wasn't what was important right now.

Still looking at the floor, JV tried to decide how to start, before meeting the other woman's gaze. "My name is JV. I've known Steve since I was a child. He was my brother's best friend the whole time we were growing up. He was always around when I was little. I wasn't a teenager yet when he joined the military, but I was older when he got out and came home. There was something new between us then, a draw that I don't know if I could have fought at seventeen.

"Then, suddenly I didn't have to. He was gone. It took me a long time to realize he was right to leave. I waited for him to come back for ten years, now I'm through waiting." She was leaving a lot out, but Rebecca wasn't the one she needed to share it with.

"So you decided to come after him?"

"Pretty much."

"What, exactly, do you have planned?" Rebecca looked intrigued, "If you don't mind my asking, that is."

"I don't really have a plan. I only had one thing in mind when I left Austin yesterday. Now that I've seen him, I've got to figure out what my next step is."

"Is that what you had in mind, to see him?"

"Not entirely, but that was part of it." JV hesitated, "It had been so long since I'd seen him, since I'd felt it, I had to see him again, see if it was really there."

"And---?" Rebecca's interest seemed genuine.

JV looked at the ceiling a moment, then back at Rebecca, "I was right. It's there."

"You feel the instinct don't you?"

She knew what the clan leader meant. She'd heard about it growing up, but it hadn't been all that important. Her family hadn't pushed her to find a mate, they were more concerned that she make a good match. A mate was someone a shifter could form a bond with that is as magical as their ability to change shapes, JV looked away again, then swallowed and met her gaze. "Yes, ma'am."

"What about Steve, does he feel it too?"

"From the way he reacted today, I think so."

"So, what are you going to do about it?"

"I don't know. I didn't think that far ahead."

"Do you want him to go back with you?" Rebecca tilted her head to one side and watched JV.

JV, still lost in thought, gave her head an absent shake, "No, I don't expect that. He has a life here. I have no intention of making him leave it."

"What about your life, in Austin, didn't you say?"

"What life? I grew up in our tiny hometown and left to go to school. I've only been back for visits, to both my family and his, since I was nineteen. I've lived in Austin since I got out of school, a little more than five years ago. I've had a couple of jobs and there are a few old coworkers I talk to now and then, but I don't have any real friends, nothing to keep me there."

Rebecca nodded slowly, thinking, "What if he says no?"

"He already said no. He told me," she glanced at the clock beside the bed, "not two hours ago that I'm wasting my time. I should go home."

"Of course he did," Rebecca wasn't surprised. "He's too used to everyone, including me, doing whatever he says. What I meant was, in time, if he doesn't see things differently, then what?"

JV took a deep breath, "I honestly don't know," she paused, "I didn't come all this way to give up. He left to get away from me. I knew it then and I actually understand it now. I was a kid, and it was more than just being underage. I was sheltered and naive. He was ten years older and far more mature. To me, he was larger than life and I was awed by him. If he'd stayed, I would have pursued him. I was as tenacious then as I am now, but I was still a child, with simple ideals. I think he saw that and left. I respect that, but I'm not a child anymore."

"You don't mean to take no for an answer?"

JV was silent a moment, "I won't force him, but I'm not going to give up easily, either."

"Are you sure he feels the instinct too?"

JV understood why she asked. It wasn't unheard of to feel the mating instinct for someone who didn't feel the same for you. It wasn't really a big deal, most just stayed away from each other and kept looking for another potential mate. It wasn't like the instinct was flawless; it just helped shifters find the ones they could form a deeper bond with.

She looked at the other woman for a long minute, then decided to hell with it, she might as well tell her everything. "When I pulled into town this afternoon, I wasn't even sure I'd felt it. For all I knew, I had imagined it or thought it could have been the wishful thinking of an infatuated teenager.

"Then I saw him. The moment I caught his scent it came back, stronger than I remembered. I tried to get him to admit why he left, but he acted like he didn't know what I was talking about." She looked down, refusing to look at Rebecca as she made her confession. "So I threw myself at him. I kissed him with everything in me. I could have believed he doesn't feel it if he hadn't, just for a moment, returned my kiss with the same hunger."

Rebecca was silent a moment, "All right." She stood, taking charge, "first things first. You can't stay here. Gather you're things." She issued orders like she was used to having them followed without questions.

"Of course I am. Where else would I stay?"

Rebecca gave her a questioning look. "JV, how can you seduce a man from more than thirty minutes away? Steve comes into town once, maybe twice a week, less once snow falls and that's not far off. If you stay here, it'll be too easy for him to avoid you." Her voice softened, "Come back out to our place. We have a spare bedroom. You can stay there until you can convince that stubborn man to open up."

"How will the Kahn feel about me staying there?" JV asked.

Rebecca gave a secretive smile, "You leave him to me. Honestly, he won't have a problem with it. He's got more insight than people realize."

"I don't know," JV hesitated.

"If you don't do it, you'll never know if you lost him because you didn't do everything you could."

JV had to admit, at least to herself, Rebecca was right. If she had any hope of wearing him down, she couldn't give him the option of retreating or hiding. She had to be close enough to be in his face all the time. She had to be where she could catch him with his guard down.

JV nodded, picked up her pistol, retrieved the holster from where she'd kicked it under the bed and stuck them both back in waistband of her jeans. She grabbed her jacket and slipped it on, making the gun invisible. "You convinced me." She looked around the room once more, checking for anything she might have missed before picking up her suitcase. "Give me a couple of minutes to load up and check out. I'll be right behind you."

Rebecca opened the door and held it so JV could get by with the bag then closed it behind them. Her enforcer fell into step beside her as she walked away.

JV carried her bag to the truck and headed for the office. After checking out, she met the Karhyn and her bodyguard beside the newer truck she'd seen in front of the cabin earlier.

"Thanks again for this." JV said.

"It's no problem," Rebecca said, "I'm happy to help."

"Is there anything I can do? Anything I can bring?"

"You're our guest, just bring yourself."

"Are you sure?"

"I'm sure. It'll be nice to have another woman around for a change"

"All right." JV agreed. She climbed back into her pickup and waited while they pulled out of the lot, then followed them back to the cabin.

Chapter 3

"What are you doing here?" Steve's angry voice startled JV.

"Unpacking," she continued what she was doing without looking up.

"I can see that. Why?"

"Rebecca invited me to stay," she was determined not to let him see how shaken she was by his sudden appearance behind her.

"Why? What did you say to her?"

"The truth."

"You mean your version of it," he snarled.

"I mean the truth." She flinched, but kept her voice even and her back to the man she'd come so far to see.

"What kind of sob story did you tell my Karhyn to get her to invite you to stay here?"

The accusation flipped a switch inside her. It turned her fear and nerves to fury. She fought to keep her anger off her face and out of her voice. "I didn't tell her a sob story. I was content to stay at the motel in town. Rebecca showed up at my door and asked a bunch of questions. All I did was answer her. Then she insisted I check out of my room and stay here."

"If you manipulated her so you could sponge off of my Chanat leaders-" he didn't get a chance to finish the threat.

JV spun around, fire flashing in her eyes as she advanced on him. "Is that what you think of me? You think I came here looking for someone to take me in?" It was all she could do not to poke him in the chest as she spoke.

"Well, ..." he verbally backpedaled, realizing he'd let his anger carry his mouth too far.

She interrupted him again, "I don't need someone to take me in. I'm quite capable of looking after and supporting myself, thank-you-very-much. I've been taking care of myself for the last eight years. You know why I am here." She went back to pulling things from her suitcase and hanging them up as if he hadn't interrupted her, though her movements had grown sharp and angry.

"What are you talking about?" he said, but his voice held no confusion.

JV turned and eyed him for a moment, "Do I need to kiss you again to remind you?"

Steve turned on his heel and left without another word.

JV couldn't help a small smile. She could tell he knew exactly what she'd meant. His leaving proved it. Now she had no doubts, he felt the draw between them, the same yearning to touch her that she felt for him. She suspected he'd do everything he could to resist the attraction. Odds were in her favor though, from what she'd been told, the more time they spent near each other, the stronger the desire would become. Her smile grew.

Glancing at the clock, she hurried to finish unpacking in time to join the others for dinner.

***

Seated around the small table situated on one end of a combination kitchen and dining room, JV was unsure what was proper. Her family had never been invited to eat with the Khan back home. They hadn't been close friends or high enough ranking for that. She was uncomfortable letting Rebecca wait on her while she sat at the table. However, she didn't know these people very well and she didn't want to offend anyone by insisting she help.

"Here we are," Rebecca placed a large pot of spaghetti in the middle of the table then turned away long enough to grab a platter stacked with slices of garlic bread before placing that, too, on the table and taking a seat.

JV waited while Nick served himself a plate of the pasta, then Steve. She planned to wait until after Rebecca had helped herself, too, but Steve handed her the pot, frowning at her as he did. She served herself and passed it on, then waited, watching to see what everyone else did before doing anything else.

"So, where are you from, JV?" Nick asked, grabbing a slice of bread and digging into the plate in front of him.

"Tenaha, Texas," she kept her voice low, knowing everyone at the table had enhanced hearing and she didn't need to speak up to be heard.

Creases appeared on his forehead, "Where is that? I don't think I've ever

14

heard of it."

JV looked at Steve for a second; curious why he'd never told his Khan where he was from. "I'm not surprised. It's a tiny town on the eastern edge of Texas, not even as big as Springerville."

"Wow, that is tiny," the pack leader spoke between bites. "What brings you here?"

"I came to see Steve."

"You said that, but I missed why."

She'd assumed that Rebecca would have told him, or possibly Steve, in an effort to get the leader on his side. She didn't see any reason not to tell him. Hell he might even be willing to help her, but then again, he also might side with Steve. "I had to see him again."

"Again?"

"Yes, sir. Until this afternoon, the last time I saw Steve was ten years ago when he left the last time."

The Khan's confusion grew, "You've been in this Tenaha?" he asked turning to Steve.

"Yes sir. I grew up just outside of town. I went to school there."

"How did I not know this?" The clan leader's brow creased as he frowned at Steve.

"You knew. I told you I grew up outside a small town in east Texas. I may not have mentioned the name of the town, I don't remember, but it hasn't been a secret."

Nick turned back to me. "You said you needed to see him, have you tried between now and then?"

She looked back down at her plate, then out at the darkness in the window beyond the clan leader. "I haven't spoken to him since he left, but I've tried to see him several times. I know his parents have begged him to visit, holidays, school reunions, that kind of thing. The mayor once tried to get him to come for the Fourth of July. They were going to make him the Grand Marshal in the parade, to honor him as the local hero he is.

"From what I've been told, no matter what's used to lure him home, his answer is always that he can't. Not that he doesn't want to, or he can't get the time off, just he can't come back." She looked down at her plate before looking back to the Khan. "I know he left because of me. I suspect I was the reason he wouldn't come back, as well. I'm sorry about that, because his parents miss him. I finally decided he was never gonna, so I took matters into my own hands and came after him."

15

"Why would he leave town because of you?" Nick didn't seem to understand.

"While I can't prove that he did, somehow I knew." She looked at Steve, meeting his gaze as she spoke, "He wasn't home for long before he left again. I have a lot of memories of him before he joined the Marines. He and my brother were inseparable. But you know how the memories of a child are; they're tinted with what you thought you knew and childish impressions of people and events.

"He visited several times during his military time, brief visits while he was on leave. As I got older, he became less of the larger-than-life figure he'd been when I was a kid, more of a person.

"I still remember the first time I saw him after he got out of the military and came home. I didn't recognize him at first, but the new man in town intrigued me. There was something about him that made me want to get close and rub up against him." She looked at Nick as she answered the question, but she watched Steve's reaction out of the corner of her eye. "I didn't, of course. I didn't have the self-confidence to be that bold. Before I could gather enough nerve to do much more than say hello, he left again."

Nick scowled, "How old were you the last time you saw him?"

"Seventeen."

"Good God," he muttered, his brows shooting up, "that explains a lot."

"It does. But I'm not seventeen anymore, nor the naive child I once was. I'm through waiting." She let a slow smile spread across her face.

"What makes you think I'm attracted to you?" Steve finally spoke.

She didn't answer. Instead she turned to meet his eyes, then lifted one brow, still smiling, challenging him without a word.

"Even if I was then, you and I both know a prolonged separation breaks the bond between potential mates."

"The bond yes," she admitted, "but until one or both of them seals a relationship, the attraction remains, as does the potential for a mating bond. Since I've never even met another potential mate, and from what I hear, you've never mated, so the potential is still there." She sat back in her seat, her look daring him to argue.

"Are you trying to steal my Shaku away from me?" Nick asked, drawing JV's attention back to him and changing the subject.

"Not at all," she assured him.

"You're not planning to convince him to go home with you?"

"No," she said.

"So, should things work out between you, are you willing to stay here? To leave your life in Texas behind and build a new one here?"

"Should something more develop, I have no problem staying here." She didn't tell him she had no life to leave behind. She'd sold most of her furniture and what little she had left was in storage. She didn't even have an apartment to go back to, she'd let her lease lapse before leaving.

"Even leaving your career behind? You've seen our little town, there's not all that much to offer here." He seemed to believe she wouldn't want to stay.

She shrugged, "Your little town is bigger than where we grew up. Besides, I don't need to leave my career. I can work from anywhere, as long as I have electricity and an internet connection."

The Khan looked confused, "You work online?"

"You could say that. I run my own web design business."

"Hmm. That's different." Nick seemed to be at a loss for words.

Steve scowled at her.

JV refused to let his stubbornness get to her. She'd known when she made the choice to come after him that it wouldn't be easy. He was proving her right, so what?

"So what do you do around here?" JV asked Nick, wondering how they lived. How they kept the secret of what they are from the humans in the area.

"Welcome to the X open A." He said, a grin spreading across his face as he made a flourished flip of his hands, leaving them open and welcoming.

"The X open A?" She frowned, confused, "What is the X open A?"

Nick dropped his hands and casually reached to lay one on top of hers. She suspected it was because he would be better able to sense how honest she was being with a little contact, "It's a ranch," he said.

She evaded his touch, making the move look like habit, "No way. This isn't a ranch."

Nick frowned for just a moment, "Why do you say that?"

"Where is everything, the buildings, the horses, the equipment?" All that sat in the small clearing was the cabin. JV had seen nothing to let her believe this was a ranch.

Nick smiled and gave a short laugh, "About a quarter mile past Steve's place, through the woods. The bunkhouse is there, too. I built the houses away from the rest of the ranch buildings on purpose. I wanted more privacy, especially since some of the hands are human."

JV turned to Steve, "How do you rate a place of your own?"

"Foreman." Steve gave the one word answer with a scowl, almost like he was sulking.

JV frowned, not understanding.

Nick took mercy on her, "He's my foreman, so he gets a place of his own."

"Are all the hands human?" JV wanted to know.

"No, just a couple." Nick said.

"Bobby, who was with me earlier," Rebecca spoke up, "is one of the hands, he's also another of our enforcers."

JV ate in silence. She thought for a moment before something occurred to her, "I thought ranchers shot cougars?"

Nick chuckled, "Some do, but most let them be unless they become a problem. They take an attitude of live and let live, at least until the cats start hunting livestock. That's not really a problem here since natural cats avoid us and our territory."

"I make sure I keep the area we roam marked, so naturals stay away and there's a standing order not to kill anyone else's cattle. It works for us and other ranchers."

"Anyone else's?"

"A few of us are ranchers. I don't care if someone wants to hunt their own animals. Occasionally, I cull out one or two that won't survive the winter and let the Chanat have them. It's not really hunting, but it's something that brings the clan together, though we're careful to do it where the human hands won't find us."

"We used to hunt deer back home, not often, maybe once a year, but it was a big deal. Everyone loved it." JV was starting to like these people. She hadn't been sure when she'd started out how things would work out. The more she got to know the people Steve had built his life with, the more she could see herself here in the future. Now she just had to convince him. "I bet having the house set away from the main workings of the ranch makes shifting easier, too."

"That's part of why I did it," Nick grinned. "Plus, sometimes the business that comes to my door doesn't think about Kitsune secrecy or the possibility of humans being around."

***

18

After dinner, JV insisted on helping Rebecca clean up, then she went out on the back porch to enjoy the cool evening air. Austin is warmer, and she thought it was early yet for it to be this cool, but temperatures in the mountains are always cooler than at the lower elevations. She stood, watching the last glimmer of the sunset thought the trees, hugging herself against the chill in the air.

"Why are you really here?" Steve's voice behind her startled her.

She tried to hide how badly he'd scared her as she turned to look at him. "I told you why I'm here."

"I'm supposed to believe that you've been waiting for me to return to podunk Texas for the last ten years. Now, suddenly, you're tired of waiting and came looking for me." He scoffed, "I don't think so, there has to be more to it."

"I don't know what to tell you." She looked away, turning back to the trees, not willing to tell him more, not yet.

He looked at her for a long minute, "How about the truth?"

"I've yet to say anything that's not true, to you, or your Khan or Karhyn."

"I don't believe you."

"Fine, don't believe me. I can't make you see the truth," she turned away, back to the trees.

"You really expect me to believe that you've been sitting, waiting for me to come back, for ten years?"

"No, not sitting and waiting. I tried to get on with my life, I went to college, graduated, got a job, more than one actually, and I built my business. I tried to forget. I almost succeeded. I'd half convinced myself I'd imagined the feeling." With the last sentence, her voice turned soft, distant.

"Are you blaming me?" He sounded angry and JV wondered if maybe he blamed himself.

She was quiet for a moment, when she spoke again her voice was still soft, but no longer distant. "I did blame you, for a long time. I was angry and I wanted to hate you for leaving me like that. As time went by and I got older, I realized that at seventeen a ten-year age difference is a big deal. I was twenty-one when I realized I wasn't the same person I'd been at seventeen. I was still angry then." She looked at him again. "Over time, I came to realize that not only was it illegal, which I knew at the time, but didn't care about, but it was wrong as well. It took me even longer to realize you left as much for me as for you."

She took a deep breath and let it out in a rush before continuing, "I'm embarrassed to admit it took me longer than it should have to understand that. I tried to build a life there, to find someone to settle down and build a life with. There was something missing, though. I couldn't get past that, no matter how hard I tried."

Steve stood there watching her. He looked at her face in the fading light as he tried to figure out what she wasn't telling him. He could tell there was something she was holding back, something big, but at the same time, he couldn't sense any lies. "What did your parents have to say about you coming out here after me?"

She looked at him a moment before looking away again, back toward the setting sun. "Nothing, they don't know I'm here."

"Oh?" he seized the opening. "Afraid they wouldn't approve?"

She spun around. "Not at all. I have no doubt they would encourage me to do what makes me happy, but they would worry, and call, and drive me nuts."

"So where do they think you are?" his voice changed, softened some until he was talking to her as a friend, not some kind of suspect.

She shrugged. "On vacation, then headed to L.A. for an on-site job."

"Do you do that often?"

"Do what?" she glanced at him, confused.

"On-site jobs."

"Not often but, once in a while a big job comes up and they want me to go see things in person so I can set up the kind of site they need, with the feel they want."

"How about lying to your parents? Do you do that often?" He challenged her but his voice was still friendly.

"Not often, and I probably didn't have to this time. I haven't lived in Tenaha for the last nine years, not since I left to go to school. I just didn't want the added distraction of them calling and worrying about me while I tried to focus on something."

"Something?"

"You." She looked at him again, wondering what he would say next.

"Ah," he was silent for a moment as he moved toward her from the other end of the porch that ran the length of the cabin and around the side. "You know you're wasting your time, don't you?"

"I know you're stubborn and you're trying to convince me you don't feel it." She countered, not backing down.

"What makes you think I feel anything?"

"One," she flipped a finger into the air as she counted, "if you felt nothing, you wouldn't have left all those years ago."

"I've already admitted that's why I left, but that was then. I 'm talking about now."

"Two," she continued as if he hadn't spoken. "If you really felt nothing, you wouldn't be trying so hard to get rid of me. You'd let me stay and find out on my own. Three, that wasn't the kiss of a man who feels nothing. That was the kiss of a man so hungry he couldn't stop himself without at least a taste." She turned on her heel and went back into the house, without giving him a chance to respond.

Chapter 4

It was late when JV stepped onto the back porch for a second time that night. She'd tried to sleep but instead had lain restless. Nick had given her permission to roam the property and run whenever she wanted, so she didn't hesitate before starting to strip.

She shivered when the cold night air hit her skin. Once the last of her clothes were off, she ran to the edge of the porch and dove. Shifting in midair, she landed on all fours. She shook her entire body, trying to rid her skin of the tingle caused by shifting, then took off into the woods at a run.

Her cat eyes picked up far more light than her human ones would have and she saw everything around her clearly. She ran through the thick woods with ease, dodging low hanging branches, ducking under a bent trunk, leaping over a downed tree. She ran hard, leaving what haunted her somewhere in the night.

Two days in the truck had left her tense. She'd been sure that Steve wouldn't be happy to see her and more than once she'd considered turning around and going back. Now, she was glad she'd had nothing to return to, it had made her stick it out. Seeing him again had been worth it.

JV continued to run, letting the uncertainty and nerves fall away. She loved spending time in this form, but living in Austin, she hadn't had the freedom to it as much as she'd craved. When she was a cougar, she felt free, fearless. In the city, there was always too much risk of someone seeing and shooting at her.

She ran until her muscles ached and her sides heaved with her every breath, but she kept going. She didn't know how far she'd gone or how long she'd been moving when she slowed to a walk. She had no idea where she was. She knew she could follow her own trail back to the cabin, if she wanted, but that didn't feel right, not tonight. She gazed up at the trees around her.

Did she dare?

Why not?

With ease, she leapt into one of the trees, settling into the Y of a branch about ten feet off the ground, she relaxed and started to doze.

***

The snap of a twig woke her. JV was instantly alert. It was still dark, but someone, or something, was close. She moved slowly, so whatever it was wouldn't see her as she looked for whatever had made the noise.

On the ground below the tree she was perched in was another cat, a cougar even larger than she was. The wind was blowing the wrong direction for her to be able to pick up the newcomer's scent, but she knew he had to be a Kitsune, she would have scented a natural cougar if she had wandered into their territory, and a natural wouldn't brave her scent if she wasn't invading.

Who are you? She thought at him, using the telepathic talent that she'd developed after her first shift to cougar. She watched him circle the base of the tree she still hid in.

Should I be hurt that you don't recognize me? Steve's voice whispered through her mind.

How would I know it's you? She demanded. *I've never seen your cat before and with the wind, your scent hasn't risen this far.*

She didn't know how he managed it in this form, but he shrugged, *What are you doing up there?* He looked up at her.

I was sleeping.

Something wrong with your bed?

She bristled, *I was too keyed up, and I thought a run might help.* She couldn't tell him she slept better in this form. Living in the city, she was always afraid someone would come in and find her, so she didn't get to do it often.

I realized you were gone when I found your clothes on the porch. Why are you up there?

By the time I got out here, I felt better and I didn't want to go back. I've never been able to run as much as I wanted to spend the night out if I wanted. I thought, why not now.

He snorted. *Are you ready to head back?*

Sure, why not? She hopped out of the tree and started back along the trail that now held both their scents.

23

Is there a reason you're going the long way?

Only that I don't know where we are. I'm going back the way I came.

Steve somehow managed to roll his eyes. *Follow me.*

He turned and started in the opposite direction, continuing in the direction JV has been going before she'd stopped to sleep.

A few minutes later, as light started to appear in the sky, JV saw the clearing where the houses sat. *I'm going to have to learn the area better.*

Especially if you plan to continue running at night, Steve sent, his mental voice dry.

Thanks for showing me how to get back. She leaned over to rub her head against his neck but Steve sidestepped, avoiding her touch.

That's my job, he left her beside the porch to go in the house on her own and he turned and headed for his cabin.

She made her way up the steps and stopped beside the chair where she'd left her clothes. She held still, concentrated on her human body and willed herself in to it. Her skin tingled as it stretched and absorbed her fur. She felt her bones move and pop as she shifted. JV shivered and hurried to pull on her clothes, the temperature had dropped since she'd undressed, hours earlier. Still shaking, she fumbled with the doorknob for a moment, then slipped inside.

Leaning against the closed door, she took a deep breath and sighed. It was chilly inside but much warmer than outside. She headed for her bedroom, hoping to burrow between the covers for a little while and warm up.

"You're out early," Nick said from behind her as she made her way through the dark kitchen.

JV jumped. She spun around, eyes wide with panic, to find him sitting at the table they'd eaten at the night before.

"You always sit in the dark?"

Nick smiled, "Actually yes, every day."

"I didn't expect anyone up this early."

"There's coffee, if you're interested."

"That sounds good. It'll help warm me up." She'd smelled the coffee, but the same scent had been in the kitchen the night before, the pot had been hot then too.

"It's a little chilly out there." He watched her move around the kitchen. He hadn't missed the scent of her fear or how she'd tried to hide how afraid she'd been.

24

"Cups?"

Nick pointed to the cabinet over the coffee pot.

JV poured herself a cup, "You really get up this early every day?"

"Mostly. Ranching means early mornings more often than not."

They sat in comfortable silence until Nick finished his coffee and headed out to get started on the day's work. JV emptied her cup and headed to the other end of the house to shower and change.

Chapter 5

That afternoon, after JV had unpacked everything she planned to, she felt unsettled. She couldn't focus on her work. Besides, it would be rude to lock herself in the bedroom and ignore her hosts. Not sure what the proper protocol was, she decided she should treat the Karhyn like anyone else. She'd show her the respect her position demanded, but treat her like a friend. She hoped, if things worked out with Steve, that she and Rebecca could be friends. It would be a little awkward to live so close and not at least be civil.

After straightening her things she went in search of the other woman. She found her in the front room, a notebook computer on her lap.

"Hey," Rebecca said, looking up from the screen as JV entered the room.

"Hey, what's up?"

"Not much, just doing a little window shopping. I'm going to need some new winter clothes and there's not much to choose from in town."

"I haven't seen much of town yet," JV sat on the end of the sofa nearest Rebecca's recliner. "But I didn't notice anywhere to get clothes."

"There are a couple places, but the selection is limited. If you want more to choose from, you have to go into Show Low, past that into Phoenix, or order it online."

"Ah," JV fell silent for a moment, "how far is it to Show Low?"

"It's not too bad, only about an hour, but it's on the other side of Springerville from here, so it's about an hour and a half from here, in good weather."

JV's eyes widened, "How often do you make the trip?"

Rebecca shrugged, "Once a month or so, less if I can manage."

"Don't you hate being so far away from everything?"

"Not really. It's a tradeoff. We have to drive for shopping, but we can shift and run whenever we like. We have our privacy and a level of security out here I never felt that I had in a more urban area."

JV tilted her head to one side as she thought about it, "I experienced that in Austin."

Rebecca closed the laptop and set it on the table beside her chair. "I'm starving, how about you?" She pushed herself up and headed for the kitchen.

"I could eat." JV followed.

"I've got some cookies we can have for a snack while I get dinner started." Rebecca pulled a couple of plates from the cabinet, handing one to JV.

"I can't keep on like this," she took the plate and set it on the counter in front of her.

"Like what?" Rebecca looked confused.

"I can't let you wait on me, especially if I'm going to be here very long." She looked away for a second, then back at the woman in front of her. "It feels like an imposition, you've got to let me help some."

"But you're a guest."

"I know, but it makes me uncomfortable. I'd like to be friends, not treated like a stranger," She smiled, hopeful.

Rebecca looked at her a moment, "All right, how do you want go about it? When?"

"Now, instead of you starting dinner, we do it together."

"Works for me, but first, cookies. Do you want milk with yours?"

"I'm good."

"I need milk." Rebecca poured herself a glass and they took their cookies to the table.

***

It didn't take long to get used to the routine of ranch life, and JV soon realized that she and Rebecca were never completely alone. There was always one of the men nearby, even if it was just someone working outside, near the house. After the first day or so, she noticed Bobby seemed to spend his afternoons in front of the house, working on the old pickup parked beside the one he and Rebecca had been in at the motel.

"Is something wrong with it?" JV asked that afternoon, watching the man through the big picture window in the living room.

"It started giving us trouble last week. He's trying to get it running smooth again."

"It must be a pain to be down to just one vehicle."

Rebecca laughed, "We're not down to one vehicle, there's several more at the barn. But generally, we only take the newest one into town, unless it's to do something messy, like pick up feed."

She scowled and turned to look at the other woman, "If you don't use the truck up here, why's he working on it here?"

"To cover me," Rebecca smiled at the shocked look on JV's face. "It's been a couple years, but my family wasn't happy about my mating with Nick. We had someone show up and try to force me to go back. Because of that, there's always someone around, in the house with me or close by, just in case."

"What if you want to be alone?" JV was horrified at the idea. The thought of someone around all the time made her skin crawl.

"It's not as bad as it sounds. Steve and Bobby are like family, but if I want to be alone, or need some space, I ask for it. They can protect me without smothering me. In fact, they're pretty good at it."

JV shook her head, not knowing if she could handle constantly having someone else so close.

Chapter 6

JV's eyes snapped open.

Something woke her. What?

She glanced around and it came back to her. She was in the guest bedroom at Nick and Rebecca's, alone in the house because Rebecca had an appointment and Nick and Bobby had taken her to town. They'd offered to let her tag along, but she suspected it was personal, so she'd plead exhaustion. After they'd gone, she lay on her borrowed bed, hoping to get a little sleep.

She looked at the alarm clock on the nightstand, 3:37. She'd slept less than half an hour. Looking around the room, she wondered again what had woken her.

The floor outside her door creaked.

Someone was in the house.

There hadn't been enough time for the others to make the appointment and be back. Panic raced through her, turning her body hot, then cold. She slid one hand silently under the spare pillow and pulled her pistol from the holster she'd hidden there.

Rolling onto her back, she aimed at the bedroom door. It wasn't an ideal position to shoot from, but she could make it work.

The rapid thump of her heart was the only sound in the room as the knob turned and the door swung slowly inward.

"Jade?" Steve's voice was soft.

Recognizing his voice, Jade let out the breath she'd been holding and lifted the barrel of her .38 until it pointed at the ceiling, "Yeah?"

The door swung open and revealed Steve standing in the hallway. She saw a look of concern on his face for an instant, then it darkened as he marched to the side of the bed and took the .38 from her loosened grip

"What are you doing in my Khan's house with a gun?." He scented the air. "How did you get it in here without anyone smelling it?"

"I'm a woman who's lived and traveled alone for a number of years. I learned some time ago being armed isn't a bad idea."

She rolled away and off the opposite side of the bed, landing so she stood facing him. "As for no one scenting it, I've had a problem with shifters trying to tell me I don't need it, or trying to take it away. I figured out how to mask the scent so that's no longer an issue."

"What if it had been Rebecca at your door?" he scowled.

"Rebecca had an appointment in town. Nick and Bobby went with her. They left a little over an hour ago. They said they'd be gone for two to three hours. I was alone, sleeping. The sound of someone else in the house woke me. It couldn't have been Rebecca, but I didn't know it was you. All I knew was that I wasn't alone and I should have been."

Steve faltered. He looked down at the weapon, it looked small in his large hand, then back at her. "All right, I'll grant you that one. But I can't have anyone other than my Khan having a gun in his house." He held one hand up, stopping her from protesting. "I know you have no intention of hurting them, but I can't allow anyone, not even you, Jade, to have a gun in the house."

She took a deep breath and let it out in a rush. She wanted to argue. She wanted to insist she wasn't giving up her gun, but she knew it would only give Steve a reason to run her off. "I can lock it in my truck. Will that be good?"

He was silent for several heartbeats, his eyes never leaving her. "I'll accept that. Do you have any other weapons? Knives? Anything?"

JV rolled her eyes, "No. What need do I have for knives? I have claws."

His brows lifted, "You're carrying a gun, but no knives. Are you worried about anything specific? Are you being followed?"

"No other weapons and I'm not being followed." she ignored the part about what she was worried about.

"Do you know how to use this thing?" Steve looked at the revolver again. He thumbed the release and flipped the cylinder open. He pulled one round out and looked at it a moment, laying one finger against the tip of the bullet before putting it back in the chamber and, with a quick twist of his wrist, flipping the cylinder closed. He looked up at her, waiting for her to answer.

"Of course I know how to use it. My father taught me how to handle a pistol years ago. As for that particular one, I've put a lot of rounds through it. I'm comfortable with it."

"All right, whatever you're worried about isn't one of us, or this would have silver rounds." He held the pistol in her direction. "Keep it in your truck."

She flipped the pillow closest to her and picked up the holster, then rounded the bed, took the pistol and holstered it.

"Unless someone is on your tail and followed you here, you should be safe in the house. We haven't had much trouble in the last couple of years, other than usual clan crap, and that's no danger to you."

JV looked away, trying not to let him see how badly the thought of being unarmed bothered her. She poked the holstered weapon in the top of her purse so she could take out on her next trip. "Did you need something?" she looked back at him, expectant.

"I came in to see if you needed anything, but you didn't answer when I called out and I got worried."

"I was asleep."

"I realized that when I found you on the bed."

Chapter 7

Two days later, JV sat in her room, considering how poorly things seemed to be going. Steve would still barely look at her and that was only when he wasn't avoiding her all together. She knew in order for their attraction to grow, they needed to spend time near one another. That was the way the Kitsune mating instinct worked. The more time they spent together, the more they would be drawn to each other. She didn't want to force him into anything, but she had hoped with time, he would come around.

She sighed and looked back down at her laptop. She needed to finish this project and send it to her client for approval, but she was having a hard time concentrating long enough to get anything done. Setting the computer aside, she stood and stretched, hoping better blood flow would help her settle her mind.

Going into the kitchen for something to drink, she found Rebecca already there, putting together a stack of sandwiches.

"You about ready for lunch?" Rebecca asked.

"Sure, but you should have let me know you were making lunch, I would have helped. This is too much like waiting on me."

"Nonsense," Rebecca waived one hand in dismissal, "I do this all the time. Here," she set several sandwiches to one side, "why don't you take Steve his lunch?"

JV brightened. The idea of spending a little time with him was far more appealing than going back to the frustrating laptop. "Sure, where is he?"

"I saw him head back to his place about fifteen minutes ago," she grinned.

JV flashed a grateful smile, packed the sandwiches and a few other items into a bag, and headed down the trail that disappeared behind the house.

Sitting less than two hundred yards from the back steps of the Khan's house, through a small copse of trees, JV found herself standing in front of another smaller home. This one was slightly newer and gave her a sense of being unfinished. She couldn't quite put her finger on why, but she knew there had to be something.

She stepped up on the porch that stretched the entire front of the building and raised her hand to knock. Before her knuckles struck the wood, the door opened beneath her fist.

Chapter 8

Steve had gone back to his house to get some rest, since he'd been up most of night waiting for her to return. Since she'd arrived, Jade had made a habit of shifting late each night and spending several hours in the woods before returning to the house. He waited up for her each night and the lack of sleep was catching up to him. He might not get more than a few hours each night normally, but recently he hadn't even gotten that.

He didn't know how much longer he could handle this. He'd left Jade once before because he wasn't sure he could keep his hands off her. Now, here she was again, and though he hadn't thought it was possible, she was even more attractive. She'd grown into her body. It sounded backwards, but it was true. Now she had a confidence that hadn't been there before.

Then there was the way she stood up to him. Every time she stood there, confronting him about something he'd done or said, he got hard. He fought to control his dick every time he saw her. Now he had less reason to keep his hands to himself. Yes, she was still ten years younger, but at nearly thirty, he could no longer tell himself that she was a child.

There was something under all that attitude though, something that had her flinching every time she was touched or startled. It made him want to find out what it was, to protect her and take that haunted shadow from her eyes.

He had to fight to remain where he was every night as he watched her step on to the porch and take off into the trees. The temptation to follow was strong, but he'd managed each night, at least so far, to stay hidden in the shadows.

He'd been surprised by her mid-air shift that first night, it was an uncommon skill, one that took a lot of practice to master, especially as smoothly as she'd done it. He could do it, as could the Khan, but he didn't know anyone else who could, not until now. That she'd taken the time and effort to learn, surprised him.

That night he'd waited for hours for her to come back, only going out to look for her when dawn approached and she hadn't yet returned. Finding her asleep in the V of a tree had thrown him. He never would have taken the city girl who'd shown up that afternoon for someone as comfortable with herself, and her cat, to do something like that. Few people, even Kitsune, were that comfortable in the wilderness.

He'd been trying to avoid Jade until she gave up and went home, but his duties wouldn't let him stay away. He ended up seeing her every day, if not several times a day, even if she wasn't aware he was near. It affected him. He didn't know if he could hold out, it was already a real struggle to keep his hands off her. He longed to touch her, to comfort her, and his skin itched to touch her.

The only way he was managing so far was to stay quiet and use his anger to keep her at a distance. He had to, because he knew, once he let himself touch her, not just letting her touch him, but if he gave in and initiated the touch, he might not be able to stop.

He'd left all those years ago because he knew, eventually, his control would snap. He'd feared he would scare, or worse, hurt the innocent girl she'd been. He hadn't trusted himself to keep his distance. He still didn't, but did he have a choice?

He heard footsteps approaching the cabin and looked out the window to find the object of his thoughts headed in his direction. Cursing under his breath, he went to the door. He jerked it open and her scent hit him like a punch in the gut. He felt it immediately, that pull, the instant need to touch her, to pull her close, to protect her with everything he had.

"What do you want?" Steve snapped, his voice sounding harsher than he'd intended.

"I brought lunch," she lifted the bag.

"What makes you think that I haven't already eaten?"

She seemed to deflate before his eyes, "I assumed since Rebecca sent me out here, she normally made your lunch."

Steve flushed and looked down, "She does."

"Then here it is," she handed him the bag and turned to go, "I'll let you eat in peace." She sounded dispirited and it made him feel guilty.

The bag rustled as he looked inside. "Wait," he reached out and grabbed her arm, "don't go."

35

He noticed how she jumped at his touch but her face revealed nothing as she turned to look at him, "Why not? You've made it abundantly clear that you don't want me here." She used anger and snide comeback in an attempt to cover the flash of terror he'd scented from her.

Chapter 9

JV tried to hide the panic that rushed through her as memories threatened to come alive. It hadn't lasted. His hand on her skin didn't feel the same as anyone else's. Somehow, she knew he wouldn't hurt her. She reveled in knowing his touch didn't burn.

Over the years, she'd almost gotten used to the biting sting that touching men caused. The only time she didn't feel it was with her brother and father, but she didn't see them often. She ached for the causal touch of others, even just friends. After it had happened and the burning started, JV had pulled away from her college friends. She hadn't made any close friends in Austin.

She wanted to lean into him, to beg him to wrap his arms around her and just hold her, but he was too angry. She couldn't ask for fear of how he might react.

"I'm sorry I've been nasty," he pushed the door open to let her in, "Rebecca sent more than enough. Come in and have lunch with me?"

His sudden change of heart made her wary. She narrowed her eyes, "I'm not sure I should."

"Please?"

Hopeful that he was warming toward her, she nodded toward a group of chairs on the porch "It's a nice day, how about we eat out here?" For some reason she was reluctant to go inside. She wasn't afraid of him. She didn't think he would hurt her, at least not physically, but she felt better out in the open.

"All right," he agreed, "do you want something to drink?"

"A soda or water would be good," she shrugged.

"Here, have a seat. I'll be right back." He handed her back the bag and ducked inside.

She sat in one of several chairs scattered along the length of the porch and started pulling out the food, setting it on the table between her chair and another while she waited.

"How do you like our mountain?"

She jumped as Steve's voice startled her. Looking up at him, she smiled and hoped he hadn't seen it. "I like it. It's beautiful here, a lot cooler than I'm used to, but it's a nice change."

Steve frowned for a second, then his face cleared, "You ever move back to Tenaha?" He handed her a can of Pepsi and popped the top on his own as he sat on the other side of the small table.

JV shook her head and swallowed, "I've been in Austin since I graduated."

He blinked. "You live in a city?" he gave a slow shake of his head, he'd hoped she'd just taken to dressing like a city girl. "Never thought I'd see that."

"It's not my favorite place, but it was a good place to set up a business. Plus, it was far enough away that my family's not in my back pocket 24/7."

"That's an advantage. Are you sure leaving Austin won't hurt your business?"

She shrugged, "It might. It shouldn't though, since I have very few clients in Austin anymore, but who knows? Right now, I don't care."

Steve looked surprised. "You don't care?"

"I don't care. I've got some money set back and enough of a client list that I can take the hit if I need to."

He frowned, "You said your folks think you're on vacation before going to LA for a job. Is there really a job waiting in LA?"

"Not this time," she looked away.

"I hope you're not thinking we could have anything more than friendship between us."

"Why?" She frowned.

"We're too different."

"How so?"

"We just are."

She knew he was hedging, "I hope you're not talking about our ages."

"What if I am?" He wouldn't look at her.

"I'll grant you, it was a valid argument the last time, but no longer. I'm not seventeen to your twenty-seven anymore."

"I disagree. I'm sure your father would too. It just won't work." He met her eye this time and seemed to be trying to convince her.

"I think my father's feelings on the age difference would surprise you," she met his eyes. "He once told me that ten years can seem like a lot, especially when you're young, but the older you get the less age and age differences matter."

"I'm not so sure." He looked away.

"Will you at least give it a chance? Don't fight the instinct. Give us a chance to see where this goes?"

He hesitated, "I don't know."

"I'm not asking for a lifetime commitment, not yet. Just a chance. See if we can get along."

"I'll try. That's the best I can give you."

"That's all I can ask for," she gave him a heartfelt smile. "I'm not sure if it'll work," she laid a hand on his arm, delighting in the ability to touch someone without pain, "but I have to see what happens. I can't just walk away knowing we both feel it."

Steve ducked his head a moment, "I'm not sure I'm cut out to be with anyone. I've been alone for so long. I'm afraid you're setting yourself up to be hurt just by getting your hopes up."

"I wouldn't say I've gotten my hopes up about anything, as much as I'm interested in what could be and I'm willing to take a chance."

"I'll try not to fight it, but I'm not sure how receptive I can be anymore."

"Just let it happen." She leaned close and pressed her lips against his, then got up and headed for the main house, leaving him with that light, gentle kiss.

Chapter 10

After lunch, and her talk with Steve, JV still couldn't settle her mind. She gave up on getting any work done after only thirty minutes. She closed her laptop and set it aside, before starting to pace her room.

Soon, a soft knock interrupted her. "Come on in," she called, never slowing in her relentless walk back and forth.

The door opened and Rebecca stood in the opening, "You sound a little restless, dear, is there any way I can help?"

JV gave her a wry smile, "I don't think so. I'm fine, really, I just can't settle my mind enough to work."

"How about a walk?" she suggested.

JV was quiet, thinking about it, "That sounds like heaven."

"Why don't you go down the road past the house? Just a little ways past Steve's place you'll find the barn and corrals. I don't know if you'll run into Steve back there," Rebecca gave JV a knowing grin, "but if not, you'll still get some fresh air and you'll feel better." JV nodded and quickly pulled on her shoes, grabbed a jacket to ward off the chilly wind she heard blowing, then set out. She wasn't sure she wanted to see Steve again. Not now. If the little bit of time she'd spent with him at lunch had stirred her this much, seeing him again certainly wouldn't settle her.

Not in a hurry, she walked at a steady, comfortable pace and in just a few minutes, she found another break in the trees. From the buildings and things scattered through the clearing, she now saw how this could be a working ranch. She glanced around, wondering where she should go next. There was a man inside a corral with a horse, she headed in his direction.

Moving slowly, because she didn't know how well trained the horse was, and she didn't want to startle him, she leaned against the rails of the corral and watched the old man work. Even over the acrid odor of horse manure and the sun kissed scent of hay, she could tell the man was a shifter. He looked a little old, to her, to be an enforcer but that didn't mean he wasn't one. She guessed he was somewhere in his mid-sixties. His mustache looked like something out of an old western movie, except it hadn't been trimmed in a while. He reminded her of a cartoon walrus she used to watch when she was a kid. She couldn't tell much about his hair because he wore an old gray cowboy hat that had seen a lot of better days, but it got the job done.

"Is there something I can do for you, little lady?" he kept his voice soft; she assumed it was so he didn't spook the horse.

"No. Rebecca suggested a walk. I saw you working and I was intrigued. I'd like to watch, if you don't mind." She kept her own voice soft in reply.

"As long as you don't make any loud noises or sudden moves, I've got no problem."

She watched as he brushed the horse, talking to him and telling him what was going on around him. JV got the feeling it was more about the man's tone and the sound of his voice than what he had to say when, in the same tone he'd used with the horse, he asked her name.

"I'm JV. You?"

"Frank, Frank Willis."

"It's nice to meet you Mr. Willis."

"None of that Mister stuff, just call me Frank, everyone does. What brings you to our neck of the woods, JV?"

"I came to see someone, and Rebecca insisted I stay here instead of in town," she shrugged very slightly, so she didn't spook the horse, "so here I am."

"Let me guess. You came to see our bull-headed foreman."

"How did you know?" JV frowned, confused.

"You carry his scent; you've been near him recently."

"Yeah, it was him I came to see." She looked away, staring sightless across the meadow for a moment.

"You gonna to be around a while?"

"For a while, I like it here." She glanced around, "It's a lot different than where I'm from."

"Where you from?" he asked.

"East Texas," she was quiet a moment, "don't get me wrong, it's pretty there and I love my home, but it's beautiful here."

"I's born and raised on this mountain. I've traveled a little, but I keep coming back. I s'pect I'll die here." The old man was still talking in the same gentle tone he'd used all along.

JV looked around, taking in the view, "I can't say as I blame you, it's nice here. But I'm sure you have a good long time before you need to worry about dying."

"It's nice to think so, but things happen to people all the time on a ranch. Horses, even the most well trained animals, are unpredictable creatures and accidents happen. A man can be hale, hearty and healthy one day and gone the next." He continued to run the brush over the horse's side as if he wasn't talking about dying.

JV watched the skin twitch and shudder after each stroke. He finished brushing down one side and went back to the horse's head, ducked under the lead rope tethering the animal to the fence to the side JV stood on, then began below the horse's head and brushed. She now saw the ponytail that hung from under the hat and reached half way down his back. For some reason it made her smile.

"He seems to like it." JV continued watching.

"She's learning to. She's not really used to people yet, but brushing and talking to her help. She's getting used to being touched and the sound of my voice." Frank said.

"She?" JV had assumed the horse was male; that it was female threw her.

"Yep, she's a mare. I take it you've never spent much time around horses?"

"No. There were a few around Tenaha, but none of my family or friends had any."

"That's too bad, there's a lot to be learned from a horse."

She watched him work a while longer. Listening to the soft constant chatter he kept with the horse while she lost herself in thought.

"Hey, Frank," Nick said, stepping up to the rail beside JV, "I see you've met our visitor." Nick's voice stayed soft, but friendly.

"I have, we talked for a bit while I worked, but I think she has more on her mind than talking to an old man."

"Could be Frank, could be." Nick looked at her, as though he wondered what was on her mind. "How's it going?" He nodded in the direction of the horse Frank had begun leading in circles around the corral.

"So far so good," Frank said, "She's coming along."

"That's good to hear."

They continued to talk about how much longer they thought it might take to train the mare, before moving on to other things that needed to be done on the ranch. JV watched the older man walk the horse, not really paying attention to what she was seeing. Instead, she was thinking about how similar what Frank was doing with the mare was to how JV had been dealing with Steve. Was it really that simple? Was he really as skittish as a green horse or was she being too careful?

"How has your afternoon gone, JV?" Nick asked.

The sound of her name pulled her from her musings. "Oh," she snapped back to the present. She quickly glanced around, realizing Frank had left the corral, taking the mare with him.

Nick was looking at her, waiting for an answer.

"Good," she paused, "I was having a hard time concentrating. Rebecca suggested I walk some. I think it's helped."

"Good. It's nearly dinnertime, I'm headed up to the house, care to join me? Or do you want to wander around out here for a while longer?"

"I'll walk back with you. I feel like I'm imposing on you and Rebecca."

"Don't," Nick's tone turned serious. "I think Rebecca's missed having other women around." He was quiet for a second, "I don't mean that she doesn't have friends, she does, but there's no one close, no one she sees or talks to all the time."

"I take it you two haven't been together long?" she felt like she was prying just by asking.

"Almost two years, but she's not from around here and we've had some trouble with her family. Having you around, even for the short time you've been with us, has really lifted her spirits."

"I'm glad. I like her, but letting her do things for me makes me uncomfortable. I keep trying to get her to let me help with the cooking and dishes, but she keeps forgetting," she made air quotes with her fingers as she said the last word.

A small smile formed on Nick's mouth. "She likes to take care of people. She took over my kitchen from the day she appeared on my doorstep. If it'll make you feel better, keep offering to help, but don't be surprised if she refuses. I'm sure, given a little time, you'll settle in fine."

"You're assuming I'll be around long enough for that."

"You're welcome to stay as long as you like. I'm sure Rebecca feels the same way."

"Thank you, sir." JV looked away, trying not to let her uncertainty show.

"None of that sir crap call me Nick." He sounded a little annoyed.

"All right." She looked back, "I'm not sure if it's going anywhere, but I'm not ready to give up on him yet."

"You've only been here a few days. Give him some time, I think he'll come around."

She took a deep breath and let it out in a rush. "He's stuck on our age difference."

"If that's the only thing stopping him, things are on your side. Give him a little more time."

"I'm not giving up, not yet."

***

A couple days later, JV felt like she was retracing her steps as she walked down the road, past Steve's cabin and around the bend that kept the rest of the ranch out of sight from the main house. She didn't have a destination in mind, just getting her body moving as she tried to make her brain work again. She still couldn't focus on her project and she was supposed to have it done by the end of the week.

Reaching the clearing where the ranch buildings stood, she veered away from them, heading instead for the open space of a nearby pasture. She stopped at the gate that looked like it was simply one of the fencing panels that made up the corral. Looking across the pasture, she didn't see anything and assumed it was empty. She climbed the metal pole gate rather than try to wrestle it open, before setting out across the open field.

In the distance, she heard the sound of an engine, the high pitched buzz of an ATV, but she didn't think much of it. She knew they used four-wheelers on a lot of ranches. The buzzing continued getting louder, but JV barely registered the noise as she continued to think about the project she was working on and made her way across the pasture. She was startled when one of the vehicles zipped past her, whipped into a turn and stopped sideways in front of her, blocking her path.

"Fool girl. Get on, quick." Frank said from his seat on the machine.

Without questioning, JV stepped on the running board and threw one leg over the seat. Her butt had scarcely hit the seat when Frank hit the accelerator and they shot forward.

As he turned the machine again, she saw a large bull, easily a ton of angry flesh, hooves and horns, headed straight for them.

She gripped the bars that made up the rack on the rear of the machine as Frank out ran the animal and pulled into an open gate leading to another corral. He moved faster than she thought someone his age could, as he scrambled off the still idling ATV and closed the corral gate, effectively blocking the animal. JV gave the gate a dubious look. She thought the bull could smash through the gate if he wanted, but he seemed content to leave them be now that they were no longer in his territory.

"What on earth were you thinking, girl?" Frank demanded now that they were safe. "That bull is the meanest creature on the property and you just go traipsing across his pasture?"

"I didn't seem him. I thought the field was empty."

"Just so you know that field is almost never empty. We only move him during breeding season."

" I'll remember to avoid it from now on," she said contritely.

She climbed off the four wheeler, and watched Frank get back on. He pulled it across to the other gate in the corral, this one opened into the yard. JV opened the gate and let him through. She watched as he parked the machine outside the barn and killed the engine.

"What were you doing out there anyway?" he asked.

"Walking," JV said, "I was trying to clear my mind. I need to get some work done but I can't think." Actually, her problem was that she was thinking too much, about the wrong things.

Frank shook his head, "You need to be more careful. There are a lot of ways to get hurt around here. Hell, you didn't even look up until I was stopped in front of you. You need to be more aware of what's going on around you."

"I heard the engine," she shrugged, "I assumed it was someone working and not something I needed to be worried about."

He blinked at her, as if he had no words for a moment. "Be more careful, girl." He turned and headed into the barn, leaving her standing there, confused.

Not wanting to cause more trouble, JV headed back for the main house, hoping maybe she could finish the project and get it over with. She wasn't holding her breath.

Chapter 11

Restless, JV gave up trying to sleep. She didn't want to disturb her hosts, not again. She quietly slipped on some clothes and tip-toed outside, planning on shifting and going for a run, as she'd done every night since she'd arrived. She gently closed the door behind her and padded barefoot down the length of the porch, the cold wood freezing her toes.

Wrapping her arms around her stomach, she thought she should have grabbed a jacket and socks as she looked out into the woods not fifteen feet from the edge of the porch.

"Please don't. I'd like to get at least a little sleep tonight and I don't want to have to go looking for you again," Steve's quiet voice startled her and she jumped.

Spinning around, she saw him standing at the bottom of the stairs on the other end of the porch. "What are you doing out here?" she whispered, still trying not to wake Nick and Rebecca. She knew he could hear her even at a whisper.

"I could ask you the same thing."

"I couldn't sleep."

He lifted his brows, "I've noticed."

"I was going to shift," she looked back out toward the trees. She could see their outlines in the darkness, but not much else.

"I suspected as much when you came out. I've been watching you every night, waiting for you to return before going in."

She looked back toward him. "I can't settle," she admitted, "I sleep for an hour or two then I wake up and can't go back to sleep."

Steve sighed, he seemed caught in an internal battle, "Come on, we can watch a movie or something."

She padded toward him, planning to follow him to his place but let out a startled squeal when Steve swept her off her feet and started toward his cabin.

"Fool woman. Were you planning on walking on this freezing ground barefoot?" he grumbled.

"I was planning to shift, so of course I would have been barefoot, but when I decided not to shift I couldn't go in just for shoes. I might wake someone."

Steve growled and carried her the rest of the way in silence. He didn't let her down once they reached his porch, instead, he waited until he'd opened the door and set her down on a soft, warm rug.

"You need to start keeping a pair of shoes next to the door. It's too cold up here to wander around barefooted."

She nodded, distracted as she saw the inside of his home for the first time. It was a mix of styles, not decorated but comfortable and lived in. Somehow, it worked. She found it a bit masculine, but not overwhelming.

Steve stepped in behind her and closed the door, "It's cold out there." He shook all over and pulled his coat off. "I can't believe you were out there without a coat or even socks."

JV tried to stop shivering. She didn't want him to see it, but he noticed anyway. He moved close and rubbed his warm hands up and down her arms trying to help her warm up. The unexpected contact sent sparks of heat through her body.

"Movies are on that shelf," he pointed, "there, pick one. You want some hot chocolate? I'd offer coffee, but that's not gonna help you sleep."

"Cocoa would be great." She went to the bookshelf where she found a large selection of DVD's neatly lining several shelves. "You watch a lot of movies?"

"Sometimes, the snow gets pretty deep in the winter; it can knock out the satellite for days sometimes. I keep enough movies around that I can generally find something I'll listen to." He spoke from the other room. She heard him moving around and making their drinks.

"What do you want to watch?" she asked.

"Whatever you want is fine. If it's there, I'll watch it."

She looked through the titles, recognizing most of them. There were a few dramas, but more comedies, and a lot of action films. "You don't have a single romance here." She wasn't surprised but was curious how he would react.

He came back in the room carrying a pair of steaming mugs, "Yeah, oddly enough, I'm not really into chick flicks."

She couldn't stop her laugh before it tumbled out. She pulled a movie off the shelf and gave it to him, trading him the disk for her cup of cocoa.

He looked at the cover, "That's an old one,"

"But a good one," she took a sip, "I've seen it at least a hundred times. I'm not sure it's possible to see that one too much."

He chuckled and got the disk ready to watch. He turned back and picked up the remote off the coffee table. "Sit, make yourself at home. You're not gonna stand for the whole movie, are you?" He sat on one end of the sofa, moving so smoothly his cocoa didn't even slosh.

JV didn't want to sit on the other end of the long piece of furniture, it felt like she was putting distance between them, plus, she would only get colder over there. Instead she sat in the middle. This way she wasn't smashed up against him, but still not too far away.

Once she settled in, Steve started the movie. She sipped the chocolate and it warmed her, but she still shivered occasionally. Before the previews ended Steve got up and disappeared into another room.

"Is something wrong?" she called after him.

"No," he appeared in the doorway, "I thought you could use this." He lifted a thick quilt and began unfolding it. "You're still cold."

"Thank you," she took the blanket and pulled it over her legs, "I'm chilled."

"You'd be a lot more than chilled if you'd been out there much longer. There may not be snow yet, but that's only because we haven't had a storm come in yet. It's plenty cold enough."

"Snow, this early?" She was surprised.

"Not early here, it's about average."

"Wow. I haven't seen snow in years." She looked toward the TV while he sat back down beside her. "I'd love to see snow."

"Don't worry, you stick around long enough and you'll see some. If you're still around in the spring, you'll be sick of it."

"Yet, you stay," she said, knowing he might be right about the snow, but it wasn't enough to make him move home, or anywhere else that didn't get as much of the stuff.

"Yeah, I stay." The movie had stopped on the menu while they'd been talking. He hit play and the movie started, preventing him from having to continue the conversation.

There wasn't much to see on the TV yet, the picture was filled with fog while a child's voice sang about a pirate's life. The fog began to clear and the bow of a ship became visible. JV sat enthralled, holding her mug in both hands as she drank. She set the empty mug on the coffee table in front of her when she was finished, then curled in the blanket enjoying the movie and the company.

Chapter 12

The movie was only a little over half over when Jade slumped and leaned against him. That's when he realized she'd fallen asleep. Looking down where she lay against him, so innocent, he thought about how much she looked like she had when she was younger.

This was why he had left. He was too old for her, even now. What did a nearly forty-year-old man have to offer a twenty-eight-year old woman? He was sure she'd soon realize he had nothing for her and move on. The hard part was going to be going on without her once she did. He could only hope that when she decided she had no reason to stay, she didn't take his heart with her.

He turned back and watched the movie a while longer, trying to put Jade out of his mind until she sighed and moved in her sleep. Looking at her again, he decided she had to be in the most uncomfortable position he'd ever seen, but he didn't have the heart to wake her. Instead, he stood and picked her up. Holding her in his arms, he lay on the sofa and let her curl up on top of him. He made sure the blanket still covered her, then turned his attention back to the TV.

***

He woke the next morning to a knee in his groin.

"What?" Jade's voice was thick with sleep, "Where am I?"

"You're at my place," Steve murmured, wrapping his arms around her as he tried to keep her still, "now quit moving before you geld me."

She stilled. "I remember now," she said softly. "I fell asleep watching the movie. How did we end up like this?"

"You looked uncomfortable, so I moved you. I intended to get you another blanket when I went to bed, but I fell asleep too."

"What time is it?" she asked.

Looking at the clock on the wall, he was surprised at how late it was. "Crap, almost seven. I need to get moving."

Jade started moving again, more carefully this time, trying not to hurt him anymore than she already had as she climbed off him. She stood beside the sofa stretching.

He stood and realized the room had grown chilly. He couldn't help noticing Jade wasn't used to the cold as her nipples beaded and pressed against her shirt like small, hard buttons. His jeans suddenly got tighter. "Let me get my boots on and I'll take you back to the main house." He turned toward his bedroom.

"No need, I can walk," she tried to put him off.

"Not barefooted you can't. Even if it wasn't cold, there are sharp rocks and sticks. It's one thing to shift and run around; cat's paws are designed to walk over those things. Those delicate little feet aren't." He nodded down at her bare feet with toe nails painted bright purple. Why hadn't he noticed that last night?

Her shoulders slumped and she wrapped the blanket around herself, "All right."

He went in to the bedroom and got a clean pair of socks.

"Um, Steve?" He heard her call as he sat down to put on his boots; there was something different about her voice. Sighing, he picked them up and went to see what she needed.

"Yeah?" he asked, stepping back into the front room.

"You're right. I won't be going up to the main house myself." She turned away from the window to look at him, her eyes wide.

"What's out there?" he asked, his brow furrowing.

"Snow."

"I knew it was getting close, any idea how much?"

She looked out the window again then back at him, "I'm going to guess about six inches."

Steve lifted his brows, "That's a lot for one night, especially without a big storm."

Jade looked back out the window, she looked a little concerned.

Steve finished lacing his boots and stood, "Don't worry. I'll get you back up to the house, no problem."

"That wasn't what I was thinking about."

51

"What is it then?"

"You, Nick, Frank, everyone else that has to work in that."

Steve chuckled, then realized she was serious. "It's nothing," he looked over her head out the window. "Wait until January when there's a couple of feet, at least. Anyway, we're used to it. We'll dress warm and do what we have to to make sure the animals are safe and have feed, break the ice on their water, then we'll come in where it's warm. We don't spend a lot of extra time out in the cold."

Jade let a breath out in a rush, "That's good."

"You ready?" Steve stopped next to the door and pulled on a heavy coat.

"As ready as I'll get, I guess." She lowered the quilt from her shoulders and started folding it.

"Keep it on. It's gonna be a lot colder out there now than it was last night, you'll need it."

JV wrapped the quilt back around herself, pulling it snug as she went to the door.

Steve picked her up and swung her easily into his arms. Outside, he pulled the door shut and headed down the stairs. He took extra care because of ice as he stomped toward the main house, breaking a trail as he went.

"A couple of trips and the path will be well beaten again," he said as he made slow progress over the short path. He stomped his way up the stairs, knocking the snow off his boots as he went, and to the back door. He opened the door without knocking and set her on her feet just inside. "I've got some things I've got to do, I'll see you later," he said, then turned and walked away.

Chapter 13

Not sure what to do, JV closed the door and headed for her room. The couple in the kitchen stopped her.

"Someone had fun last night," Rebecca said, her voice teasing.

"It's not what it looks like," JV cringed at the sound of her own words, that only made it look more like what it already looked like.

Rebecca lifted one brow and looked her up and down, "How on earth did you end up at Steve's last night barefoot? Did you shift?" She took in the clothes JV still wore under the quilt now hanging open. "No, you didn't shift or you wouldn't have clothes. No shoes and no coat? What were you thinking?"

JV took a deep breath and let it out in a rush, "I couldn't sleep, I went out to the porch planning to shift and go for a run, but something stopped me. Then Steve was there, saying he didn't want to stay up again or have to go looking for me."

"Again?" Rebecca asked.

"So he invited me over to his place to watch a movie," JV ignored the question, "I fell asleep, then he did too."

"Steve fell asleep with someone in his house?" Nick asked from his seat at the table.

"He said I'd curled up against him before he fell asleep." She glanced out the window. "Anyway, we woke up to this," she motioned outside, "and he wouldn't let me come back on my own."

"I don't blame him," Nick said.

"If you'll excuse me, I'm gonna go take a shower and get dressed."

"Go ahead. I'm headed out to help with the animals anyway." Nick said, standing.

JV left the couple and made her way to her room.

JV finished her shower and went back to her room to dress, and hopefully get a little work done. She'd made the bed she'd only tossed and turned in the night before and picked up her laundry when a soft knock sounded on the door. "Yes?" she knew it had to be Rebecca. They were the only two in the house, she'd heard Nick leave as she got in the shower and she hadn't scented anyone new when she came out.

"Am I bothering you?" the other woman pushed the door open.

"Not at all, what's on your mind?"

"I wanted to ask you something, if you don't mind," she leaned against the door frame, "I hope I'm not being too nosy."

"Well, I don't know." JV gave her new friend a mock serious look, "Why don't you ask and I'll tell you if it's too much."

Rebecca laughed as she stepped into the room. "You said Steve fell asleep, do you have any idea what time that was?"

"Oh, hang on," she looked up at the ceiling and talked her way through the evening before. "It was about eleven when I went outside, and it couldn't have taken us more than thirty minutes to start the movie, that movie is about two and a half hours. He said he fell asleep before the movie ended, so before two."

Rebecca blinked. "All right. When did you wake up?"

"He said it was seven when I asked, and he needed to get to work, there was maybe twenty or thirty minutes, max, between when we woke and when he dropped me at the door."

Rebecca looked intrigued.

"Why?" JV asked.

"Come on in the other room. I'll fix us some breakfast while we talk," Rebecca suggested, giving herself a minute or two to figure out how to explain. In the kitchen, she started pulling things from the cabinet, "Pancakes sound good?" she asked.

"Great," JV fixed herself a cup of coffee and sat at the table and waited for Rebecca to start talking.

Rebecca started mixing the batter, "It caught our attention when you said Steve fell asleep. I've been here a little over two years, and while I wouldn't say Steve sleeps around, it's safe to say he never lacks for female company."

Jealousy flashed through JV. She ignored it. She knew it was stupid, but she couldn't help it. The thought of him sleeping with someone else hurt. He had no way of knowing she'd never found anyone she'd been willing to go that far with.

"But I've noticed, no matter who Steve spends his time with, no one sleeps over. Ever," Rebecca continued.

"It wasn't like that-"

Rebecca held up one flour-dusted hand, stopping JV mid-protest, "I'm not saying it is. I'm telling you what I know."

JV blinked, "Okay."

"Also, he's had a couple of visitors since I got here. They either stay in the bunkhouse or in town. Nick tells me Steve doesn't sleep much, maybe two to three hours a night and never with anyone in the house."

JV was silent for a moment, considering Rebecca's words. "But he slept at least five hours last night."

"Exactly. With you *in his house*." Rebecca flipped several pancakes and looked at JV to see if she understood.

JV's heart soared. The idea that he couldn't, or wouldn't, sleep with anyone in his house, yet he'd not only fallen asleep with her, but he'd slept longer than usual, a lot longer, gave her hope. It made her believe he might let something develop between them. "I see what you're getting at. Does Nick have any insight?"

"Not really. He said it was interesting, but that's all."

"It is interesting, and encouraging. It gives me somewhere to work from."

***

JV spent the day in her room. She was finally able to focus, and she worked straight through lunch. Her dedication paid off and resulted in a finished product. She sent it to her client for approval just in time for dinner. She closed her laptop and stood. She was stretching the stiffness out of her neck and back when she sensed him nearby. Steve was in the house.

A knock sounded on her bedroom door, different from Rebecca's.

"Yes?" she called.

"Rebecca sent me to tell you dinner's ready," Steve's voice was muffled by the door.

JV opened the door, "I was just on my way."

55

"I hope you had a good afternoon," Steve said as they headed for the table.

"I did. I finally finished my project; I just sent it to my client."

"That's great. I hope he likes what you've done."

His sudden friendliness made JV suspicious, but she wasn't going to question it. She might ruin it. "Me too, I don't want to have to re-do it. I had a hard enough time getting it done the first time."

"You think you're done with the restless nights?" he asked.

JV could have sworn he seemed disappointed, "I doubt it. I haven't really slept well in a long time."

"How long?"

"Years."

"One, two?" he scowled.

"Closer to five or six." She looked at the floor, avoiding his gaze.

"That's a long time to not sleep."

"It is." She didn't let on that she knew that he didn't rest much either, or that last night had been the best night's sleep she'd had in a long time.

They joined Nick and Rebecca at the table, talking and getting to know each other better. Over the last week, JV had spent more time with Rebecca than anyone else and she liked her. She got along well with Nick, too, though she'd spent less time with him. She felt sure, if things worked out with Steve, she could make a home in this Chanat. She respected these people as pack leaders and thought they would make great friends, too.

"We're supposed to get more snow in the next few days, we need to make sure we're prepared," Nick said. He and Steve were discussing ranch business.

"I've got all the cattle in the east pasture, we just have to make sure they're taken care of and don't jump the fence."

"Sounds good, how are we doing-"

The conversation was interrupted by a knock on the front door.

Steve looked at Nick, then Rebecca, "Are you expecting anyone?"

"No," said Nick.

Steve frowned slightly when Rebecca shook her head. Without another word, Steve stood and went to the door.

JV heard a high-pitched voice, young and threaded with panic, then Steve's deeper tone, but she couldn't make out what was being said.

A moment later, Steve came back to the kitchen, a girl who looked about 16 trailing behind him. "Sir," he said, "I'm going to have to go, we've got a couple of kids fighting. I've already called Bobby, he's on his way up. He'll stay until I get back."

"Go," Nick didn't argue or ask for details, "fill me in later."

Steve nodded once then herded the girl back toward the door.

Chapter 14

JV hoped Steve would make it back before bedtime, but it got late and he still hadn't returned. She hoped he hadn't had much trouble as she said goodnight to her hosts and headed for her room.

She lay in bed, wondering what could have happened to keep him out so long as she tried to fall asleep. She dozed a little, but spent more time tossing and turning than sleeping. It was just after midnight when she heard his pickup pull in.

Giving up on sleep, she tossed the blanket back and pulled on a pair of warm socks in addition to her sweats before heading for the back porch. She slipped silently from of her room and waved to Bobby where he sat reading as she crossed the living room, then went out through the kitchen to the back door. Steve was almost to the tree line, where he would disappear from sight, when she stepped out the door.

He stopped and turned at the soft click of the latch. He spotted her instantly, her bright running clothes standing out against the darker shades of the cabin. He was too far away for her to read his expression in the dark but she could tell by the way he moved as he turned and headed her way that he wasn't happy.

"What are you doing out here again, with no coat?" he demanded, his voice low.

"I couldn't sleep and I heard you pull in."

"So you came outside, in the snow, without a coat or shoes?" he didn't sound happy.

As JV got closer, she saw a bruise darkening his cheek. He'd been hit. The skin had split and the wound was red and angry looking. "What happened?" She reached for him.

"Don't change the subject. I asked why you don't have shoes on, again.

You're going to catch your death if you keep this up."

"I'm fine," she waved away his concern, "tell me what happened here." She reached out one hand and gently cupped his cheek, trying to get a better look.

Steve sighed, and almost reluctantly, wrapped one arm around her thighs, pulling her snug against him before lifting her off her feet and heading for his cabin. "If we have to do this, we might as well get warm first, and you, fool girl, are barefoot again."

"I'm not barefoot, I have socks to keep my feet warm."

"Socks that will get wet the instant you step into this snow, then they're worse than nothing. You'll end up with frostbite."

JV was glad he couldn't see her because she couldn't stop the smile that spread across her face. He was concerned with her health and he kept picking her up and carrying her around. It was a sign he was opening up.

Again, Steve didn't set her down until they got inside. Loosening his grip around her thighs, he let her slide, slowly down his body. JV felt heat pool in her core. He stepped back, closing the door before peeling out of his jacket.

"What happened?" JV asked again.

"I had to break up a fight. They weren't ready to stop yet," he growled. "I got in the way of a fist."

"Come into the light and let me look." She pulled him under an overhead light and stepped into the seat of a nearby chair so she could get a better look at the wound under his left eye.

"It doesn't look too bad, but you're going to have a hell of black eye." She touched his face, her fingers resting lightly just below the wound, then closed her eyes and concentrated. His cold skin heated beneath her fingers and she knew it was working. She opened her eyes and found the cut scabbed over and half healed. It looked days old instead of hours. "There, that should help."

Steve scowled, "What did you do?" He pulled away and went in the bedroom. Coming back into the living room he looked surprised. "You can heal."

JV shrugged, "Some. It's not very strong, but I've been working on improving. I'll never be as strong as Hannah," she referred to the healer from their Chanat in Texas, "but I do what I can."

"I'd forgotten how nice it can be to have a healer around," he reached up and ran his fingers over the swiftly healing wound.

"You don't have a healer here?" she asked, her surprise clear.

"No."

"Then how?" she was at a loss. To the Kitsune, a pack or clan healer was as important as a doctor to humans. It was someone they could trust to treat their wounds, set bones, whatever was needed, and not ask uncomfortable questions about their increased healing and fast metabolisms.

"One of the clan is married to a doctor, she treats us when we have to see someone," he dismissed the issue.

"But you have no one to push healing, or to find the deeper problems?"

"Nope."

"Wow, I can't imagine." She could, but she didn't want to think about that. She'd been living pretty much on her own since she left home for school. After moving to Austin she'd met with the local Khan but hadn't joined the clan. She hadn't been refused access, but she'd kept to herself, it had been what she'd wanted at the time.

"It's not that bad. We have a few who can share energy, when someone's hurt; we push energy to help 'em heal. It's not the same, but it works in its own way."

JV understood that the clan had found a way to deal with their lack of a healer. It wasn't the same, but it got the job done. She looked at the wound and the bruise developing behind it once more. "That shouldn't sting as badly anymore either," she had to give herself something to focus on.

"It does feel better," he dropped his hand. "Thank you."

"Can I ask what happened? Or is it none of my business."

Steve rolled his eyes, and sat heavily on the sofa, "Two teenage idiots got into it over the girl who came and got me. She panicked and went for help. They were still at it when I got there, both bloody and bruised." He shook his head. "I don't get it, they're not old enough to have any clue what's gonna happen with the rest of their lives and they're fighting over a girl who's even younger."

"You put an end to it?"

"Sit. I'm tired and looking up at you makes my neck hurt."

JV sat in the middle of the couch where she'd been the night before, one knee up in the seat as she faced him, waiting for him to continue.

"Yeah, I put an end to it. It didn't take long, but I had to wade in and pull 'em apart. That's how I got this," he motioned to his face, "but that was only the beginning. I took all three of them to her parents and made them explain what had happened, then to each of the boy's folks. Then I had to get 'em all home." He shook his head again. "Their parents were not happy. I'd be willing to bet they'll think long and hard about doing something like that again or at least before taking their petty fight to the Khan."

"I hope so." She wasn't sure what else to say.

He glanced around, looking up at the clock then over at the TV on the wall. "Wanna watch another movie?"

"Sure, why not?"

"Pick one. I'll go get comfortable then fix us something to drink." He stood and headed into the bedroom.

JV took her time, looking over the titles carefully before selecting one.

"You ready?" Steve came back with two steaming mugs.

"Yep," she took her mug and settled onto the couch while Steve changed the disk then disappeared into the bedroom for a few seconds, returning with another quilt.

"I should have brought your quilt back. I was going to give it to you after dinner."

"Don't worry about it, I have several. I'll get it later." He sat beside her on the sofa, spread the quilt over both their laps, then started the DVD player.

JV sipped her cocoa while Steve skipped the previews and started the movie. The opening scenes of a woman disembarking from a plane and starting a trek through the jungle came on the screen while the woman's voice narrated, talking about the company she worked for and a botanist who works for them.

After they finished their cocoa and set the cups aside, Steve turned out the lamp, leaving the only light in the room coming from the TV. "Come here," he pulled her against him.

JV was surprised. He'd touched her first again. Maybe he was actually giving the attraction between them a chance. She slid closer, leaning against his side while he wrapped one arm around her. She sat curled against him, covered by the quilt, until she couldn't keep her eyes open any longer. Then she laid her head against his side and closed her eyes, planning to listen to the movie, but his warmth beside her and the security of his arm around her lulled her to sleep.

Chapter 15

Steve knew the instant she fell asleep but he finished the movie anyway. He turned off the TV and briefly considered waking her up and sending her back to the main house. Then he remembered she didn't have any shoes, he didn't want to go out in the cold again. He considered easing out from under her, making sure she was covered and letting her spend the rest of the night on the couch, but it felt wrong. He thought for a moment, thinking about how much better he'd slept the night before, with her in his arms, than he had in longer than he could remember. He wondered how much better he might sleep somewhere comfortable, as he moved them both until he would be able to sleep, then closed his eyes.

***

Steve eased out the front door, closing it as gently as he could. He was trying not to wake her. Stepping silently off the porch, he headed for the main house. He needed to talk to Nick. Knowing the Khan would be up already, he let himself inside. He fixed himself a cup of coffee and sat down at the table without a word.

"Well?" the clan leader asked.

"Stupid teenagers fighting over a girl." Steve rolled his eyes.

"All ours?"

"Yeah."

"You break them up and tell their parents?"

"Took 'em to speak to all three sets of parents then delivered 'em to their homes."

The clan leader nodded, "Any trouble?"

"Not really."

"What's that under your eye?" Nick motioned to Steve's face.

"Oh," Steve reached up and touched what remained of the wound from the night before. "I took a hit while breaking 'em up. It's nothing."

Nick lifted one brow and hit the light switch on the wall beside him, throwing light into the kitchen and making Steve duck away from the sudden glare. "I might believe it was nothing and you'd just been bruised, if it weren't for that nearly healed cut under your eye."

Steve looked down, knowing he was going to have to confess. It wasn't that he was hiding something, he just hadn't wanted to advertise it. There was no way to hide that he'd been near Jade recently. He could smell her scent on his skin and he knew that the Khan could too.

He took a deep breath and explained, "It was after midnight by the time I got in. I knew you'd be asleep so I headed home. I was almost to my place when I heard Jade open the back door. I stopped to talk to her and she saw the cut. She wasn't dressed to be outside, especially as cold as it was last night, so I took her to my place. When we got there she took a good look at the cut and the next thing I knew, it felt different. When I checked, it had scabbed over, healed more than it would have in a couple days. When I asked her about it, she said she has some healing talent, it's not strong, but the more she uses it the more it grows."

Nick looked at Steve a moment, his expression giving nothing away, then out the window into the darkness. "It would be nice to have a healer in the clan. How are things going otherwise, between the two of you?"

"I don't know."

"You don't know?" Nick seemed amused.

"I don't know if I can do it," he clarified.

Nick was confused, "If you can do what?"

"If I can let this continue," he sounded miserable, even to himself.

"Why not? Is the instinct not there? Don't you like her?"

"I like her, and yes," Steve nodded, "the instinct is there, but we're just too different."

Nick looked confused, "Different how?"

"We just are."

"I hope you're not talking about the age thing."

"So what if I am?" Steve scowled.

"Man, I really don't think it's that big of deal."

"Think of it this way," Steve took a different tack, "remember when you met Rebecca? What if when you met her, you were the same age you were

63

then, but she wasn't. Consider how you would have felt if she was seventeen. How would you feel about it then?"

"I honestly can't say. But the fact remains, she's not seventeen anymore."

"She may not be seventeen anymore, but I'm still ten years older. That's never going to change. When she's fifty, I'll be sixty. By the time she's sixty-five, I'll be damn near eighty. Is it really fair to her to saddle her with someone she's going to have to take care of?"

"Do you think she hasn't thought of that? Do you really think she came all this way, came hunting for you, without considering that? Is it fair to assume she hasn't?"

Steve sighed, "She probably has. She's not an idiot."

"So, I'll ask again. How are things going between the two of you?"

Steve took a deep breath and stared into his cup, "I haven't slept more than two hours in a stretch and four or five hours on a good night, in about fifteen years." He looked up, focusing out the window at the faint glow from his porch light as it twinkled through the trees. "And I haven't been able to sleep with someone else in the same house, much less room, for quite a while. With Jade it's different. There's something about her that calms me.

"It's certainly not the reverent way she talks to me, I swear," he scoffed, sarcasm heavy in his tone. "Everyone around here has always treated me with, I don't know, an air of respect, almost fear, even the females, but not Jade." The ghost of a smile curved his lips as he thought about the way she'd stood up to him about the pistol.

"It's like she has no fear. She stands there chewing me out or issuing orders and expecting me to listen," the smile faded as he looked at the other man. "When she's around, and not in my face about something, I'm more relaxed than I've been in a long time. Hell, I don't even mind when she *is* in my face." He grinned for a moment.

"I can sleep with Jade in the house, and night before last, when we fell asleep on the sofa during the movie, I slept for five hours straight and I probably would have slept longer if we hadn't been on the sofa."

"And last night?"

"We fell asleep on the couch again, not entirely on accident this time." A slight smile formed at the memory, "She curled against me and was out in less than five minutes," he turned serious again, "but nothing's happened, not really."

"Hey, you're both adults. You've known her a hell of a lot longer than I knew Rebecca before we ended up in bed. Heck, she's been here longer than I knew Rebecca."

Steve looked down, embarrassed, "I wasn't nice about it either."

"I guess what really matters is, if you forget about the age difference and just focus on her, do you like her? Are you drawn to her? Can it go anywhere and do you want it to?"

Steve was silent for a moment, "I don't know."

"You have some thinking to do then, don't you?"

"I guess I do."

"While we're on the subject, have you noticed the way she avoids me when I go to touch her?"

"I have," Steve scowled, "but she doesn't do it with me, it's strange. I'm not sure what's going on, I'm waiting for her to trust me enough tell me what it is."

"On another topic," the Khan said, "it's probably a good idea for you to stay away from the humans until that mess on your face is gone. There's no way we can explain why you were fine yesterday and today you have a bruise that's already green and yellow. It looks weeks old. I'll go make sure everything's taken care of, you go back to that girl you left asleep in your house."

"But-" Steve tried to protest.

"Nope." Nick stopped him. "It's settled. You can't be seen and there's no reason for us both to stay out in the cold, so go back to her and enjoy."

Steve took a deep breath and let it out in a rush. He sat in silence, looking into his coffee. After a couple of minutes he picked up the cup and drained it in one swallow. "All right then. I'll go back to my place. Enjoy your morning in that cold white shit." He pulled his coat back on and headed home.

Chapter 16

JV was going crazy. She'd spent the last week going between the main house and Steve's cabin, seeing only Steve, Bobby, and clan leaders. She hadn't been able to walk outside more than that, because she didn't have anything warm enough to be outside in for very long. She'd never, in all her twenty-eight years, experienced anything like it. She felt trapped and found herself pacing through the house, then bundling up in what little warm clothing she had, to go outside and pace back and forth on the porch, returning only when her face and hands started to ache from the cold.

She'd tried to shift and run through the snow, but she'd soon discovered that even as a cat, moving around in foot-deep snow wasn't an easy prospect. When the ice had caked on her paws she'd given up, going in and taking a hot shower to warm up.

Today was no different. She came in from the back porch, taking off the coat and the scarf Rebecca had loaned her upon discovering she didn't have either. There really hadn't been much call for cold weather gear in east Texas, it might snow occasionally, but it never lasted more than a few days and she'd never seen snow this deep.

"Come on, let's go to town." Rebecca said, as soon as JV stepped into the living room where she had been sitting.

"Town?" JV was instantly interested. "What about the snow?"

"Bobby will take us," Rebecca answered. "The truck has four-wheel drive and good tires. The snow's no problem."

"Are you sure?"

"Yep, I've been working on a list of things that I need and I've watched you pace about all I can take. Let's get out of here for a while."

"Normally I'd say don't do it just for me, but I'm just grateful for the opportunity to get out."

66

Rebecca laughed. "It's only November, get used to it."

JV shook her head and muttered something under her breath as she went to change clothes.

***

"Wow, how often do you go shopping?" JV was trying not to be rude, but the volume of food Rebecca was adding to the cart awed her.

"Every couple of weeks or so. It means big trips, but not this big." Rebecca laughed, not at all offended. "Most of this is for Thanksgiving."

"Thanksgiving?" JV repeated, "that's still weeks away."

"It's next week."

JV blinked at the other woman, having a hard time believing it. She stopped, took out her cell phone, and pulled up the calendar. "Well I'll be damned. I totally spaced it."

"I'm not trying to run you off, you're more than welcome to stay. But doesn't your family expect you home?" Rebecca asked gently.

JV gave her a wry smile. "My family's never made a big deal about Thanksgiving."

"That's too bad. It's my favorite holiday," Rebecca kept moving through the aisle. "Nick had a habit of doing a big meal every year, the hands are all invited. Most of the hands generally spend it with their families, they're all somewhat local, but we also invite any kin without family in the area. I took over cooking the year before last. I'm not really sure how it worked before that. Last year we had twenty-five show up for dinner, with more turning up later for dessert."

"You cook for them all yourself?" JV was horrified and knew it showed.

"It's not that bad. I enjoy it."

"Don't get me wrong," JV laughed, holding her hands up in front of her, "I don't mind cooking, but wouldn't know where to start, cooking for that many."

"It's not that difficult, you just make a lot of food." Rebecca laughed. "Most of the ones who show up are men. Men aren't known for being picky about their food, as long as there's plenty of it."

"Hey, I take exception to that." Bobby said from where he'd been trailing behind the two women.

"You are the epitome of that," Rebecca rolled her eyes. "It might be from living in the bunkhouse and eating your own cooking most of the time."

"I'll have you know, I'm not a bad cook."

"You're not a good one either." Rebecca quipped, moving through the aisle. She pulled items from the shelves and dropped them into the cart she pulled along behind her, marking the list she carried as she went along.

"Yeah, well," he was silent a moment, then grinned, "I got nothing."

"That's because you know I'm right," she said in a singsong voice, cracking up as she finished.

Bobby shook his head and went back to following the women in silence, watching for anything or anyone who might be a threat. Before they'd left, Rebecca had told JV that her family hadn't been in favor of her leaving her clan, or picking her own husband. They'd started trouble in the past. It had been a while since anyone had tried anything though. Nick was still worried. While he didn't insist on it, he asked that she take one of the enforcers with her whenever she left the ranch. Since he'd never tried to stop her from going wherever she wanted, she felt it was a minor thing to take someone he trusted with her, in case someone showed up, or she had problems. That was why they had an escort.

"Anyway," JV tried to steer the conversation back on topic, "I'd like to help cook, for Thanksgiving that is, if you don't mind."

"That would be great." Rebecca was a little distracted as she looked for something, "making that much food is a lot of work, but it's worth it." She found what she was looking for, grabbed two bottles and dropped them in the cart, then started down the aisle again.

By the time Rebecca finished with her list they had filled three shopping carts.

"We're gonna cook all of this?" JV was awed by the sheer amount of food they'd gathered.

"No. This is Thanksgiving plus the next couple of weeks, too." Rebecca said as the two women worked together, loading the groceries onto the belt.

It took more than thirty minutes to get through the register, get everything bagged and head out to the truck. Together they loaded the groceries into the back of the pickup so they could get out of the wind and cold.

"Anywhere else you need to stop?" Bobby asked, climbing behind the wheel while the women got in from the other side.

"Stop at the drug store, please," Rebecca said, "I have a few things I need."

Less than five minutes later, Bobby parked the pickup in front of the store. Inside, they separated. It wasn't a large store, more of an old fashioned variety store than a modern drug store. Rebecca and Bobby both knew if anything happened, he could hear them, even from the far end of the store. Besides, he had a few things he needed, too.

Rebecca grabbed a cart on her way in and pushed it through the store. She knew exactly where to find everything and quickly gathered what she was after.

"Is there anything you need while we're here?" Rebecca turned to JV.

"A couple of things," JV said, her face heating, "I need to find some warm clothes."

"I'm sure you can find something here. If they don't have what you're after, they'll probably order it. Or, if you want, we can look online and have anything you need delivered to the house."

"Okay," JV said, looking for the few things she knew she needed. She realized she should have put together a list, because she knew she was forgetting something but had no clue what.

After the drug store they headed back out to the ranch, the sun hanging low in the sky.

"It's going to be nearly dark by the time we get back," JV said.

"Nearly? We'll have to hurry to get everything in before it's completely dark," Bobby said. "Once the sun sets the temperature's gonna drop fast and there's another storm on the way. We'll have fresh snow before we get up tomorrow."

JV groaned.

"Are you sick of the snow already?" Rebecca laughed.

"Not really. I was just hoping for a break before we got more." JV watched out her window as the trees flew by. "I don't think I've ever seen more than six inches at a time, until this week."

"You spend the whole winter here and you'll see more," Bobby said. "Give us a few more inches and you might even convince Steve to take you out on one of the snow mobiles."

"Snowmobiles?" JV brightened, "That sounds like fun." She watched the white dusted trees sweep by for a few seconds. "Why do you have snowmobiles?" She was suddenly curious.

"For winter work on the ranch, four-wheelers for the summer, snowmobiles for the winter. It makes checking on and finding lost cattle easier and faster," Bobby said.

JV didn't know what to say. She spent the rest of the trip back wondering what Steve was up to, if he'd noticed she was gone and if he'd want to watch another movie tonight.

Chapter 17

Wednesday, JV helped Rebecca bake more than a half-dozen pies. By the time they were done, they had two pumpkins, an apple, pecan, cherry, mincemeat, banana cream, coconut and a chocolate. At the end of the day, they were both exhausted. Their legs ached from being on their feet and when Steve and Nick offered to wash dishes after dinner, they gladly accepted. Sitting at the table, they sipped hot cocoa and watched. Nick dried the last of the dishes and put them away while Steve drained the sink.

"Want to play something?" Nick asked.

Rebecca looked at JV then back to him and asked, "What do you have in mind?"

He paused a second, "I guess it depends on what everyone knows how to play."

"Cards, board games, what?" JV wanted to know.

"Cards we have, board games are a little iffy. We have a few, but not much of a selection."

"I can play cards." JV said, hesitant.

"Do you play Canasta?" Nick asked.

JV made a face, "Sorry, never had an opportunity to learn."

"Actually, I don't know that one either." Rebecca put in.

"Me either." Steve put in.

Nick shook his head. "Where's the youth of this country going to, that no one knows how to play Canasta anymore?"

Steve shot Nick an unhappy look, "Youth? Really?" He was several years older than the clan leader and everyone knew it.

"I can play Pinochle." Rebecca volunteered.

"Me too." JV offered.

Steve nodded, "I probably learned the same place Jade did."

71

"Why do you call her Jade?" Rebecca asked.

"Because it's her name," Steve said.

Rebecca scowled and looked back and forth between them, confused.

JV couldn't take it anymore. "He's always insisted on calling me his shortened version of my given name. It started when I was little, maybe four or five. I'd done something to make my mom call me by my full name and as soon as he heard it, he quit using JV and started calling me Jade." She smiled slightly at the memory.

"Why JV?" Rebecca was even more confused.

JV sighed and rolled her eyes, "Jaiden Victoria. My parents named me Jaiden Victoria. My grandfather dubbed me JV while I was still in the hospital, it stuck. I've been JV to everyone since; everyone but Steve." She sent him a fond look.

Rebecca turned back to Steve. "So why Jade?"

Steve stood beside the island, watching JV as he answered his Karhyn, "Because I took one look at the grubby, grinning little girl running from my best friend's mom and I didn't see the tomboy, instead, I got a glimpse of the woman she would be. Strong, confident and beautiful, JV didn't fit that, Jade did."

JV looked back at him, a mystified smile on her face as she heard, for the first time, why he'd given her the nickname.

"So, do you play pinochle, babe?" Rebecca asked Nick, continuing as if the discussion hadn't been side-tracked.

"It's been a while, but yes, I play pinochle."

"All right," she rubbed her hands together, "who wants to play?" She looked around.

JV shrugged, "As long as I don't have to stand, I'm in."

Rebecca laughed, "I agree."

"I'm in," Nick said. "It was my idea."

Steve shrugged, "Why not?"

"I'll get the cards." Rebecca jumped up and headed in the other room.

"I don't think we have a pinochle deck, better grab two." Nick called after her as he took three glasses and a mug from the cabinet. "Who wants something to drink?"

"What do you have in mind?" JV watched Steve fold the dishcloth on the edge of the sink then use the towel on his hands. Her eyes never left him as she spoke to the Khan.

"You've already had cocoa. I was thinking something with alcohol, but whatever you want is fine."

"Is there enough eggnog for me to have some tonight?" JV asked.

"I'm sure there is, and if not, oh well," Nick went to the refrigerator, pulled out a gallon jug and poured a little more than half a glass. "You want rum in it?"

JV was quiet for a second, considering, "Why not?"

He put the jug away and added a liberal amount if rum from a large bottle before going to the cabinet where Rebecca kept the spices and added a small sprinkling of nutmeg. Without asking, he poured a liberal amount of whiskey into the other two. He served JV the eggnog and handed Steve one of the whiskeys before heating water in the mug and making more cocoa in Rebecca's empty mug.

Rebecca came back with the cards as Nick carried the cocoa and the other whiskey to the table.

"How do we want to do this? Men against women? Couples? Mixed couples?" Nick asked, before taking a seat.

JV looked at Rebecca, who was already seated beside her at the small table. "What do you think?"

"Couples." Rebecca's voice was certain. She quickly separated the two decks to create a single deck for pinochle.

They played for nearly an hour before Rebecca plead exhaustion. "I'm done in guys, I can barely hold my eyes open and JV and I have to get up and start all over in the morning."

"I agree," JV stacked her cards neatly before passing them to Nick, who had dealt the last hand.

Rebecca put the cards away on her way to bed, while Nick gathered up the glasses and mugs and put them in the sink.

"I guess I'll see you in the morning then," he left the room to catch up with his wife.

JV turned to Steve, "I guess-"

"Where's your coat?" Steve looked at the rack beside the back door.

"In my room." JV frowned, confused.

"If you'd hang it next to the door with the rest of 'em, you could grab it on your way out, even in a hurry, and I wouldn't have to worry about you freezing your butt off."

JV scowled.

Steve sighed, "Are you coming to my place tonight?" His voice was a little calmer.

JV looked surprised. "I'd like to, but I didn't want to assume-"

He cut her off, "I sleep when you're there, and I don't when you're not. It's the same for you."

"I'll get my coat," she turned away so he wouldn't see the grin that she couldn't keep off her face. He hadn't just found her outside and allowed her to stay tonight. He was inviting her to spend the night in his cabin. "I'm ready," she said, returning to the kitchen.

"Is that the warmest coat you have?" He frowned at her.

JV looked down at the thin, cotton lined, denim jacket. "Yeah, I've been borrowing Rebecca's when I have to go outside, but I don't want to leave her without one."

Steve shook his head, "That's not enough for winter here. It'll do for short trips, but we'll have to see about getting you something warmer."

JV wasn't concerned, she planned to order something warmer soon, she'd been waiting to see how things went. Now that he seemed to be softening she didn't think it would be a waste of money. Waiting patiently while he pulled on his own gear JV then followed him outside and through the trees between the houses.

The crisp scent of pine in the cold night was becoming familiar and comforting. Something moved to her left and JV froze, narrowing her eyes as she watched the spot, trying to identify the source of the movement. After a moment she spotted as small rabbit huddled in the snow. A small smile spread across her face as she continued along the path.

"What's up?" Steve asked as she reached his side.

"It's just a cottontail."

He nodded once and hurried toward the house. "Inside," he held the door open. Once inside, they both kicked off their snow-covered shoes. He added wood to the old-fashioned stove that kept the place warm, before taking off his coat and helping her tug hers off her arms. "It's a little cool in here, but it will warm up soon. In the meantime, I think I can keep you warm." He tugged her against him, sliding his arms around her body as he lowered his mouth to hers, taking possession of her mouth. He teased her at first, then deepened the kiss until she melted against him, leaning in, trying to get closer to him.

Steve's arms tightened around her an instant before he straightened, lifting her as he went.

"Come on, baby." He picked her up and carried her to the sofa, where he sat, pulling her onto his lap as he did. He placedhis mouth on hers once

74

more, just for a moment before he pulled away.

"You fell asleep in the middle of the movie again last night. Do you want to find a new one or start this one again?"

"Whatever you want," she covered a big yawn, "I probably won't last for the whole thing again anyway."

"How about we start it where you left off, what's the last thing you remember?"

She blinked, "I don't know. It wasn't long, maybe thirty minutes in?"

"All right, I can work with that." He used the remote to navigate through the movie.

"Stop," she said, "there, that's where I fell asleep."

He hit play, wrapped one arm around her, where she still sat on his lap, and turned his attention to the screen.

Chapter 18

Rebecca stood on one side of the kitchen island, cutting ingredients for the dressing while JV sat at the dining room table, peeling potatoes. With as many people as they expected, there were a lot of potatoes to peel. The two women chatted while they worked, comparing favorite movies and music. Steve had pulled out a paring knife and was helping with the potatoes. Nick had asked him to stay close to the house. There would likely be people in and out for most of the day and he didn't want to have to worry about Rebecca while he was working.

As he'd left, he'd said something about lost cattle that had to be found, then he'd disappeared through the back door. A few moments later, JV had heard the buzz of a snowmobile as he'd headed for the barn.

Several hours had passed when Rebecca turned to Steve, "I take it from what you said last night, you've known JV a long time."

"Almost all her life."

"Are you close with her family?"

"Her brother was my best friend all the way through school," he didn't seem to mind Rebecca asking questions and he answered them without reserve.

"But not anymore?" Rebecca was curious about her new friend and she had no issues asking what she wanted to know.

"Not for a while, really."

"You two fight about something?"

The buzz of a snowmobile grew louder, telling them someone was coming from the barn.

"No, I was gone for a long time with the military and only home for a little while before I left again. We simply grew apart. We're still friends. We see each other now and then, just not best friends." He tossed his peeled potato into the bowl that was half-full of similarly naked ones and picked up another.

Nick came in the back door. He shed his snow gear in the mud room and went to the refrigerator. He pulled out a can of beer, popped the top and took a drink before sitting at the table across from JV.

A knock sounded on the front door. Steve dropped his potato back in the bowl of unpeeled ones and got up. From where they were working, Rebecca and JV heard Steve open the door and every word that was said.

"What are you doing here?" Steve's voice was clear in the silence as they waited to see who was there.

Instead of another voice, they heard the sound of someone being hit.

"Why'd you do that?" Steve asked.

"That's JV's truck outside and I can smell her on you. You told me you left home because you wouldn't be able to keep your hands off her. Nothing's changed and you've touched my sister."

Rebecca and JV both dropped what they were doing and rushed into the other room, Nick barely in front of them.

"She's sweet and innocent and you're too damned hard for her." the new voice continued.

"Matthew Joseph Wilkins! What the hell do you think you're doing?" JV was shocked to realize her brother was standing in the doorway glaring at Steve, who actively blocked him from entering.

The man in the door looked past Steve, to JV, "I came to take you home."

"You've wasted your time. I'm not going anywhere."

Matt's look darkened and he turned his attention back to the man between them.

"If you hit him again I'll make sure you regret it." JV snarled, advancing on the pair.

Matt looked at her, the anger in his eyes unchanged, "You wouldn't dare."

JV lowered her voice, moving closer, until Steve put out one hand and stopped her from getting nearer the angry man. "Do you want to try me? Really? I've been waiting a long time to prove to you I'm not in diapers anymore. I'm a grown woman. I make my own choices, my own decisions. I decide who I work for. I decide where I live. I decide who I sleep with. I decide where I go and where I don't. I'm damn near thirty, none of this is any of your business. It never was."

"Did you know your sweet and innocent sister," Steve's voice was filled with sarcasm as he threw her brother's words back at him, "carries a gun and has a concealed weapon permit?"

Matt gave a short laugh, "No way, JV couldn't hurt a fly. Besides, we'd smell a gun."

"It's not in the house anymore. I couldn't let her be armed in my Khan's house, but believe me, she carries. She's also found a way to keep us from scenting it."

Rebecca coughed, drawing everyone's attention. She turned pink, "I knew she had it. I knew before I brought her back to our house."

Steve and Nick looked at her, shocked.

"You knowingly let a stranger bring a gun in the house?" Nick asked.

"Well, yeah." Rebecca said, as though obvious. "It made her more comfortable," she shrugged.

Nick turned to JV, "Where's the weapon now?"

"Locked in my truck, like he said." She waved one hand in Steve's direction.

Nick turned to Steve, "If you didn't smell it, how did you find out about it?"

"A couple weeks ago, when you took Rebecca, I came in to check on Jade. She didn't answer when I called, so I went looking for her. She was in the bedroom. I'd woken her, but she didn't know who was in the house. She had the gun in her hand when I opened the door." Steve looked at Nick as he answered his clan leader, but everyone else watched JV.

She looked around once then spoke, addressing Rebecca, "How would you have responded if you were alone in the house when you laid down, then the presence of someone else woke you? I hadn't been asleep long enough for you and Nick to be home yet."

Rebecca was silent a moment, then lifting both brows, she turned to Nick, "She has a point."

Nick didn't bother responding, instead he turned to JV. "How did you keep us all from scenting it? We should have been able to smell the oil."

JV gave a slight smile, "I didn't keep you from smelling it, I just masked the odor with scents you're used to, scents you expected."

Steve frowned.

Nick scowled, "What do you mean?"

"I mix a few drops of essential oil into my cleaning oil."

Steve looked intrigued. "What oils?"

"Juniper, pine, and lemongrass."

"Could you teach me?" he asked.

"Sure," she shrugged.

Matt looked at JV, his eyes wide as she didn't deny carrying a weapon, hell she'd even admitted it. He stared for a moment in disbelief, then shook his head, "I never would have believed it. Do Mom and Dad know?"

"I haven't told them, but I haven't hidden it either. I keep telling you, I'm not twelve anymore, Matt. I don't need permission for everything I do."

"I wasn't saying you are," Matt said.

"But you're here to protect my virtue from your friend and drag me home. You may not be saying it, but you're sure as hell acting like it."

He had the grace to look guilty.

"Are you planning to hit Steve again?" Rebecca interrupted.

"I don't know yet," Matt looked at the other woman for the first time.

"Well, at least you're honest," she sighed. "If you can talk like adults instead of breaking down into a fist fight, you can come in. Close the door, all my warm air's escaping." She turned and went back to the kitchen and her cooking.

"Who was that?" Matt asked after she was gone.

"My Karhyn." Steve stepped back and let Matt inside.

JV waited until her brother was inside and the door closed behind him, then narrowed her eyes at him, "So, what? You think after leaving town so he could keep his hands off me, he'd lured me up here and take advantage of me?"

"Well, no, but-"

"But what?" she challenged. "Am I too stupid to make my own choices?"

Matt looked at the floor, "No, but-"

"But what?" she repeated.

"What do I tell Mom and Dad?"

"Tell 'em I'm an adult? How about you tell 'em I can find my own mate? Or, tell 'em they don't need to arrange a marriage for me, no matter how old I get? Better yet, here's a shocking concept, don't tell them anything."

Steve growled.

JV ignored it and kept talking, "I don't even want to know how you found me."

"It wasn't that hard. I called a friend and had him trace you're cell." Matt turned to Steve, "How did you convince her to come to your tiny corner of the planet?"

"Why do you assume he convinced me to come up here?" JV didn't give Steve a chance to speak. "Why couldn't I have found him and come on my own?"

"You had no way to find him," Matt scoffed.

"Hello?" JV was exasperated, "I'm a tech geek and web designer. Do you really think it was difficult for me to look him up on line and figure out where he's been all this time?"

Matt looked confused, "Why would you do that?"

" I wanted to know." JV turned and went back into the kitchen, returning to dinner preparations.

Chapter 19

Matt turned to Steve, "You didn't invite her up here?"

"I had no clue she was coming. It shocked the shit out of me when she showed up out of the blue."

"Why didn't you send her home?"

Steve looked at Matt, incredulous. "When was the last time you tried to make your sister do anything?"

"A while ago, I haven't been around her very much in a few years," Matt rolled his eyes. "How hard can it be?"

Steve stepped back, motioning with one hand for Matt to go ahead of him, "See for yourself."

Matt narrowed his eyes. "Don't think for a moment that I don't know you're sleeping with her, I can smell her on you. I knew the instant you opened the door."

Steve shrugged. He knew he wouldn't be able to convince Matt there had been nothing more than a few kisses between them, or that all they'd done was sleep on the same couch. "Whatever, you try telling her what to do, see if that gets you anywhere," he headed back to the kitchen, leaving Matt standing alone in the front room.

***

In the kitchen, Steve washed his hands before going back to the table and resumed what he'd been doing.

"Is Jade's brother staying for dinner?" Rebecca asked.

"I don't know," Steve said.

"Did you invite him?" Rebecca wanted to know.

Steve knew she'd probably heard every word they'd both said. Asking him was her way of telling him he should, "I didn't invite him here, why should I invite him to dinner?"

"Steve Romero, I thought you had better manners." She looked at him with her hands on her hips.

"My mother tried to teach me better, but I've got this strange habit of treating others like they treat me. Besides, he hit me," he said sullenly.

"You deserved it, you're sleeping with my baby sister," Matt said from the arched entrance to the kitchen.

Jade glared, "Whom I sleep with, or don't, is none of your business, Matt."

"I disagree," he stepped into the room so he could see her better.

"If you're just here to cause problems, you can leave. Now." Jade didn't bother with niceties.

"I don't know," Matt said, watching them closely.

"Would you like to join us for Thanksgiving dinner?" Rebecca invited, seeing that no one else was going to.

Matt looked at the Karyn for the first time since he arrived, "I don't know, Ma'am. I wouldn't want to intrude more than I already have."

"Not at all, we always host a big dinner for anyone without anywhere to go. One more is no big deal."

"Then I'd love to."

"Where are you staying?" she asked.

"I don't know, I hadn't planned on staying," he looked at Jade. "I was just going to gather my sister and take her home."

"Then you can stay here on the ranch, I'd offer you the spare bedroom, but my husband, Nick, and Steve would have a fit and JV's using it. Steve has an extra bedroom, or you can stay in the bunkhouse with the hands. Be careful though, some of them are human and don't know about shifters."

Matt scowled, "Why does Steve get a say in who stays in your home?"

Rebecca smiled at him, a little confused, "Because he's our Shaku. He's in charge of making sure that I'm safe when Nick's not around."

Matt looked back to Steve, realization dawning. "That explains why you answered the door."

Steve nodded and finished peeling the potato in his hand, then dropped it into the bowl with the others. He picked up the bowl of peeled potatoes and carried them to the sink. After turning on the water to run over them, he turned to look at Matt again, "It does. Now, you think you can behave this afternoon, and not upset Jade or Rebecca, or do I need to run you off?"

Matt looked back and forth between Steve and Jade for a moment, obviously thinking about something, "I'll behave. Staying will give me a chance to watch the two of you. See if there's something between you I can live with, or if the two of you are jerking me around for the hell of it."

Jade peeled the last of her potatoes, dumped her bowl of skins into the one Steve had used, then added the last potato to the bowl in the sink. Picking up a towel, she dried her hands as she went over to her brother. Before he had a chance to figure out what she was up to, she kicked him hard in the shins.

"Hey! What the hell was that for?"

"For being an ass," she turned away. "Watch it or I'll do it again." She ignored him as she pulled out a large pot and started cutting potatoes and dropping them in the pot.

After getting the potatoes on to cook, she dried her hands again and went to stand in front of Steve.

"Let me see."

Steve pulled a chair close and sat so she could look at his lip, but his eyes never left the other man.

"It's not too bad," she placed her fingers lightly on his lip and closed her eyes.

The sting faded, replaced by heat and a slight tingle.

A moment later, she opened her eyes again, "How's that?"

He stretched and moved it, testing the lip, "Much better, thank you." He gave her a quick but thorough kiss to prove it.

Jade shot Matt an angry look as she turned and went back to work.

Chapter 20

Matt shuffled out of the bedroom the next morning, into the bathroom, glad Steve had relented and let him stay at his place instead of the bunkhouse. It wasn't until he came out and headed for the kitchen, in search of coffee that he noticed the pair asleep on the sofa. He stopped and blinked. Technically, only Steve was on the sofa, JV was curled on top of him, snoring softly.

Matt stood, staring at the couple. Steve looked more relaxed than he'd seen him in years. Matt had been aware for some time that since Steve had gotten out of the Marines, he'd been on edge, as though he was always waiting for an attack. Haunted was the only way he could describe it. Now, the troubled look was gone, he looked like the guy he'd gone to school with.

Matt watched the two of them sleep for several moments. Noting the way Steve held her, protecting her even in his sleep. He took a deep breath and let it out in a silent rush before continuing past the sofa into the kitchen. Opening cabinets until he found the canister of coffee, he filled the percolator and put it on the stove. On his way back through the living room he saw that Steve was awake. The man on the couch met his look and placed a single finger against his lips, letting Matt know his sister was still sleeping, as if the quiet noise still coming from her wasn't enough.

Matt nodded, looked at the pair for another long moment then started for his room. After just a few steps he stopped, turned on his heal and went quietly out the front door. On the porch, he quickly shed his clothes, dropping them on a porch chair, and shifted. Once in his cougar form, he bounded off the porch and into the nearby trees.

***

Later, after returning from his run to find the small house empty, Matt showered and dressed before going back to the kitchen for some of the coffee he'd made earlier. He poured a cup and focused his attention out the window over the sink, sipping the steaming liquid and thinking.

He'd come here to take his sister home. To protect her from a man he believed was too hard for her tender heart. He'd been sure it was the right thing, but after what he'd seen this morning he was having second thoughts.

He'd been sure they were too different. Growing up, Steve had been kind of wild, but so had Matt. They'd partied and run around together throughout high school. The Steve he'd known then would have been a better match for his sister than the dark, angry version that had returned after his time with the military. Matt didn't know what had happened to his friend while he'd been gone, only that he'd spent time overseas. He'd returned a different person than the happy, teasing young man who'd left.

Come to think of it, JV wasn't the person she'd been then either. It had been years since he'd lived in the same house with her. She'd barely been a teenager the last time he'd spent more than a few days with her, usually when home visiting. She'd been a vivacious, outgoing kid. Somewhere along the line, something had happened to change that. Matt didn't know exactly when, only that it had been sometime while she was in college. Since then, she'd been reserved and far more careful than before. The JV he'd known would never have carried a pistol, much less have been able to point it at anyone.

Matt drained the last swallow from his cup and refilled it. He needed to spend more time with his sister and this was the perfect opportunity. The night before, the clan leaders had invited him to stay for the weekend with them; it was a good excuse not to have to go home to his empty apartment. It was a little late now to spend the holiday with their folks. Besides, they would only ask if he was seeing anyone and he wasn't ready to face that. It had been two years since he'd lost Connie and while they hadn't been mated, he'd loved her. He still couldn't think about another woman. He frowned. Perhaps that was what had happened to Steve, maybe he'd lost a woman, maybe even a potential mate.

Matt shook himself from his dark thoughts. He took his cup with him as he went up to the main house to see what everyone was up to.

Chapter 21

JV had been annoyed when Rebecca invited her brother to stay for the weekend. She'd been surprised when Steve decided to let her brother stay at his place. It meant she'd started the night in her own bed in the house for the first time in over a week. As before, she'd dozed restless for an hour or so before waking confused and panicked, knowing she wouldn't be able to sleep. She'd gotten up and tip-toed out to the porch. She hadn't been there five minutes before the crunch of snow and Steve's growl made her turn in his direction.

"Damn it. I knew it," he'd snagged her off her feet and marched back to his house. "I can't leave you on your own for one night." He'd carried her into the house and put her on her feet. Without a word he'd kicked off his boots and removed both their coats. He led her to the sofa, where he settled on his back then pulled her to lay on top of him before flipping the quilt off the back over them both. She'd lain there, warm and secure, and in no time she'd fallen asleep.

This morning, she'd woken to the sound of the front door closing. She'd been confused for a moment, remembering going to bed alone, then waking to find Steve still lying beneath her. Then she'd remembered Matt and knew he had to have seen her there with Steve, sound asleep. She thought about it for a few seconds then decided she didn't care. She'd let his presence affect her behavior. She'd let it stop her from going home with Steve in the first place, but it would be the last time. From now on, she would pretend he wasn't there and life would go on for the rest of his visit.

Steve had taken her back up to the main house before heading to the barn to help with the animals. She'd watched until he'd disappeared around the corner then went inside.

Stepping out of the shower, she toweled the water from her skin and rubbed it from her hair on autopilot. After dressing, she opened the door and a puff of hot air and steam rushed ahead of her. She was still lost in thought as she gathered her things and headed for her room.

She'd been here nearly two weeks and she'd yet to spend a full night in the bed. It would be more convenient to move her things to Steve's but it felt wrong without him asking her to. Besides, as easy as it might make some things, it would complicate others. As awkward as it sometimes was, it was better to keep things the way they were. She straightened things up then went to help Rebecca with breakfast.

She found the kitchen empty, but poured herself a cup of coffee. She leaned against the counter and took several sips. Closing her eyes, she waited for the caffeine to hit her system. It did more to wake her up than the icy cold outside or the warm shower had done. When the cup was half empty, she topped it off and went looking for the Karhyn. When JV came in, Nick had told her she wasn't up yet, but it was nearly 8:00 now and really late for her not to be up. JV was getting worried.

After looking through the entire house, she ended up at the clan leader's bedroom door. Knocking softly, she called out, "Rebecca, are you up?"

"I'm awake, come on in."

She pushed the door open and found Rebecca sitting on the edge of the bed, her face white.

"Are you all right?" she rushed to the Karhyn's side, afraid her friend was hurt.

"I'm fine," Rebecca said, one hand against her belly, "just sick to my stomach."

"Is it a bug? Something you ate?" JV hated to see her new friend feeling bad. "Is there anything I can do for you?"

Rebecca shook her head, "No, it'll pass. I could use a couple of saltines, though, if you know where they are."

"I do. I saw 'em yesterday, above the microwave. I'll be right back." She rushed into the kitchen and came back with a tube of the crackers.

"Thank you." Rebecca took the package. She pulled out a single cracker, set the package on the nightstand and took a small bite.

"Isn't Bobby on duty? Where is he? I'll have him get Nick."

"No, don't. I'll be fine," Rebecca stopped JV with a hand on her arm.

She turned back and looked at the other woman again, "Are you sure?"

Rebecca clamped her lips together and nodded, "Just give it a little while. It'll pass."

Skeptical, JV sat on her heels and looked her friend's face, "Is there anything else I can get? Anything I can do?"

"No, just give me a bit. I'll be fine, I promise."

JV wasn't so certain, but she couldn't think of an argument that would convince Rebecca to let her get Nick.

Rebecca ate three more crackers with small bites and her color improved. Nearly an hour after JV knocked on the bedroom door, Rebecca stood, only looking slightly ill.

"I think the worst is over," she said. "Thanks for the crackers, I think I'll keep these here for a while." She closed the tube and left them on her nightstand. "What do you want to do for breakfast?"

"Are you sure?" JV was worried. "Will your stomach handle it?"

Rebecca smiled, "I'm sure. I only get sick if I go too long without eating. When I first get up is the worst, since I haven't eaten all night."

JV frowned, confused, "All right."

"What do you want to eat?"

"We had some mashed potatoes left over yesterday, how about I make you potato pancakes?" she offered.

"I've never had those." Rebecca said with a small frown.

"All the more reason to let me make them."

"All right, I'm in." She laughed. "Why don't you go get started, I'll get dressed and be right there."

"You sure you're all right?" JV asked.

"I'm sure. I'm fine."

JV looked at her friend for a long moment before relenting and heading for the kitchen.

***

JV stood at the kitchen sink, washing the dishes from breakfast when a soft thump outside drew her attention. She looked up and out the window in front of her, spotting the small brown squirrel running across the snow.

She watched as the curious animal raced from the tree line to the porch and back again. She couldn't figure out what he was up to. There wasn't anything on the porch that would interest him, at least not that she remembered. She couldn't help but grin as he made several more trips dropping something on one then racing back to pick it up, making her laugh out loud at his silly antics before he disappeared up one of the trees.

She still wore a silly grin when Steve rose from under the window. His appearance reminded her there was a bench there. Realizing how strange she must look, her smile quickly faded.

Chapter 22

Steve sat on the bench under the kitchen window, as he did almost every afternoon, a handful of acorns in one hand. He dropped them one at a time in his right hand and sat very still. He waited while the squirrel he'd been taming for the last several weeks came up and took the seed. As the squirrel scampered away with his prize Steve dropped another acorn into his hand and waited.

He'd been sitting there about fifteen minutes when, half way across the yard, the animal dropped his nut. He scurried back to get it and Steve heard a soft tinkling laugh through the window above him. He knew it had to be Jade, though it wasn't the same laugh she'd had as a child. She and Rebecca were the only ones in the house and he knew Rebecca's laugh. That wasn't it. The sound stirred something deep inside he hadn't been aware still existed. He resisted the urge to stand and look at her, instead, he forced himself to stay where he was and finish feeding the animal.

It wasn't until the little guy took the last acorn and skittered his furry butt home that Steve stood and turned. He met Jade's gaze, the happy smile she wore made his heart skip a beat and his jeans tighten. As she sobered and the smile faded, he realized he wanted to see it again; more so, he wanted to be the one to put it back.

He gave her what he hoped was a pleasant smile and went inside to warm up. He'd been out in the cold long enough, his nose had gone numb.

He pulled off his jacket and scarf, and hung them both on the hooks beside the door. After kicking off his snow-caked boots he went into the kitchen for a cup of coffee.

"Were you feeding him?" Jade asked.

"Mm hm," Steve answered as he cupped both hands around his mug, letting the warmth seep into them.

"Are all the animals around here so tame?" Jade's eyes were wide.

"No, I've been working on him a while to get that. I started out leaving a small pile on the edge of the porch while I sat there. He had to brave getting close to get the treat. Each day I moved it a little closer, until I could hold 'em and he'd snatch 'em out of my hands. Eventually, I won't have to be so still, he'll just come take them."

"That's amazing."

"It just takes patience."

"But why, most people wouldn't bother."

"It amuses me." He shrugged. "It started out as something to do while I kept close to the house one afternoon."

"But it wasn't just once, you keep doing it. You've put a lot of time into taming that squirrel."

He shrugged again, and looked away not really knowing what to say.

"You hungry?"

"You offering to cook for me?"

"I thought something hot might help warm you up."

"It would. What do you have in mind?"

"I don't know there's a lot of left-overs from yesterday in the fridge, what do you want?"

"What would be nice to warm people up in this weather would be some turkey soup. Have you ever made it?"

She scowled, "No, but I'm willing to learn."

He stood, "I'll show you. Get out the turkey and the veggie tray from yesterday. We'll start there." He pulled the biggest pot Rebecca had from under the kitchen island. "First we bone out the turkey. Make two plates of meat, one dark, one light and drop the bones in the pot."

"Are you sure Rebecca won't mind us using things up like this? What if she has plans for something else?"

"She's been the one to make it the last couple of years. We're just saving her some work." He glanced around. "Where is she?"

"She wasn't feeling well, so she went to lie down for a while."

"Let me go check on her, then I'll help with this." He left her to get started and headed down the short hall to the Khan and Karhyn's bedroom. Knocking on the open door, he peeked inside, "Are you all right?"

She rolled over and looked at him, "I'm fine, my stomach's bothering me a little, that's all." She laid one hand low on her abdomen.

"You're sure it's nothing to be concerned about? Want me to call Nick?"

She shook her head, "It's nothing to worry about. Don't bother him."

"You're sure?"

"I am."

"Jade and I are putting together turkey soup; do you want me to check in when it's done? See if you want some?"

"If I'm not feeling better by then, that would be great."

"All right, call if you need anything."

"That's what JV said." She smiled, "I will."

He watched her a moment longer then went back to the kitchen.

Nick came in and looked around the kitchen. Steve and Jade sat playing cards while they waited for the broth to cook.

"Where's Rebecca?"

"In the bedroom. She's not feeling well." Steve said as he dealt another hand of gin.

"What? Why didn't you call me?" His eyes widened and he headed for the back of the house.

"She said not to bother you, she was all right," Steve called after him.

Nick didn't say anything as he disappeared down the hall.

"Maybe we should have called him," Jade said, looking after Nick instead of at her cards.

"It'll be fine." Steve suspected he knew what was wrong with Rebecca's stomach, but he wasn't going to say anything, not yet.

Jade looked at her cards and started rearranging them, "How much longer do you think the soup will take?"

"Not long now, we're just waiting for the carrots to cook, then we'll divide it up and add noodles to what we'll eat today."

She frowned, "Why not add the noodles first?"

"They don't store well, as the soup freezes and thaws the noodles absorb all the extra water and then they're just mush. It works better to wait to add them."

She nodded her agreement then she picked up the top card from the discard pile and put down one out of her hand.

They kept playing until Nick returned, Rebecca with him.

"How much longer until that soup's ready?" Rebecca asked, rubbing one hand over her belly.

Steve turned to Rebecca, "Give it another ten minutes and you can have some."

"That sounds great," Rebecca said, turning back to the table. "What are you playing?"

"Gin," Jade said. "It's too cold to go outside and I didn't want to leave you, in case you needed something. Plus, this way we could keep an eye on the soup. I hope you don't mind, Steve told me where to find the cards."

Rebecca smiled, "Not at all. I told you to make yourself at home. I just thought we all could play."

Steve looked at Jade and shrugged, letting her know he didn't care, it was up to her.

"Sure," she said, "or we can play something else, it's up to you." She frowned, "Where's Matt?" She turned to Nick, "I thought he was with you, helping feed."

"He was, but before we headed back to the house he said he had something he had to do in town and he left."

She blinked, "I didn't hear a car."

"I wasn't sure what the road's like, so I sent him in one of the ranch trucks. He left from the barn and took the other road."

Jade went back to the table and started gathering cards. "Do we want to play gin, or something else?"

"Gin or Rummy is good with me, then when Matt gets back we can just deal him in, if he wants to play. If we're playing pinochle it's not that simple," Rebecca said.

Steve moved to the cabinet, "Who's gonna want soup?" He pulled out enough bowls for everyone and took them to the stove, stirring the pot while he was there. "Go ahead and deal, I'll take care of this and we can play while we eat."

They joked and laughed until they heard a vehicle pull into the yard. Thinking it was Matt, they continued until someone knocked on the door. When Steve went to the door, he was happy to discover it was Walt, the local UPS driver. "Thanks," Steve said, "Be careful, it's icy out there."

"Will do," Walt replied, "Have a good weekend."

"You too." Steve glanced at the address on the box and knew what was inside. He took it with him into the kitchen. He kept his face carefully blank as he handed the box to Jade, "It's for you."

She frowned, "For me?"

"It's got your name on it."

Her frown deepened, "I didn't order anything. How can it be for me?"

"Why don't you open it and find out," Steve suggested.

She frowned, then cut open the top of the box. Pulling out the puffy coat inside, she looked at it a moment, then at the people around her. "A coat? I know I needed one but I didn't order it. Did you?" she looked at Rebecca.

"Not me," the other woman said, "but it matches your eyes perfectly."

"I didn't do it," Nick said. He looked like she shouldn't need to ask.

She turned back to Steve, confusion filling her eyes, "Did you?"

"You needed a coat," he shrugged. "I was worried about you wandering around in the snow without one."

"That's sweet," she put it back in the box and set it aside as she stood. "Thank you," she stretched up and kissed him on the cheek.

He looked down into her smiling face. The smile sent a sense of peace through him. The knowledge he had put it there stirred him. "You're welcome," he bent and laid a light kiss against her mouth. Her taste distracted him. He coaxed her mouth open and drew her closer against him.

The sound of Nick clearing his throat drew Steve back to his senses. He broke away and gently set Jade back on her feet. "Come on, let's play." He steered her toward her seat and went back to his. "Rummy?" he asked, picking up the deck.

"That's what we settled on," Rebecca said, a spoon of soup halfway to her mouth.

He started dealing.

They were well into the second game when they heard another truck pull into the yard. Continuing to play they waited to see who would come in. Two brief knocks sounded then the door opened.

"Hello?" Matt's voice called. "Anyone in here?"

"We're in the kitchen Matt, come on back," Nick said.

Matt appeared in the doorway, "What are you guys up to?"

"Playing rummy, wanna join in?" Steve offered.

"Maybe in a bit. I have some things I need to take to my room first; I just wanted to check in before I went out there."

"There's some turkey soup on the stove, too, if you're interested," Rebecca said.

"I'd like some, but after I finish. I'll be back in a bit."

Steve didn't bother looking up from his cards. He picked up half the discard pile and started making plays. "We'll be here."

They continued to play and Steve was in the lead by more than a hundred points when Matt came back. He came into the kitchen, twitching as a shiver ran through him.

"I'm ready for some of that soup now, if it's still hot," he said.

"If it's not, I'll heat it up," Jade went to the stove, and pressed one hand against the side of the pot, "it's warm, it'll only take a few minutes." After turning on the burner she pulled out a bowl, "Anyone else want some?"

"I'll have some," Rebecca said.

"No, thanks," said Nick.

"I'm good," was Steve's reply.

She grabbed another, left the pair of bowls beside the stove, and went back to the table. "I think Steve's about won this game, want us to deal you in for the next one?" she asked Matt as she gathered up glasses and took them to the island to be refilled.

"Sure, if no one minds," he said.

"The more the merrier," Rebecca smiled, happy.

"There's another chair in the mud room," Steve told him, scooting his chair toward Jade's to make room for him to add a seat.

While Jade filled drinks and served soup, he got the chair and put it in the opening between Steve and Nick. Jade set one bowl of soup in front of him, then moved around to give Rebecca the other before going back to her own seat.

"Who deals first?" she asked.

"I will." Steve took the deck and quickly shuffled it several times before passing them out, one by one.

"What did you think of operations, Matt?" Steve asked after the last card was dealt and the top card had been turned to start the discard pile.

"Cold," he said between bites. "I don't know how you guys do it."

"We like the freedom," Nick put in. "I spent a couple years in Phoenix, like to drove me crazy. I much prefer rural life."

"Living in a city is a challenge for us," Matt admitted, "but it has advantages."

"I've spent nearly ten years in large communities, first at school, then in Austin," Jade said. "I'm pretty new here, but so far I like it. I love being able to step out the door and shift. I missed being able to shift as often as I wanted. I was terrified if I shifted in my apartment someone would see or hear me. I had to drive for more than an hour to find somewhere I felt safe running."

"Didn't the local clan have somewhere you could shift?" Nick asked.

"They probably did, but I didn't have much to do with them. They were friendly enough and they invited me to join, but I wasn't interested. I wanted to be left alone and, for the most part, they let me have my way."

Nick looked at her and Steve knew he was shocked the clan leader in Austin had let her live on her own, without at least checking in with her regularly. It wasn't something he would allow, but then, life around here was lot different from in a city, any city. The clan had a few single women who lived alone, he had no problem with that, but he made sure they were checked on regularly. It wasn't that he worried they would do anything, more to make sure they were safe and didn't need anything. It was just how he was.

"What if you needed something?" Steve asked.

"What could I need that I couldn't get myself?" she countered.

"Medical help, the touch of another shifter," he suggested.

"I didn't have much need for medical care. When I did, I managed on my own. As for touching another Kitsune, I've avoided touching people, anyone, for years."

Steve's brow furrowed as he frowned, this was important. "Why?" He hoped she would answer.

"Because the touch of any man not related to me, hurts."

Steve's scowled deepened.

Matt frowned, "What? How long has this been going on?"

"Years."

"How many years, Jade?" Steve asked, trying to keep his voice calm. He didn't want her to hear how badly he needed to know.

She was quiet a moment and Steve wasn't sure if she would answer, but finally in a soft voice she spoke. "Almost six."

"You've avoided touching people for almost six years because it hurts?" Rebecca asked, clearly astonished. "Hurts how?"

Jade looked down at her cards, then at her lap, as if avoiding looking at anyone, "It makes my skin burn."

"You shook my hand when you first got to town," Nick said, "I smelled your pain, but I didn't think I was the one causing it."

"Sometimes I just have to deal with it. I've learned not to let it show."

"You touch me all the time." Steve looked at her. He knew his confusion was clear on his face.

"You don't hurt me," she met his look.

"That's why you're determined to see if we can make it work." New understanding dawned across his face.

"That's part of it." She looked down again.

Steve reached out and lifted her chin with one finger. "Don't look away from me. I like your spirit. I love that you stand up to me and not let me tell you what to do simply because I'm the Shaku."

"Just because you're in charge of security around here is no reason for you to boss me around," she shot back, some of the spark returning to her eyes.

"I'm curious," Rebecca interrupted, "have you let anyone but Steve touch you since you got here? Since you started spending time with him?"

Jade looked at her a moment, as if surprised by the idea, "I don't think so. It's become a habit to avoid being touched. It usually takes conscious effort to let it happen."

"I have a theory, but you'd have to let Nick touch you to test it. Do you mind?"

"I don't think so," Steve protested, not giving her a chance to answer.

"Why not?" Jade looked at him, her eyes wide.

"You just said it hurts when someone touches you. You're not gonna to do it on purpose."

Jade rolled her eyes, "It's not that bad. Besides, I'd like to see if anything's changed and what her theory is." She reached one arm across the table in front of her friend. "Go for it, sir."

"What did I tell you about that sir crap?" Nick said, his voice stern as he stretched his arm out and laid his hand on hers for a few seconds, then pulled back. "Well?"

"It hurt, but not like before," she drew her arm back, her brow creased with confusion. "It's not as strong as it was." She turned to Rebecca, "What's your theory?"

"I think it may be some kind of severe skin hunger, triggered by a traumatic event. If you think back, I'll bet it started after something happened, I won't ask what it was. But it's gotten worse the longer it's gone on. Am I right?"

Jade looked at the table again, then her gaze flicked to Matt for a second before back to Rebecca, "About something happening and this starting afterward, yes, but that's all I'm gonna say."

"I'm not asking you to tell us your secrets, I'm just trying to help you. I think the more you're around Steve, or possibly any potential mate, the more contact you have with him, the better it will get, but honestly? I don't think it will completely fade until after you've sealed a mating."

Jade frowned, "You really think so? Have you seen something like this

97

before?"

"Not exactly like it, but I saw something similar in my old Chanat. They didn't care about mating or potential mates. It was common for parents to arrange marriages for their own benefit. It's why I left."

Jade looked like she wanted to ask something but stopped herself. She glanced around the table, "Enough about me, let's play?"

"In a minute," Matt said, speaking for the first time since early in the discussion. "You said this has been going on for six years, do Mom and Dad know?"

"No. It's my problem and I didn't want to trouble them. There's no need for you to tell them either." She shot him a menacing look and Steve had no doubt that if he did, she'd find him and make him pay.

He held both hands up in front of himself, "Okay, okay, I was just asking."

"Now you know," she turned her attention back to the cards in front of her, carefully pretending that being the topic of conversation hadn't bothered her.

Chapter 24

It was still early in the evening, barely 8:30, when Rebecca pled exhaustion and headed to bed. Nick went to help and check on her. Matt said he had some messages he needed to answer and he went out to the cabin.

"Go get your clothes and come on out with me," Steve said once they were alone.

She hesitated. "I don't know. I don't want Matt to hit you again."

"I don't think it'll be an issue. He saw us on the couch this morning," Steve said pulling her into his arms. "He knows where you spent the night, so why not start out there instead of making the trip at 2:00am?"

She thought about it a moment. "All right, let me get clean clothes and I'll go with you."

She fetched her things, pulled on her new jacket and went out with him.

***

At the smaller home, they found Matt in the living room, a notebook computer on his lap. JV was surprised to find the house warm and comfortable.

"Thanks for adding wood to the stove, Matt. I was afraid it was gonna be chilly in here," Steve said, taking off his coat and gloves.

"No problem." Matt looked at them, his eyes flickering to the bundle of clothes in JV's arms. He closed the computer, put it in the bag beside his chair then watched as they moved to sit on the sofa.

JV could tell he was waiting to say something.

"Spill it," Steve said, dropping his arm around JV's shoulders and pulling her against him. Apparently, he saw it too, she thought.

Matt took a deep breath and let it out slowly. "I'm willing to consider that I could have been wrong."

JV looked at Steve but his focus was on her brother. His arm tightened around her, letting her know he wasn't unaware of her attention.

"And?" Steve prompted.

"I'm not going to apologize for hitting you, if that's what you're after. You'd do the same if it was your sister."

Steve stiffened slightly beside her and JV knew he was biting his tongue.

Matt continued without noticing. "I'm still not happy with the age difference, but it's not my life. After what I've learned over the last couple days, I won't fight it." He looked at Steve and spoke directly to him. "As long as she's happy, I have no issue with you. You no longer have an excuse to stay hidden away here. I'd start expecting family visits if I were you."

Steve looked at him, silent.

"With that," Matt pushed himself out of the chair, "I think I'll go to bed." He grabbed the computer bag and disappeared into his room, closing the door behind him.

"You about ready for bed?" Steve asked once Matt's door clicked shut.

"I am. What do you want to sleep to tonight?"

"I thought we might try something different."

"What?" she blinked, surprised.

He took a breath and let it out in a rush. "I sleep better with you, better than I have for years. But honestly?" He hesitated, as though nervous. "This sofa isn't the most comfortable thing I've slept on, and the only way we both fit is one on top of the other."

JV nodded, following him so far.

"I'd like to sleep on the bed, see if we sleep better there."

"I am alright with that," she said. "But what about Matt? Will he pick another fight if we do?"

"After the way he found us this morning, I don't think so. Between that and what he just said, I'd say it's unlikely."

"We'll just sleep?" She hesitated.

"I'll behave myself. I just want to get some sleep," he assured her. "No pressure. We can sleep here if you'd rather, or I can take you back to the house."

JV's mind spun. This was huge. He wanted her to go to bed with him. Granted, he wasn't offering to be her mate, but it was a start.

"I'll get my boots." Steve assumed from her silence that he'd made her

100

uncomfortable.

"No." She put a hand on his arm. "I haven't slept so well in years either. I'd love to sleep in your bed."

"You're sure? I don't wanna push you into something you don't wanna do."

"I'm sure," she said with a small smile. "I trust you, Steve, or I wouldn't keep falling asleep against you."

"I'm glad," he nodded. "Come on." He led her into the bedroom carrying the quilt they'd been using along with them. He'd been leaving it folded over the back of the recliner. "How do you normally sleep?"

"Fitfully."

He looked at her, one brow lifted, and waited.

"On my stomach, my left side, or a combination of both. Why?"

"So I know where to sleep."

She blinked twice and shook her head. "Whatever. Where do you want me?"

Steve flipped the quilt from his arms and spread it over the bed before pulling back one corner. "Here."

JV looked down at her sweats and shrugged. She didn't have anything else with her except what she'd brought for the next day. She climbed in and pulled the covers up under her arms.

Steve went to the attached bathroom, turned on the light, pulled the door close, before shutting off the bedroom light. There was only a sliver of light left and a pale glow in the room. "Can you sleep with that?" he asked.

"Yeah, no problem."

He nodded once and went around the other side of the bed. He peeled off his sweatshirt, leaving him in only a thin tee shirt and sweatpants. Sliding into the other side of the bed he lay on his back. "Come over here."

JV slid across the king sized bed until she came up against him. "Where do you want me?"

He lifted one arm. "Here."

She curled against his side, resting her head on his shoulder, "Like this?"

Steve wrapped his arm around her. "Perfect."

JV closed her eyes and let his scent envelope her. The comforting sensation of him holding her against him quickly lulled her to sleep.

Chapter 25

Steve woke early the next morning, surprised at how good he felt. He lay still a moment, enjoying the feel of Jade lying in his arms, so trusting, as she let out a soft snore with each breath. He hated having to wake her but he needed to get up, to go take care of the animals. He glanced at her sleeping face again and realized that since she wasn't on top of him, he could leave her sleeping and come back to her later.

He slipped out from under her, careful not to wake her. Quietly gathering his clothes, he went into the living room to dress. Matt was sitting on the sofa. Placing one finger against his lips he beckoned the other man to follow him and headed for the kitchen.

"I take it JV didn't go back to the other house last night?" Matt asked once they reached the kitchen, careful to keep his voice low.

"No. She's asleep in my bed." Steve watched his old friend's reaction

Matt took a deep breath and let it out in a rush. "I really ought to be pissed, but I'm not. Even before finding out that it hurts her to touch people, I knew I was wrong. She's been, I don't know… unsettled, I guess is the word, for a long time. Even I could see it, and I haven't seen her much since you and I got out of school. Something happened to her. I don't know what. Hell, I don't even know when, but it changed something inside her. She doesn't laugh anymore." Matt met Steve's eyes. "Hell, I've seen her smile more in three days than in the last five years. I think being here with these people could be part of it, but I think the biggest part is you."

"I don't know-" Steve started to protest.

"You didn't see her after you left." Matt held both hands in front of him. "I'm not blaming you, it was the right thing at the time. She was too young then, but that's not true anymore. She's different with you." Matt's eyes moved in the direction of the bedroom where his sister slept.

Steve didn't know what to say. He'd never expected her family, or his for that matter, to approve of a relationship between them. What Matt said gave him hope. Maybe, just maybe, if things worked out between them, he could go home and see his family. He'd never have admitted it, but he missed them.

"Just take care of her," Matt said before turning to look out the window over the sink.

"I'll do my best," Steve said the only thing he could. "Let me get dressed and feed the animals, Bobby's on house duty this morning. You want to go with me or stay here?"

"I'll come, I'll be ready when you are."

Steve went into the bathroom near the guest room to change. Once dressed, he wrote a quick note, slipped into the bedroom and left it on his pillow. He braced himself for the cold and headed for the barn, wishing he were still snug in the warm bed with her in his arms.

Chapter 26

That evening, after Matt had headed home, JV could see how tired Rebecca was. *She's exhausted,* she sent to Steve telepathically. *We don't need to stay and keep her up.* They went to his cabin early, curled up on the sofa and watched a movie to pass the time.

"Why don't you move your things down here?" Steve asked as the music rose and the final credits rolled up the screen. "You spend every night here anyway. Why keep making the trip back and forth every time you need something?"

The idea both thrilled and terrified her. She was happy he thought things were going well enough that he wanted her in his home every night, even if all they did was sleep. She hoped it would become more, but she'd have to come clean first. That part terrified her. She had to tell him what had happened. What had triggered her intense skin hunger. She didn't know if she could. She'd never told anyone.

"You don't have to," Steve said, seeing her hesitation. "It was just an idea."

She looked at him a moment. "It's not that I don't want to. I'm thrilled you asked." She paused, looking for the right words. "It's me. There's something I've got to tell you before we can go much further, but I don't know if I can. Not yet."

He looked at her for a long minute, concern creasing his forehead. "We can move at your pace. Move what you're comfortable with when you're ready to move it, just know that I want you here."

She smiled up at him. "I'll do that. Thank you." She stretched up and gave him a kiss on the cheek before settling down beside him. "Do you want to watch another one? Or do something else?"

He glanced at the clock on the wall. 9:21. Still too early for bed, but he didn't want to stay up for another movie. "How about we play some fact poker."

"Fact poker?" She frowned.

He smiled. "It's like strip poker, only instead of winning pieces of clothing, you win facts about your opponent. Stuff we don't already know."

She was quiet a moment, considering. "Loser gets to choose the fact? You can't make me tell you something I'm not ready to share?"

"Loser gets to pick what they share," he agreed.

"Then I'm in."

"Why don't you refill our drinks while I get the cards?"

They settled onto the sofa, facing each other and started playing,

"Two pair," Steve said, revealing his hand.

"Hah! Full house, I win! Give it up," JV bounced in her seat, eager to find out what he would reveal.

"Hm…" he drew it out for a moment, enjoying her impatience. "After I got out of the Marines and left Tenaha, I wandered around the country for a couple of years. I lived as a loner while I tried to decide what I wanted to do with my life."

"Okay, my deal." She gathered the cards and shuffled, wondering if she could manage to keep winning and not have to tell him anything.

Steve won the next hand. "My turn, what do you have for me?" he asked without the triumphant tone she'd had.

"You know I went to Texas A&M, but did you know I graduated with honors?"

"I didn't. That's a big accomplishment." He picked up their cards, shuffled and started dealing again.

Steve won the third hand and waited quietly for JV to pay her debt.

"Okay," she said. "You know that after school I moved to Austin. While there, I worked a couple of office jobs, while I got my business off the ground. In the three years it took me to do it, I never had any close friends. There were a couple of girls I'd go for drinks with after work once in a while, but after I left the company we lost touch."

"You had no friends in Austin?"

She shook her head. "No. None."

"Then why stay so long?"

She shrugged and dealt again. She was relieved when she flipped her cards and saw three queens. After discarding the four and seven, she gave Steve the three cards he asked for, then took the two she needed. Triumph flashed through her when he turned over his cards, revealing a pair of sixes. She flipped her own hand, revealing her queens and watched him.

"I miss my family," he said. "My parents and grandparents. I've stayed away because I didn't want to run into you and not be able to keep away from you." He looked up from his lap.

Her eyes softened. "I'm sorry I've kept you from your family."

"It wasn't just you," he reassured her. "I mean, yeah, you're why I didn't go home, but there's been nothing to stop them from coming to see me, and yet they haven't. Matt's the only one who's made any effort to see me. He'd never been here before, but every now and then he'll call and we meet somewhere, spend a couple days together. Our relationship's not what it was while we were growing up, but it's *something*." She thought she heard some resentment in his voice as he talked about his family.

She felt bad that she'd kept him from seeing his family and the sorrow in his voice touched her. Reaching out, she took his hand and squeezed it gently, trying to make him feel better. "I'm still sorry."

"Don't be. It's been my choice, not your fault." He held on to her hand a moment then picked up the cards again.

"The good news is, now you can go see 'em. Whether it works out between us or not, you can see your family."

"That's true," he said without commitment.

JV picked up her cards and considered them. They weren't much. She held on to the ace of clubs and king of hearts, then tossed the other three to the discard pile and waited for Steve to deal her new ones eight of spades, five of clubs and the deuce of diamonds. She knew she'd lost this one and she didn't know what she was going to tell him. Glancing up, she saw he was ready and showed him her cards. "Ace high, that's it."

He chuckled. "I thought you had me beat for sure." He flipped his hand over, revealing a pair of two's.

"You're lucky day." She sighed and looked at the cards in her lap, then turned a blank stare toward the television. "Before I left Austin I sold almost everything. What I couldn't let go of, I put in storage. I let my apartment go. Other than to get my things, I have no reason to go back." She couldn't look at him, she wasn't sure she wanted to see his reaction.

He tugged the cards from her hand, stacked them on top of the deck and set it on the table in front of the sofa. Reaching across the space separating them, he tugged her into his arms. "Come here." He turned her so she sat sideways on his lap and pulled her against his chest. Dropping a

106

soft kiss on top of her head, he spoke again. "There's something I should probably tell you," his voice was soft. "As hard as I tried, I couldn't get you out of my mind. I've thought about you every day since I left."

She looked up at him, "For ten years?"

"No, sweetheart. The first time."

Her eyes widened and she stared at him, shocked. "You felt it that long ago?"

"It wasn't the same mating instinct we've got now, but there was something about you, even then, that drew me. I wanted to be near you, to protect you. It may have nothing to do with what we feel now. I don't know." He shook his head.

"Does this mean you're not gonna fight it anymore?"

"Sweetheart, I quit fighting it the first night you fell asleep against me right here. When you moved in your sleep, curled against me, I was lost."

Not knowing how to respond, she placed a soft kiss against his cheek and laid her head against his shoulder. She let his arms around her sooth her.

He sat, holding her for several minutes. "You about ready for bed?"

"I'm ready when you are," she murmured against his neck.

Chapter 27

In the bedroom Steve gave her one of his tee shirts and she went into the attached bathroom and changed. Once they were both ready, they crawled into bed. JV lay on her side with Steve lying behind her. She drifted to sleep feeling safe with his arm holding her against him.

***

Steve woke alone. Jade's spot in his bed empty. He glanced at the clock. 2:13am. Too early for her to have gotten up for the day. He lay there a moment, waiting, thinking maybe she was in the bathroom. He realized the light was out and he couldn't hear movement anywhere in the house. She couldn't have left the house without him hearing it. He got up, pulled on a sweatshirt against the chill, and went looking for her. Room to room, he searched the dark house. After finding nothing on the first round, he started turning on lights. He'd been through the entire cabin twice when he heard a soft shuffle and a sigh. The sound came from the bedroom. He frowned and went back where he'd started, flipped the light on and looked around again. Nothing.

"Jade?"

Nothing.

"Jade?" A little louder this time.

Something moved. No. It couldn't be, could it? He bent down and looked under his bed. "Jade? Are you under there?"

Soft golden eyes opened. She was in her cougar form.

"Jade, baby, it's okay. Come on out, please."

The eyes blinked and she started moving.

He moved back and waited. Once she was out, he ran his hand along the top of her head, petting and soothing her at the same time. "You all right, baby?"

She shuddered then her body blurred as she shifted. Once human, she curled against him, burying her face in his chest as he held her tight.

"You all right?" he repeated.

Shivering, she nodded against him.

"Come on, let's get you warmed up." He stood, lifting her as he went, and set her on top of the bed. "Climb in." He watched as she slid between the sheets, then turned out the light. He went to the bathroom and turned that light on. Nearly closing the door he left them a little light, but not enough to keep them from sleeping. Back on his side of the bed, he pulled the sweatshirt off, slid in and pulled her against him. "Wanna tell me about it?"

"Nightmare," she whispered.

"A nightmare woke you, so you shifted and crawled under the bed?"

She nodded.

He sighed. He wanted to push her for more but he was afraid it would only make her pull away. He rolled towards her and wrapped both arms around her. "Come here, I'll keep you safe."

She snuggled into him. Slowly, she relaxed and fell asleep.

Steve held her in his arms and wondered what she'd been through to give her nightmares that made her hide under the bed.

It was a long time before he fell back to sleep.

Chapter 28

JV woke feeling safe in Steve's arms. Something wasn't right, but she couldn't remember what. Blinking, she tried to make her mind function enough to remember.

It came back to her in a flash. A nightmare. Shifting. Hiding. Steve. He'd coaxed her from under the bed and held her while she fell back to sleep. She usually didn't sleep for hours, sometimes days after a nightmare.

Opening her eyes, she realized it was late morning. She twisted and his arms tightened around her. Looking at his face, she saw he was awake. "You're late. Who's taking care of the animals?"

"It's taken care of," he said after a moment. "After last night, I didn't want you waking up alone." He looked her in the eye. "You all right?"

She heard the concern in his voice, saw it on his face. She buried her face in his chest to get away from it. "I'm fine, it just caught me by surprise. I haven't had one in a long time." She knew her words were muffled, but she couldn't look at him.

"You want to share? It might help."

"Not now, I just want to forget." She started to roll away.

"You sure?"

"I am." She got out of the bed and realized she was naked. She'd lost the tee shirt and panties she'd started the night with when she shifted. It was too late to worry about it now, she'd spent half the night this way. She figured it was too late to worry about now, and headed into the bathroom where she'd left her clothes the night before.

Chapter 29

After breakfast, Steve told Jade to bundle up. He had a surprise. He watched as she dressed as warm as she could, two layers of pants, a tee shirt, and sweater, then told him she was ready to go.

"How many pairs of socks do you have on?" he asked, looking down at her stocking feet. Her boots were beside the door, she'd put them on on the way out.

"One," she frowned, confused.

"Hang on." He disappeared into the bedroom and came back with a pair of bulky socks in one hand. "Here, put these on too. They're wool, they'll keep your feet warmer than plain cotton, even two layers of it."

When she got the extra socks on, she stood. "Now what?"

He looked her over, from head to toe. "You have a hat?"

"Just the one on my jacket."

He shook his head and rolled his eyes. "Come on." At the door he handed her a knit cap. "Here's one of mine, you'll need it."

She pulled on the tight cap then started on her boots. After she'd put on her jacket, she looked at Steve, who handed her a pair of insulated gloves.

"You'll need these too." He adjusted her hat so it covered her ears and rested low over her forehead. He checked her clothes once more. "Okay, let's go." He led her, not onto the porch, but through the house and out the back way.

Not far from the back door sat a snowmobile.

"You ready for a ride?" He turned and watched her reaction.

She grinned, looked at the machine a moment then back at him. "Hell yeah!"

"Put these on." He handed her a pair of goggles out of the pocket of his jacket and pulled a second pair over his own head. He swung one leg over

111

the low machine and turned. "Climb on." He waited for her to settle behind him before starting the engine. *Hold on tight,* he sent to her, after her arms tightened around his middle, he hit the accelerator and they took off. He steered the speeding machine down the lane that led to the barn, but when they reached the meadow, he made a quick turn. Running them parallel to the tree line for a while, he increased their speed until the wind would have made their eyes water if not for the goggles. He twisted the handlebars from side to side, making the snowmobile weave as if on a slalom course and Jade's laughter bubbled around him.

Reaching the trail he'd been headed for, he turned, aiming into the woods once more. It was a path they used often with the four-wheelers and Steve knew it well enough that he didn't hesitate to keep it at full speed, slowing only for the sharpest of turns.

They rode for quite a while, twisting and turning around trees, testing the limits of the machine. Jade alternated between delighted laughter and clinging to Steve's back as they quickly made their way through the woods. The feel of her arms around his waist, and the sound of her laugh, made him hard. He wished he could stop and take her here, but not yet. Out here in the snow and cold was not how he wanted their first time together to be.

He continued along the trail, knowing it would lead them back to the meadow where the main workings of the ranch sat. *Are you warm enough?* he asked.

My face is cold, otherwise I'm fine.

Are you having fun?

This is great, She squeezed his middle, punctuating her words.

We're almost back to the barn. You wanna go back to my place or up to the main house?

The main house would be good. I wanna check on Rebecca. See how she's feeling today. We can do something about lunch there, too.

Sounds good to me. He gunned the engine again and they shot down the trail.

***

On their way through the meadow, he spotted Frank and a couple of other hands near the barn.

Wave, 'cause I'm not stopping. as he lifted one arm to do the same. Her laugher echoed in his ears when she caught sight of the shocked look on a couple of the hands faces. He knew he'd catch hell later over speeding through without stopping but he didn't care. Her laughter was worth it.

***

That night when Steve woke alone again, he didn't bother searching the house. He turned on the lamp beside his bed, climbed out and looked underneath.

"Jade, are you under here?" He didn't reach under into the space or try to grab her. If something had scared her badly enough to make her shift and find a small place to hide, he didn't want to scare her more by suddenly touching her or grabbing her. "Jade," he heard her shuffle. "Come on out, baby."

Her golden eyes opened and he gave her room to crawl out.

"Come on, baby, on the bed." He didn't wait for her to shift, but invited her up in her cat form. "Lie down with me." He waited while she curled up on top of the bed then lay down beside her, wrapping his arm around the mound of her body and waited.

After several minutes she shifted and turned her human body into his, burrowing against him as if he were her only hope at survival. He held on, letting her reassure herself in her own way.

"Talk to me, baby," his voice was soft, he hoped calm. "Tell me what's bothering you."

"Another nightmare."

"I figured as much. What are they about?"

She shook her head.

"Talking about it will help."

"I don't know if I can," her voice was hoarse. "I... I've never told anyone."

Steve swallowed, that wasn't good. Bottling whatever it was inside, was only going to make it hurt more when she finally let it out. He had no doubt he would get it out of her, eventually.

"You can tell me. I'll help you."

"I don't know."

He squeezed her against him. "I do."

"Can you turn the light out first?"

He frowned, "Are you sure? Things often seem worse in the dark."

"I'm sure."

He turned out the lamp, then wrapped both arms around her and ran one hand up and down her back, hoping to keep her calm. "Tell me."

Chapter 30

She was silent for several seconds and when she spoke her voice was barely audible, even to his enhanced hearing.

"It was my senior year, my last class before the Labor Day weekend. I had a night class."

He wanted to ask if she meant when she was at A&M, but he kept silent. He didn't want to stop her, for fear she wouldn't start again. She needed to get it out.

"I was headed out to my car. There were other people around, people I'd seen around and after class, but only one was anywhere near me. He wasn't from my class, but there were a lot of night classes. I had my bag on my shoulder and had just gotten to my car. I was digging my keys out of my pocket when there was a blinding pain through my entire body, then nothing."

Steve's arms tightened around her. He ran his hand up and down the length of her naked back, silently assuring her he had her and she was safe.

"When I woke, I was laying on my back tied down in the back of what looked like a cargo van. I tried to break loose, I tried to shift, but I couldn't." A soft sob escaped.

"I'm right here." He kissed the top of her head and held her tight. "You're safe. It's just a memory."

"I should have been able to break free. It was just rope." She fell silent again for several seconds, gathering courage to continue. "He shoved my skirt up around my waist and ripped off my panties." Her voice changed, it became more distant. It was as if her mind wasn't here in the bed with him, but was there again, with it happening to her all over again. "I fought as hard as I could while I was tied, but he hit me. He slapped me a few times then he used his fists until I stopped fighting. I gave up. I knew he was going to kill me." Her voice had gone flat and lifeless

The dull tone made his heart ache but her words ripped him to shreds. "Shhhh. You're all right. You survived. You're here, with me, safe." Steve couldn't stay quiet any longer. He knew he couldn't let her see how angry he was. Comforting her was the only thing he could do.

"It hurt. It hurt so bad when he pushed himself inside me that I screamed. I couldn't help it." Her voice was starting to clog with tears. "I screamed until my throat was raw while he rammed himself into me over and over. When he was done, he started hitting me again. Over and over, until there was nothing."

Steve felt her tears soaking his chest where her head rested and he was glad she couldn't see the ones running down his face. "You're almost done, baby. Come on, finish it." He knew she needed to get it out, to purge it. It wouldn't be a magic cure, but it would let the pain start healing.

He could tell she hadn't dealt with the attack, not really. Instead, she'd shoved it back and tried to forget about it. It had worked for a while, but now it was surfacing again, bringing the nightmares with it.

"I woke just before dawn. I was lying on the pavement beside my car, my skirt still around my waist. My bag was on the ground beside me and my keys still in my pocket. I got in my car and went home."

"You didn't go to the hospital?"

"I couldn't. I'd already started healing. I would have given us away. Besides," she hesitated, "I couldn't tell anyone."

"What about your Khan?" Steve asked.

She shook her head against him. "No clan there, the school is neutral territory."

He sighed, still holding on to her. "You didn't tell your family, either, because they would have swooped in and taken you home."

She nodded against him.

"What about friends? Anyone?"

She rubbed her face against him. "No one."

His heart ached for her, suffering such a brutal attack all alone. "This happened what? Five? Six years ago?"

"Yeah."

"This is why you don't sleep, isn't it?"

"Yeah."

Something occurred to him. "Have you slept with anyone but me since?"

"No," she whispered. "He did something to me that night, something I don't understand."

"What?"

"I don't know. It was weeks before I could shift again. And you already know about the trouble I've had touching men."

He wondered what her rapist had done to trigger that kind of reaction? Why hadn't she been able to shift for so long? Had it been a psychological reaction?

"You don't hurt me," she whispered. "Being with you has been wonderful." She was quiet for a while. "You've shown me it's not all pain and fear. Some of it is beautiful, too."

Steve started. Somehow he knew, but he had to ask anyway. "Jade, baby, were you a virgin when he raped you?"

She nodded, fresh tears running from her eyes and hitting his skin in scalding drops.

"God, baby." He pulled her close, not knowing what else to do.

"I..." she hiccupped. "I was afraid. Afraid he would come back. Afraid he would kill me like the rest."

"The rest?" he prompted, realizing there was more to the story.

"I was his second, but by the time I'd healed enough I could go back to class, there were three more." Her arms wrapped around Steve's body and she clung to him. "I was the only one that survived. He beat them all to death."

Steve closed his eyes and tried to calm himself. His anger wouldn't help her, it wasn't directed at her anyway. "Please tell me they caught the bastard, that he's not still out there."

"They caught him. He wasn't careful. All of his victims were covered in DNA, and he had a record. It only took them long enough for the DNA to come back for them to identify him. Then they caught him within 24 hours. He didn't bother to run or hide."

"How did you get through it?"

"I healed. Faster than I could have explained to anyone. While healing, I decided I would never be anyone's victim again, ever. I enrolled in martial arts classes and learned everything I could. I got a permit and as soon as I finished school, I started carrying my pistol with me, almost everywhere."

"That's why you carry a gun?" He still wasn't sure he liked the idea. He knew her parents had taught her to handle a weapon, but the idea of her feeling as if she had to carry it, didn't sit well with him.

"It is."

He let out the breath he'd been holding. "If it'll make you feel better, you can bring it in here. My place isn't my Khan's and if it makes you feel safe, you can keep it beside the bed."

"Thank you." She placed a soft kiss on his shoulder. "But I don't think I need it. I'm safe when I'm with you. When I have your arms around me, your scent on my skin, even just knowing you're near and I feel like I'll always be safe."

"I'll protect you with everything in me," he whispered against her hair. She relaxed against him and he loosened his arms until his grip on her was more comfortable for them both. He couldn't stop himself from asking. "You said they caught him. What happened to him?"

She tensed for a moment, then relaxed again. "They killed him. He'd raped and killed four women and left plenty of evidence. The jury took less than three hours to return. They found him guilty and sentenced him to death."

"How long did it take?" He had to know. "When was he sentenced?"

"Six months ago."

"Did you go?"

"No." Her voice was distant again. "I didn't watch the trial or attend the execution. I didn't want to ever see his face again."

"I don't blame you." He tightened his arm around her shoulders, hugging her for moment before relaxing again. "It's still early yet, do you think you might be able to go back to sleep?"

She rubbed her head against his shoulder and yawned. "I don't know."

"You comfortable where you are or do you want to move?"

"I'm good if you are." Her words were slurred with sleep. She was drifting off already.

"I'm fine." He lay there a long time, listening to her breathe, while he tried to rein in his temper. He wished the son of a bitch wasn't already dead. He'd love to hunt him down and kill him himself. It was just as well, though. He'd have to leave her to hunt her rapist down and he didn't want to do that.

Chapter 31

JV woke instantly, her memory of what had happened the night before clear. They'd moved in the few hours she'd been asleep and now she lay on her side. Steve was behind her, his arm snug around her waist. She didn't want to face him. Not now. She was nervous about what he'd say after her revelation. Afraid he might see her as broken, used.

She tried to slip from under his arm, intent on getting out of bed without waking him.

His arm tightened around her middle. "Where do you think you're going?" His voice was thick and low.

"I was gonna get up. Maybe make some coffee." She tried to keep her voice calm and even.

"Not yet. You're gonna stay right here and talk to me a minute."

She stopped trying to get away, but she didn't relax. "Talk about what?"

He kept his voice calm and patient. "Last night."

"What about it?" She lay stiff against him, aware she was naked beneath the blankets. Thankfully, he still wore the sweatpants he'd worn to bed.

"How much do you remember?"

"Everything."

"Good. That'll make it easier."

She was afraid to ask but she had to know. "Make what easier?"

"The talk we're about to have."

She sighed, giving up hope of escaping. "Do we have to?"

"We do."

She braced herself for what she knew was coming. "What do you want to say?"

"Sweetheart, it's not just what I have to say, it's what we both need to say." He spoke softly, tugging at her until she rolled to face him.

119

Surprised by the endearment, she let him move her, knowing it would only make it hurt more when he told her it wouldn't work between them. What she'd told him during the night was too much. She was too damaged.

"First, look at me." He lifted her chin until she was forced to look him in the eye. "Baby, the only reason it matters is because it hurts you. It's still hurting you. If you had truly dealt with it and moved on, it wouldn't be an issue now. I would see it as something in your past, something that helped form who you are now, nothing more." He wrapped his arm back around her, not pulling her against him, just holding her, letting her feel him there in case she needed him. "The nightmares are because you haven't dealt with it, only tried to forget it. Now that you feel safe, your mind is bringing it back for you to deal with."

A shudder ran through her body.

"It's okay. I'll help you. I'll do whatever is necessary to help you get through it," he continued.

Her heart leapt. Did this mean he wasn't going to make her leave?

"I can see it in your face. You thought I was going to reject you because of something you had no control over. That pisses me off, but I'll deal with that later. Right now we're gonna deal with you." He took a deep breath and held it a moment before letting it out slowly. "Baby, I'm not equipped to be the only one to help you with this. I need you to trust me, all right?" He looked her in the eyes, waiting for her answer.

She tried to look away, but he wouldn't let her. After a few moments she answered, her voice small and quiet. "I trust you. I always have."

He placed a gentle kiss on her forehead. "Good. There's someone I want you to talk to. I'll go with you if you want, or you can see her on your own. It's up to you. She can help you."

"I don't know if I can tell it again." She looked away.

He moved her face back until she was looking at him again. "Baby, bottling it up only makes it hurt more. I know it hurts to talk about, but it *will* get easier." He saw panic flare in her eyes and swiftly continued. "I'm not saying you have to tell everyone, but see the therapist. She's helped me deal with some of my own issues, from while I was in the Marines. She can help you."

JV was silent for several moments. "All right," she said after a while. "I'll see her. Once. I'll try, that's all I can promise."

"That's all I'm asking, sweetheart." He kissed her forehead again. "Now, do you want to have breakfast here or with Rebecca?"

"With Rebecca." She jumped at the opportunity, seeing it as a chance to get away from their uncomfortable conversation.

"Then get dressed and I'll take you up there."

His voice sounded suspicious to her. "What are you going to do?" she asked, her eyes narrowing.

"I've got a few things to do around here, a few calls to make. I'll take you up to the house then come back for a little while. Don't worry, I won't be far."

The tight band around her chest loosened. "Okay." She swiftly rolled out from the bed, grabbed her clothes and headed for the bathroom. "I'm gonna need to go to town soon. If I keep shifting in them, I'll be out of panties soon." She pushed the door close but didn't bother to latch or lock it.

He chuckled. "At least my shirts are big enough they don't shred, though I don't know how you keep losing them." His voice was muffled through the door.

"When I'm a cat they feel weird. I scrape them off as I work my way under the bed," she said.

He laughed.

Chapter 32

In the house, Steve pulled Nick aside. "I had a breakthrough last night." He kept his voice low, not wanting to disturb the girls as they chatted in the next room.

"Why doesn't that sound like you finally got laid?" The Khan chuckled. "I don't know how you've managed to hold out this long."

Steve scowled. "Not funny. I need you to keep an eye on her for me while I do some things at my place."

Nick sobered at Steve's serious look. "Sure, but what are you afraid of? You think she'll run?" Steve's grimace told the clan leader he'd guessed right. "I'll keep her from going anywhere. What's the issue?"

Steve shook his head. "Not my place to tell, but I need to call Karen and see if she can see Jade today."

Nick's brows shot up. "That bad?"

Steve's face darkened with unexpressed rage. "That bad and worse. She's pushed it back and not dealt with it for six years, now it's starting to surface again."

"Anything I can do?"

"Just keep an eye on her for now. I need to make that call. I've got a few things to do at my place, but I shouldn't be more than an hour, two tops."

"Take your time. Do what you gotta do. I'll stay with the girls. You're not far if we need anything."

He headed back out, on his way through the kitchen, he stopped and kissed Jade on the head as she sat at the table with Rebecca. "I'll be back as soon as I can, okay?" He sat on his heals as he looked her in the eye. *If you need me, don't hesitate to call. I'll be here in seconds.*

"I'll be okay," she replied. "Go take care of your stuff. I'm fine." She smiled but it didn't reach her eyes. They were haunted this morning. He'd seen haunted eyes before, but seeing them in her face bothered him. He didn't like it. He wanted to see her real smile again, to make her giggle or laugh. He knew right now neither was an option, so he left to do what he could.

***

Back at his place, his first move was to call the clan's Emine, the second female in the pack. Her mate, Julio, was the Kadri, second in charge below Nick. When Steve sealed his mating with Jade, and he had no doubt he would, it was just a matter of time before hit happened, that would make her the third female in the clan, not in the chain of command but in dominance. There was no one more powerful, in any clan, than the first and second pairs, but the Shaku and his mate ranked right below them, even if they would never lead the clan.

He sat on the sofa, listening to the line ring.

"Hello?" A cultured voice came over the line.

"Ma'am, it's Steve. I hope I haven't interrupted you," he paid his respects before asking what he knew was a huge favor.

"Not at all, is something wrong?" She knew he wouldn't have called during office hours for no reason.

"Yes and no," he said. "The Khan and Karhyn are fine, but I have someone who needs to see you, as soon as possible."

"Does it happen to be that pretty girl who came all the way from Texas to see you?"

"Word travels fast."

"Not that fast. She's been there for more than two weeks. Rebecca called me." Karen was the closest friend Rebecca had in the area, despite the fifteen-plus year age difference.

Steve grunted. "Can you see her today? Please?"

"Just a second, let me pull up my schedule." She paused for a couple moments. "My last appointment for the day, at three, is open. You can bring her to the office, or I can come out there if that would be better."

Steve was quiet a moment, considering. "Here would probably be better. She's reluctant to talk. Familiar surroundings might help."

"All right, can you give me an idea what the issue is?"

He hesitated, unsure if he should tell her, then decided if she knew, it might help. "She was raped, more than five years ago. She never told anyone

123

until I convinced her to tell me last night. No one."

"Oh dear. I have a few more questions then, if you're comfortable answering them."

"I won't know until you ask."

"Was her rapist caught?"

"I asked he same thing. Yes, she was one of a string of attacks and the only one who survived. From what she said, I'm guessing that was only because she's one of us and we heal faster than normal humans."

"So he killed his victims. Do you know how?"

"Beat 'em to death."

"Do you know if she followed the trial?"

"She said no, but she knew about his sentance, and when he died. She said she hadn't watched much, she never wanted to see his face again."

She made a noise to let him know she was listening and he heard the scratch of her pen as she took notes. "Where did this take place?"

"Texas A&M campus, six to seven years ago. You planning to look it up? She said she was attacked after her last class before a holiday weekend."

"I am. If she didn't follow the case, maybe more details about what happened to him will help her get past it and heal."

"Then there are a couple other things you'll need to know. She said during the attack she tried to shift and couldn't. She said she couldn't shift for weeks afterward. I've never heard of that happening or what might cause it."

"Hmm. That's different. I'll look into what might have caused it. Anything else?"

"Yeah." He had to swallow past the lump in his throat before he could say it. "She was a virgin before he attacked her."

She groaned. "I take it she hasn't been with anyone since the attack?"

"I'm certain she hasn't. There's one more thing, since then any time a male touches her, other than blood family, it burns her skin, I seem to be the only exception."

"Hmm. Rebecca said the two of you are potential mates, is that true?"

"Yes, Ma'am."

"I understand you knew her before the attack, knew you were potential mates before her rape?"

"Yes, ma'am."

"All right. I'll be there about 3:30, I'll see you then."

"Oh," he hesitated. "I promised her that, if she wanted, I'd stay with her while she talked to you. It was the only way I could get her to agree to see you, even once."

"Not a problem. If you being there makes her comfortable, you're welcome to stay."

"All right. I'll see you this afternoon then?"

"This afternoon."

"Thanks." He knew her coming out to the ranch to see Jade was a favor for him.

"You're welcome. I'll see you later."

He dropped the phone on the charging cradle next to the sofa then headed to the bedroom.

In his room, he quickly emptied several drawers, combining their contents with others. He pushed his clothes to one side of the closet, making room for Jade to put anything she brought. He'd asked her to move in; the least he could do was make room for her. Next, he went into the bathroom and made sure there was space for her to put her makeup and toiletries.

He hoped she'd just move in, but he didn't expect it. He'd settle for her bringing a few things, for now, enough so she wasn't always hauling things back and forth to the big house. When he'd finished there, he headed for the basement. Basements weren't common in the area, but he'd wanted space for his gym and hadn't wanted to add another room to the house's footprint, so he'd added the basement instead.

Downstairs, he taped his hands first, to protect them from the beating he was about to give them. Then he went to the heavy bag he'd hung near one corner of the room and started trying to work out his rage and frustration. He started with an easy pace, right, left, right, right, left. He ignored the aching in his hands and kept going, blocking out everything but his next move.

When he finally stopped, he was out of breath and his shirt was dripping with sweat. He took a deep breath, peeled off his shirt and wiped his face. Then he unwound the bloodied tape from his hands, cursing under his breath at the damage he'd done to his knuckles.

Heading up the stairs, he knew he had to shower before going for Jade. He wasn't sure how long he'd been gone but it was probably longer than he'd intended. She wasn't gonna be happy about what he'd done to his hands.

Chapter 33

JV scowled at Steve as she fussed over his damaged knuckles, then she'd done what she could to speed their healing. She managed to heal where he'd broken the skin, but she told him they'd be sore for a few days. He'd been upset, she knew. She could only hope that he'd managed to vent the worst of his ill temper during his workout.

They were still at the main house when the Emine arrived. Steve answered the knock on the door and let her in.

"Jade, this is Karen Roberts, the counselor I wanted you to talk to, as well as our Emine." He turned to the other woman. "Ma'am, this is JV Walker, my potential mate."

JV's eyes widened at how he introduced her. Did this mean he wasn't gonna try to run her off anymore? Was that what he meant when he'd said the night before about protecting her with everything in him?

"Nice to meet you." JV extended one hand to the new woman and shook her hand.

"Welcome to the area." The Emine smiled wide, her expression open. "I'm sorry Julio and I haven't been to meet you sooner. We were out of town for the holiday, visiting his family."

"I understand."

Karen exchanged greetings with Rebecca and Nick then turned to Steve. "Where would you be the most comfortable talking?"

"We can use her room here or my place, it's up to Jade." He turned to her, "Where would you be the most comfortable talking?"

She took his hand, weaving her fingers with his. "Your place."

Steve tipped his head toward his cabin, "You want to walk or pull your car around?" He looked down at the Emine's feet and his surprise at finding sturdy boots showed on his face.

126

"I do know how to dress for the weather," she said, her voice filled with scorn.

"So you do." He nodded. "Sorry."

"No problem. Let's get started." She followed as he led them through the narrow strip of woods and let them into his house.

"How do we do this?" JV asked as soon as the door was closed behind them.

"However you're comfortable," Karen said.

Chapter 34

"Come sit down." Steve led everyone into the living room and waited while Jade sat on the couch, Karen taking a seat in the recliner. "Want anything to drink?"

"Water, please," said Karen.

"Can I have a shot of whiskey?" Jade looked up at him, a hopeful look in her eye.

Steve looked to Karen for her opinion.

"With most patients, I wouldn't recommend it," she looked at Jade when she spoke, not him. "But considering our metabolism and how much alcohol it takes to affect us, a shot or two wouldn't hurt. It might help you relax enough to get started."

Steve got the drinks, bringing a bottle of Johnnie Walker, a shot glass, and an extra glass of water for Jade. He gave the Emine her glass, then sat beside Jade on the sofa.

Jade scooted to the edge of the sofa and filled the shot glass. He watched as she closed her eyes and tipped the glass back, drinking it all in one large swallow. She refilled the tiny glass and downed the second shot with ease. Shaking her head she put the bottle back on the coffee table and leaned back. He lifted his arm and waited while she scooted against him then wrapped his arm around her.

"I don't know where to start," Jade said.

"Start where ever you like." Karen pulled a small notebook from her bag and leaned back in the chair, getting comfortable.

Jade was quiet for several moments and Steve didn't know if she was going to be able to do it, then she spoke. "I've known Steve for as long as I can remember. At first, he was my brother's best friend. It wasn't until I was a teenager that I felt it."

Steve looked down at her, surprised she'd chosen to start with him, but stayed quiet. He didn't care where she started as long as she got through it all.

She told Karen about when he'd come home after being discharged from the military and stayed less than two weeks before he left again. It made his heart ache all over again, even knowing he had done the right thing.

She explained how it had hurt her and how she'd turned the hurt to anger. "I knew I couldn't just sit in the little town we grew up in and wait for him," Jade said. "My parents wanted me to find a boy and get married. The idea held no appeal to me. The only person I could think about was him," she turned and looked up at him. "No one else measured up. So I pushed to go to school instead."

She talked about her life at school. She'd gone to class and studied, met some people but hadn't been close to anyone, not even the girls she'd shared a house with.

"It was the Friday before the holiday, Labor day. I had a late class. My roommates were already gone for the weekend when I left for class. I wasn't planning to go home. Mom would have nagged me to get married and start a family and I didn't want to hear it." She was quiet for a moment before continuing. She told the rest of her story, much the same way she had the night before, pausing now and then to compose herself.

Steve held her and stroked her arm, soothing her when her voice clogged with tears or went distant. She picked up his other hand from his lap and wove her fingers into his, holding tight as she talked. When she'd told her entire story, she turned in her seat and hid her face against his shoulder.

Karen waited several minutes, then spoke, her voice soft and reassuring. "JV, talking about it is good. By holding it in, you're letting him hold on to the part of you he took." She watched Jade, as if looking for any reaction. "Steve told me he's dead. He can't hurt you again and he can't do it to anyone else."

Jade looked at Karen, not quite meeting her eyes. "That's right."

"He's dead. There's no more reason to be afraid of him."

"I know that, here," Jade touched the side of her head, then laid the same hand against her chest. "This is harder to convince."

"I know. It will take a while but opening up, telling Steve and myself, is a good start. When he called this morning, Steve said you had some residual effects after the attack. Can you tell me about them?"

"He did something to me. I don't know what, but it kept me from being able to shift. Not just during the attack, but later too. It was weeks before I could shift again. For a while I was afraid I might never get to be my cat again."

Steve's heart ached. He didn't know how he might handle it if it had been him looking at the possibility of never shifting again. That she'd gone through it alone made him angry, but he pushed his anger away. It wouldn't help her now.

"I understand you didn't follow his case?" Karen said, her voice soothing.

"I couldn't stand to. The most I could do was look up the verdict and sentence after it was over." Jade's voice was stronger.

"I did a little research and found a few things I think might help. Would you like to hear them?"

Steve appreciated that she'd asked first, instead of just telling Jade details that would probably upset her.

Jade looked at him, as if asking his opinion.

"I trust her, sweetheart. If she thinks it'll help you, she's probably right."

Jade turned back to the Emine. "Okay, I'd like to know." She sat up a little straighter, pulling away from Steve to sit up on her own.

"In court, it came out that his M.O., you know what that means right?" She waited for Jade's nod. "It was to come up behind a woman at night, away from other students, and hit her with a stun gun."

"I heard that," Jade said, not understanding.

"JV, dear, do you know what that much electricity does to our systems?"

Jade scowled. "No. What?"

"It kind of shorts out the magic that lets us change, that's what kept you from shifting. Depending on how strong the shock, it can last for weeks, even months, but it's not permanent."

Jade sagged with relief. "What about my skin burning when I'm touched? Is that a side effect of getting zapped too?"

Karen cringed. "That one's harder. I can't say for sure but I think that was triggered by a combination of the physical and emotional trauma. Has it eased any since you got here?"

"Rebecca wondered about that a few days ago, so we tested it. It's not as bad as it once was, but it's not gone by any means."

"I suspect it will vanish when you're totally secure, when you feel safe and no longer fear that your world is falling apart under you."

"I feel safe. I have since I got here," Jade protested.

"But you aren't totally secure, are you? You're afraid things won't work, you'll have to leave here and find somewhere else, aren't you?"

Jade blushed. "Are you reading me?"

"Only on the surface, dear," Karen said. "Yes, I'm an empath and I let it help me with my work, but I never push without permission. You've got good shields though, not much gets through unless you're really afraid."

Steve frowned at Karen for not warning his mate before they started, then turned back to Jade. "I know it was hard, but you did it."

She turned and smiled at him, her eyes a little less haunted than they'd been that morning.

"I'd like to talk to you again, if you think you can," Karen said.

"I think I can do that," Jade agreed after a moment.

"It would be easier for me if you could come to my office, but if you need me to, I can come back out here."

Jade looked at him.

"I'll take you," he said.

"I'll come in to the office," Jade turned back to Karen.

"Good. How about Friday, day after tomorrow, at three o'clock? It's my last appointment for the day and we can take as long as you need."

She looked at Steve again as if to see if he could do that and at his nod, turned back. "We'll be there."

Karen stood. "I'll see you then, and over the weekend too, Rebecca called last week and invited us for dinner on Saturday. You'll get to meet my husband then." She looked down at the pair on the sofa, Steve still holding Jade close. "Will you be okay until Friday?"

Jade looked up at her, surprise plain in her wide eyes, then lowered her gaze as she thought about it. "I think so, yes."

"If you need to talk, don't hesitate to call, day or night. Steve has my personal cell number."

Jade nodded.

"I mean it." Karen's voice turned stern. "If you need to, you call."

"I will, I promise."

Karen gave her another hard look and then nodded. "Don't worry about seeing me out, I'm going to stop at the main house and spend a few minutes with Rebecca before heading out."

Once she closed the door, Steve turned and looked down at Jade. "I know it was hard. How are you feeling?"

She was quiet for several minutes, "Better, but I'm exhausted. Talking about it, stirred everything up again," she sighed, "but it helped to let it out."

"Do you wanna go back up to the house for dinner or stay here and have a quiet evening? Maybe go to bed early?"

"Staying here and crashing early sounds heavenly."

Chapter 35

After her next session with the Emine, who insisted on being called Karen, JV felt better. She was steadier than after their first talk and she realized she should have talked to someone a long time ago, but who? She still couldn't tell her family, she didn't know if she would ever be able to. Until Rebecca, she hadn't had friends she could talk to. There was no one she was close enough to share secrets with, even little secrets, much less her secret horror.

Karen had said when she met with her on Friday that it was okay that she didn't want to talk about it, but treating her attack like a secret was only letting it hurt her more. She said it would help to tell someone she was close to. Someone other than Steve. JV wasn't so sure.

Saturday afternoon, she was in Rebecca's living room with Rebecca. Steve and Nick were busy in the Khan's office. She didn't know what they were doing, she hadn't cared enough to ask. The two women sat together, laptops open in front of them as they worked on Christmas shopping.

"Do you ever wish you could just go into the store and wander through until you find what you're after?" JV asked.

"Not really," Rebecca shrugged. "I hate crowds and it's always in the back of my mind that someone from my old Chanat will see me. That they'll try to take me back."

JV frowned. "Why would they do that?"

Rebecca gave her a kind smile. "Didn't Steve tell you?"

"Tell me what?"

"How I got to be here."

JV gave her friend a confused look. "He hasn't said a word."

"I shouldn't worry anymore, but I do." She took a deep breath and let it out slowly, trying to figure out where to start. "When I met Nick I'd been

133

on the run from my Chanat for about a year. My father was the Kadri."

"Was?" JV asked.

"He may still be for all I know, I haven't spoken to any of them since I left, three and a half years ago. Anyway, I was living wild, as a cougar. I hadn't been in my human form in about six months when I wandered into his territory. He chased me down, caught me, convinced me to shift and offered me a shower. Oh my, that shower was heaven." She closed her eyes and remembered for a moment. "He convinced me that I was safe here. I didn't know if I could trust him, but I trusted my instincts. I told him I was running from an arranged marriage and that I wasn't going back.

"He said I didn't have to, I could stay with him. It took us less than a day to wind up in bed together. I almost sealed our mating that first night because I didn't know what I was doing." She smiled at the memory. "Things moved extremely fast between Nick and I, and Steve wasn't nice about it, not at first. He softened somewhat when he found out what I was running from, and more after we sealed our mating, even though that was still within a couple weeks of having met each other. When my father sent someone to take me, Steve met him with teeth and claws. He fought him off as if he'd always approved of me.

"Nick sent my father's man back with a message. He told them I was staying and the next person to try to take me away would die and he'd report the whole thing to the Council. I haven't heard from them since.

Still, it's hard to forget that year I was on the run. They tried to capture and take me back several times. I just got lucky. That's what finally drove me to live wild. I knew it was the only way. They couldn't trace me unless they were physically on my trail."

"Wow," JV said, surprised. "I had no clue."

Rebecca smiled. "Life here's been good for me. I hope it'll be as good for you." She laid her hand on JV's. "I know you've had some issues in the past. I know Karen was here to talk to you the other day and you saw her again yesterday. I won't push, but want you to know that I'm here, if you want to talk. I know first-hand life isn't always what you want it to be."

"I've sure learned that the hard way," JV muttered. "I'm sorry you had to go through that. My clan never made much of mating, but they don't do the arranged marriage thing. I didn't know anyone still did."

"Not many do. The council frowns on it, but it still happens."

"I don't know what to say."

"Don't have to say anything. It haunts me a little sometimes but for the most part I've put it behind me."

"I hope someday I can be as casual about my attack."

"Do you mind if I ask what kind of attack?" Rebecca watched her friend.

JV bit her lower lip and looked away, not entirely comfortable, but Karen had said it would help. She took a deep breath and laid it out as plainly as she could.

"Oh, dear," Rebecca responded, and laid a hand on JV's arm. "Who helped you through?"

She looked at her friend, then dropped her eyes to the hand on her arm. "No one. I didn't tell anyone. My roommates were gone and everything that showed had healed by the time they got back."

"You never told anyone?" Rebecca's concern was obvious from the frown she wore.

"Not until a few days ago when Steve worked it out of me. I did my best to forget it and go on with my life. It was how I dealt with everything. The attack, Steve's leaving, any problem I've had, I've ignored it and moved on."

"Did it work?"

"For a while, but it failed in the long term." She gave Rebecca a wry smile.

"I'm sorry." Rebecca gave her a hug. Not knowing what else to say, they dropped the heart-to-heart and went back to shopping until it was time to make dinner.

***

"This is a lot of food." JV looked at the dishes they'd laid out on the kitchen island. She knew there was more in the oven and on the stove top that wouldn't be ready for a while yet.

"Well, we've got four more people coming and two of them are teenagers. I've seen those two eat. They'll put away as much food as the rest of us combined." Rebecca didn't seem to mind, only to want to be prepared.

They were ready when a vehicle pulled up in front of the house. Together, the girls headed for the living room as Steve opened the front door. The guests hurried from the cold and Steve took his place beside JV and introduced her to the Kadri and the rest of his family.

"Jade, this is Julio Roberts, second-in-charge in the clan. You've met Karen and these are their children, Ricky and Izzy." He motioned to each of the teenagers in turn then dropped his hands on her shoulders and addressed the older man. "This is JV. I'm hoping, eventually, she'll be my mate."

JV turned and looked at Steve with wide eyes, shocked at how he'd changed his introduction. She smiled up at him, then turned back to the Kadri. "It's nice to meet you, sir." She extended one hand to shake his, but Steve grabbed her wrist instead.

"No offense, sir, but right now touching most males hurts Jade, and the scent of her pain drives me to the edge of my control. Until we can figure out how to either stop it or I can gain better control, it's best if we avoid the situation."

Julio looked back and forth between the two of them for a moment, then his gaze flicked to his wife for an instant before going back to Steve. "That's fine." He turned his attention back to JV. "It's nice to meet you, ma'am. I hope you find what you need."

JV said hello to the kids, both of whom were teenagers. The boy was obviously older than the girl, though they both looked old enough to drive. They sat in the front room and talked about the holidays, pack business, and town happenings until dinner was ready, then Rebecca and JV finished getting everything on the table and called the others.

As everyone settled around the table, Nick stood back up. "Rebecca and I have an announcement. You've probably already figured it out, but I'm gonna make a big deal about it anyway." He looked at his mate, his eyes shining with love and happiness.

JV wondered if she'd ever feel that way. If Steve would ever look at her like that. She had no clue what Nick was about to share, but she didn't let on. She remained quiet while waiting for the announcement.

"Rebecca is pregnant. We're gonna have a baby!" Nick's grin was so wide it almost split his face in two. His happiness was infectious. Beside him, Rebecca sat, smiling happily, though not as effusively as her mate.

JV couldn't help herself. She stood, rushed to her friend and hugged her. "Congratulations! You'll be a wonderful mother." She moved to hug Nick too, but Steve's growl stopped her in her tracks. She turned and looked at him, eyes wide.

He flushed, all eyes turning toward him. "Sorry, I didn't mean to. I just thought about the pain touching him would cause her, and it came out." He ducked his head. "I can't apologize enough."

"No harm done, man." Nick was good-natured, still glowing from his announcement.

"Congratulations to you both," Steve said. "I've known for a while, but didn't want to say anything until you were ready." He held out one hand for JV. She moved to his side.

"That's wonderful news," Karen said.

"Way to go, man." Julio clapped one hand on Nick's back. The children were quiet, as if they didn't know what to say, so they said nothing.

How did you know?

Her scent changed. It was just before you got here, you wouldn't have noticed.

Thanks. I felt stupid for not knowing.

There's no reason for that. There was no way you could have known.

He served himself a helping of mashed potatoes from the bowl being passed around. Conversation turned to children and babies. They ate and talked after dinner before the family left and everyone called it an evening.

Chapter 36

That night, as they lay in bed, she finally gathered the nerve to ask. "What was with the way you introduced me tonight?"

"What do you mean?"

"That you're hoping, eventually, I'll be your mate," she repeated his words back to him.

"What about it?"

"You started out telling me it wouldn't work between us, then last week you introduced me to Karen as your *potential* mate, that I understood. It was the facts without any commitments, but tonight you said you're *hoping* I'll be your mate? The change is sudden, that's all."

"Sweetheart, it's been several days since I told you I'd protect you with everything in me. Who protects anyone like that but a mate? How is that sudden?"

She was quite a moment. "I hadn't thought about it that way." Her voice was soft with the realization that he was ready to embrace what was still growing between them. "What about the eventually?"

"Jade," he ran one hand up and down her back. His touch soothed her. "We've got some issues to work through before either one of us is ready to make a lifetime commitment." He spoke slowly, "You're just starting to work out something that's been haunting you for years. I'm trying to deal with not being able to hunt down the son of a bitch that hurt you and rip him to pieces." He took a deep breath and let it out slowly. "I'll probably always be worried about you. I'll be over-protective, not just because of what you've been through, but because it's who I am. You need to be sure that's something you can deal with. That's gonna take some time."

She smiled, closed her eyes, and laid her head against his chest. She fell asleep listening to the steady thump of his heart beneath her ear.

Steve lay awake a long time, thinking about that growl he hadn't meant to make, and what it might mean.

Chapter 37

The next morning, the incident was still on his mind. He left Jade sleeping and went to the main house to talk to his leader.

After kicking off his snow-covered boots, he padded into the kitchen on silent stocking feet and poured himself a cup of coffee before taking a seat at the table with his Khan. "I don't know what's going on with me." He didn't look up from his cup.

"What do you mean?" The clan leader asked, a frown creasing his brow.

"Last night, I growled at you. I didn't mean to, hell, you know as well as I do that I'd never attack you."

"I think you would." Nick's voice was calm, as if they were discussing the weather, not beating the shit out of each other. "If I was a threat to JV, I don't think you'd hesitate to attack me." He paused a moment. "But, Steve?" He waited until the other man looked up, met his eyes. "I don't blame you. I don't know what, but I can tell she's been through something rough. It's our job to protect our mates and we'd kill our best friends, if we had to, to keep them safe."

"But Rebecca's been through a lot too, and you don't growl at every man who tries to touch her. You don't want to rip them to pieces for touching her, do you?"

"No, I don't. I want to shield her, to keep anything that might upset her, or hurt her feelings, from her, but you know what she'd do if I tried."

"You'd probably end up sleeping on the couch for a week."

"At least," Nick said with a laugh.

"Why am I so sensitive about her being touched? Why did I want to leap across the table at you last night?"

"I'm not entirely sure," the sound of a vehicle pulling into the yard interrupted him. "That's probably Julio, he said he'd stop by this morning."

Steve let the Kadri in and led him back to the kitchen.

Before sitting, Julio took down a mug, spooned some sugar into the bottom and filled it with coffee. He took a sip and sat at the table. "What's up?"

"We're trying to figure out why Steve can't control his instinct to protect JV," Nick said.

Julio took a long look at the man in question. "You said you were hoping she'd be your mate, didn't you? That means you both feel the instinct?"

"Yeah, of course," Steve wasn't sure where this was heading.

"She's been here, what? A month?" Julio looked back and forth between the two men.

Steve thought about it, counting the days before answering. "A little over a month." His brow creased as he tried to work out where Julio was going.

The older man carefully scented the air. "How much of that time has she been in your bed?"

A low growl trickled from Steve's throat before he could stop it. He coughed.

"No offense intended," the Kadri said. "But the more interaction the two of you have, the more intimate the relationship, the quicker the instinct will advance."

"We share my bed, but we sleep, that's all."

"Then it shouldn't be progressing quite this swiftly." He took a sip of his coffee and his face lit. "Unless…" he trailed off, not wanting to cause more problems.

"Unless what?" Nick wanted to know.

"Unless there's some other factor, something to stress the bond. Say for instance she was threatened in some way, or in some kind of danger."

Steve narrowed his eyes at his friend. "Would finally facing a trauma that's several years old qualify?"

He was quiet a moment, considering, "It might, if the trauma was severe enough."

Steve cursed under his breath.

"What is it?" Julio asked, looking back and forth between Steve and Nick, as if wanting to know what was up.

Steve looked at both men, debating how much he should tell them. "Damn it. I've gotta tell you because I need help, but she can't know I said

141

anything. She has to share in her own time." He looked back and forth between them, waiting for them to reply.

"Of course," Julio agreed.

"I have a good idea, but of course," Nick said.

Steve frowned at his clan leader, but continued, telling them only what they needed to know.

Nick's face turned a deep, angry red.

"That would do it," Julio said.

"It gets worse." Steve looked into his cup.

"It's already worse than I suspected," Nick said.

"How can it be worse?" Julio asked.

"I got as many details as I could from her and I convinced her to see Karen." He nodded at the Kadri at the mention of his mate. "I gave Karen as much detail as I could, before she came out. She looked up the case."

"I thought you said she didn't tell anyone?" Julio asked.

"She didn't but she wasn't the only victim, just the only one who lived. There were four others, all raped and beaten to death. They caught him, convicted and executed him, but it's not enough, not for me."

"Wouldn't be for me either," growled Nick

Steve stared down at his empty cup. "Anyway, he got to the girls by slipping up behind them coming out of a late class. He would choose one who was apart from everyone else, and zapped them with a stun gun." He looked back and forth between the men at the table. "Does of either of you know what a stun gun does to us?"

"No, what?" Nick asked.

"I've never had the occasion to be hit by one, what does it do?" Julio asked.

"The voltage screws with the magic that lets us shift. I was hit by one while I was in the military, but I didn't have the opportunity to shift often then, and I didn't notice it. Jade spent weeks not knowing if she'd ever shift again. "After she healed, she started learning self-defense. She took martial arts classes and she armed herself."

"That's why the pistol," Nick said, understanding.

Steve nodded and continued, "It's what started the burning when she touches someone, too."

"She seems to have dealt with things well," Julio said. "I never would have known she'd been through something like that, if I hadn't been told."

"That's just it. She hasn't dealt with it. She shoved it out of her mind and did her best to forget it," Steve said. "I would never have known if she hadn't started having nightmares. I woke alone and found her curled under the bed in her cat form." He looked out the window in front of him, staring sightless at the gray world just starting to brighten. "Since she told me, and I convinced her to talk to Karen, it's been a little better. She still has nightmares, as often as not, but instead of shifting and hiding she wakes me and lets me calm and reassure her."

"That's good," said Julio.

"I know, but still." He looked back down at his cup, wishing it had refilled itself while he'd talked.

"That's not everything," Nick said. "You're holding something back."

Steve looked at his clan leader, his eyes held a deep sadness. "She was a virgin."

"Fuck," Julio muttered.

"Since contact with men, shifter or human, hurts her, rape is her only experience with sex, isn't it?" Nick's voice turned rough.

Steve couldn't say it, he couldn't force the words past the lump in his throat. He nodded and wiped away the tears he'd finally become aware of.

"Fuck," Nick echoed. "That's a hell of a situation."

"You do know there's a limit to how long you're gonna be able to control that part of the instinct, right?" Julio asked, his voice careful.

"I know," Steve said. "I'm sure she does too, but since she came to me, she may be willing to risk it." He took a deep breath and let it out in a rush. "I'm not, not yet."

"Why not?" Julio leaned back in his chair to watch Steve's reaction.

Steve looked up, and met his gaze, his eyes hard. "She's just started reliving it, it's too fresh right now, too new in her mind. I'm not gonna push her for anything more than she's willing to give." He barely kept from snarling at the other man. "I'll give her time, as much time as she needs, or as I can manage. I'm hoping after a few weeks of seeing Karen, she'll approach me."

"That's a good plan." Nick looked across the table at his second for back up.

"It is," Julio agreed. "Wait, not until she says she's ready, but until she makes the first move. Let her take the lead, if you can."

Steve dropped his head again and listened to the men he respected tell him the same thing he'd been telling himself all week.

"Back to the aggression though," Julio said after a moment. "All things considered, you'll probably always be a little over-protective of her."

"Amen," Nick muttered.

"But once you seal your mating, assuming it goes that far, then the worst of it should pass." the Kadri continued as if the clan leader hadn't spoken. "The inability to control it, that kind of thing."

"That's good to know. Thanks."

Talk turned to clan business, things they hadn't wanted to discuss in front of the kids the night before. When Bobby showed up for house duty, Julio took off. Nick headed for the barn to oversee feeding and Steve went back to his place. He didn't want Jade to wake up alone.

Chapter 38

The next couple of weeks passed without much note. JV slowly moved most of her things to Steve's place, filling his closet and drawers. She'd even taken to stealing his tee shirts, not that he seemed to mind. He'd been taking her into town twice a week to see Karen, though she didn't need him to sit through the sessions with her anymore. She'd spent every night with him and had only had a few nightmares wake her. She was glad she'd stopped shifting and hiding. Instead she woke Steve. He held her, calmed her and reassured her until she felt safe enough to go back to sleep.

Now it was less than two weeks until Christmas. She'd done most of her shopping online but she wanted to look for a few things in town. "You don't have to take me to my appointment this afternoon," she said to Steve one morning. "I can take my pickup."

"I don't know." He seemed hesitant about letting her make the drive alone. "Are you sure you can drive in the snow? The highway will be plowed, but the road out isn't. Can your truck handle it?"

She was glad she'd spent the extra for four-wheel drive when she'd bought it. "I don't see why it wouldn't. I've driven in snow before. It's just been a while. I'll be fine. I have some shopping I want to do and I can't drag you along for that."

"I don't mind-"

She cut him off. "I didn't say I don't want to take you along, I said I can't. I'm looking for something for you." She pinned him with a look that said he was being dense.

He gave an unhappy sigh. "All right, but keep your phone with you. Call if you have any trouble."

"I can do that." She gave him a quick kiss on the cheek. "Thank you." She wrapped her arms around his waist and stretched up to kiss him again,

145

this time on the mouth. She coaxed his mouth open and his arms were around her, pulling her closer as he sank into the kiss. All too soon, he pulled away.

"If you're gonna go shopping before your appointment, you'd better get ready." His voice was husky as he spun her toward the bedroom they were sharing.

"I thought I'd shop after," she protested.

"No, before. After you won't have much time before shops close and it gets dark. I'll feel better if I know when to expect you home."

Chapter 39

That evening, they sat together on the bench on his front porch. A blanket covered their laps as they watched the snow fall in the swiftly fading light.

"How did it go today?" Steve asked. It was the same question he asked after every appointment since Jade had told him she didn't need him to go in with her anymore. He didn't ask for details, just how it went.

"Good," she said, her eyes still on the falling snow. "It went really well." She was silent for several minutes. "I think it's time." Her voice was soft, barely a whisper.

Something in her tone caught his attention and he looked down at her. "Time for what?"

"Time to try sex... on my terms." She used the same soft voice, but there was something strong and certain in her tone.

"Are you sure?"

She took a deep breath and looked at him for the first time since bringing it up. "I'm terrified, but I know you won't hurt me. You'll do everything you can to keep from scaring me more." She laid one hand against his cheek. "I need to do this. It's time."

He looked down at her, uncertainty filling his eyes, he knew. "Let's go inside where it's warm and we can get comfortable."

He stood and before she had a chance to do the same, he scooped her up, blanket and all and carried her inside. Once he kicked the door closed, set her on her feet and helped her take off her coat, then added wood to the stove to take the chill from the air. "Come here," he called from the living room.

"Yes?" she asked, reaching his side.

"Before we go any further, I want to get some things straight." He

147

looked down at where she stood in front of him, then sat on the sofa.

"Okay." She sat a couple of feet away on the arm of the recliner. She was too far away to suit him, but it was probably better this way, at least for now.

"First, you're in charge. I don't want to scare you or hurt you in any way, so if you tell me to stop, I stop. Instantly." He kept his tone gentle, but firm. He watched for her response and at her nod, he continued, "Second, you're in the lead. If at any time, I touch you in any way or do anything that makes you uncomfortable, say so. We'll figure out how to make it work for you. Do you understand?"

"I understand." She gave him one swift nod. "Can I touch you now?"

He spread his arms wide. "I'm all yours." He waited, holding his breath, not sure she was really ready for this.

She moved to the couch and went to her hands and knees to close the gap between them. "I've been dying to do this for days." She tugged his sweater over his head, taking his tee shirt with it, then sat on her heels, and just looked at him.

"How did I miss this before?" She ran the fingers of one hand lightly over the tattoo high on the left side of his chest. She marveled at the slightly different texture of the colored skin.

"I'm not sure you've seen me without a shirt since I was a teenager." He watched her reaction, a small smile on his mouth.

"How long have you had it?" Her fingers outlined the snarling cougar staring out at her with odd colored eyes.

"I got her not long after boot camp."

"No one asked why a cougar?"

"A couple, I just told them the truth. She reminded me of a girl back home. Pretty, but dangerous."

Her eyes finally left the amazing artwork and found their way to his face, she stared at him a moment, confused.

"Look at her eyes, Jade." His voice stayed calm and patient, the way it did when he was waiting for her to see something obvious.

"I noticed. They're an odd pale green. That's not the color of a cougar's eyes." Her brow creased and she looked back at the cat as if trying to figure out what he was telling her.

"Babe." His breath fanned against her cheek as he ran the back of one finger down her neck. "Her eyes are jade."

Her mouth fell open and she looked him in the eye again. Blinking, looked at him, her mouth moving but no sound came out.

Steve started chuckling, his body vibrating beneath the fingers still resting on his chest. "Never thought I'd see you speechless, baby. Or that I'd be the one to put you in such a state." He hugged her close for a moment.

When she could speak again, she couldn't help but ask. "You got this done when you were eighteen?"

"Most of it," he said. "I've had some touch-up work done, her eyes changed, but that's about it."

Her eyes narrowed slightly. "Her eyes changed?"

He nodded, "They started out the golden yellow of a natural cougar. But I had them changed almost ten years ago. "

"Why?"

"I'd dreamed about her for a long time, but I never got a good look at her eyes. Then I got out of the Marines, went home and saw you. The pull between us had changed and I knew she was you. I had her eyes changed after that."

She was quiet for a moment. "Has Matt seen it?"

Steve nodded. "Once, a few years ago. We'd gotten together for a few days and ended up at a hotel pool. We fought that day, probably the worst fight we've ever had. We both walked away bruised and bloody, but we'd worked it out."

She frowned. "Why did you fight? It's just a cougar."

"He knew the instant he saw her eyes that she's you, baby. He didn't like it."

"But how can she be me?" Her eyes flicked to his face then back to the cat. "I hadn't even shifted yet, I didn't have a cat then."

"But you would, I had no doubt. She's fierce and yet beautiful, just like you."

"That's so sweet."

He ran one knuckle down the side of her face again. "It's the truth."

She looked away a moment and when she looked back her whole demeanor changed. She seemed more confident, less frightened. She ran her hands over his chest. "You're so warm," she mumbled, leaning into his mouth with hers.

She coaxed his mouth open and drew him into a deeper kiss. He lifted his hands to rest on her hips and she shivered when he let one slip under her sweater and slide along the bare skin of her back.

149

"You all right?" he broke the kiss to ask.

She nodded and went back into kissing him without a word. At the same time, she ran her hands over his chest and shoulders.

His hands moved, one cupped her ass through her jeans, the other splayed against her bare back, but he went no further.

After several minutes she broke away. "I need more." Her voice had turned breathy. She pulled her sweater and tee shirt over her head and tossed them aside. "I want to feel your skin touching mine."

"This might be a little easier on the bed." His voice was thick, but not as breathy as hers as he asked if they could move.

She nodded as she lowered her mouth to his neck.

Without another word he pulled her against him and stood, trying to keep her from feeling how hard he was through his jeans as he carried her into the bedroom. He set her on the bed then let her go and lay on his back. "Do your worst."

She looked at him from head to toe, spread out like a banquet just for her. "Can I lick you here?" She touched one nipple.

He'd thought it was impossible, but his jeans got tighter. "You can do anything you want."

She met his eyes, uncertain. "You're sure?"

"Positive."

She grinned, then bent over him and kissed him again, briefly this time, before moving her mouth away. Trailing it down the side of his neck, she drew swirling designs along his chest with her tongue until she found one nipple. He jumped and tried not to hiss as she drew the tiny button into the heat of her mouth. Every pull as she sucked on the sensitive spot sent bolts of sensation to his cock.

He groaned. A long deep sound that he couldn't hold in.

"Did I hurt you?" she asked, her brow furrowed with concern.

"N-" He had to swallow to get the words out. "No, it feels good, really good." He put his hands on her hips and pulled her up his body. "Come here and let me show you."

"I don't know." She seemed uncertain.

"I do. It won't hurt, trust me." He leaned up and moved her so they were face to face and kissed her, a quick hard kiss that he poured all his longing into. "Come on, put one leg on either side of me." He dropped back to the bed and guided her until she knelt astride his chest. "Perfect." Sliding his hands up her body he cupped her breasts through the bra she still wore.

"Perfect," he said again, loving how they just filled his hands. He gently squeezed and kneaded the soft mounds of flesh then tugged one cup down to reveal the nipple. He flicked one finger back and forth over the sensitive tip until it drew into a tight bud. "You like that?"

"It feels odd, but good."

"Can I take this off?" He ran one finger under the band around her chest.

Instead of answering, she reached back and unhooked the bra with a deft flip of her fingers.

With gentle hands, he slipped the straps from her shoulders and lowered the cups away from her breasts. "Beautiful." He tossed the bra aside. Bringing both hands up, he cupped both breasts gently, then rolled one nipple between his thumb and forefinger. "Lean down here." He lifted his head to meet her half-way.

She tensed when he pulled the tender tip into his mouth, sucking hard for several seconds before playing his tongue over the sensitized skin. He bit gently then sucked the sting out and she moaned softly. He moved his hand to cover the other breast and mirrored the actions of his mouth. Then he switched breasts and gave the other the same attention.

The longer he kept it up, the more intense his touch got. His bite a little harder, his grip a little tighter.

Jade's moans grew longer, deeper and she moved against him. When her hips started grinding into his chest he thought he would burst the zipper in his jeans. He moved his mouth down her stomach and found Jade breathing heavy. "I want you on your back, can you handle that?"

"I think so." She moved off him and lay back, watching his every move.

He bent over her and put his mouth back to her belly where he'd left off. He worked a trail down her stomach and made swirls with his tongue along the waist band of her jeans. Her hips strained against him. "I want to take these off."

She nodded and reached for the button.

"No. Let me." He slowly slipped the button loose and lowered the tab on her zipper, still teasing her stomach with his tongue and the rough growth of his beard. "Lift your hips, baby."

She braced her feet against the mattress and did as he asked.

He slid her jeans off her hips and down her thighs. "You're good." He watched as she lowered herself against the bed then finished pulling off her pants and tossing them aside. He lowered his mouth to the waistband of her tiny lace panties, making teasing swirls from one hipbone to the other then pulling away.

He ran gentle hands up her thighs, until his thumbs met at the apex. He slipped a single finger between her closed thighs. Through the thin panties, he spread her nether lips and ran a light touch over the hard, sensitive nub hiding inside.

Jade gasped and her entire body jerked.

"Like that, sweetheart?" he watched her face for any sign of distress. He could smell her arousal, but that didn't mean she wasn't afraid, even if he wasn't scenting fear.

"Feels good," she said, easing her thighs apart a little.

"Want more?"

"Please?" She breathed.

He hesitated. "Just remember, all you have to say is stop and I will. All right?"

She nodded, meeting his eyes.

"Can I take these off?" He ran his fingers under the elastic of one leg of her panties.

Instead of bothering with words she lifted her hips.

He slowly tugged the satin and lace off her hips, teasing her skin with his mouth along the way, light nips with his teeth, then kissing away the sting. Once he'd tossed the slight garment aside he sat a moment, just looking at her. "You're beautiful." He ran a light touch down the side of one breast, smoothing his fingertips along the dip of her waist then his hand come to rest on her hip. He watched her a moment longer, then lowered his mouth to her breast, teasing the tip back to a hard, tight bud before moving to the other side and treating that nipple the same.

Jade whimpered beneath him and her hips moved, restless against the bed.

"You doing okay, baby?" He watched her face, looking for signs of fear or distress.

"It aches," she said with a moan.

"Is it a good ache or a bad ache, baby?"

She whimpered again. "A good one." Her hips moved again. "I don't know what to do."

"That's easy, sweetheart. Stay there and enjoy." He lowered his mouth once more, teasing her breasts in turn before he started moving down her body again.

He kissed his way down her stomach and noticed for the first time that she kept the hair between her thighs trimmed short. He kissed lower, easing her thighs apart with careful hands as he lowered his face to her center. He inhaled softly, taking in the scent of her arousal and wondering what she'd taste like when she exploded against his mouth.

Steve ran the flat of his tongue up the length of her slit, spreading her and tasting the moisture flowing from her core.

She jerked and looked down her body at him, "Steve?" Her voice shook with uncertainty.

"What is it?"

"Are you sure you should be..." She trailed off, unable to finish.

He tilted his head to one side, like a curious cat. "Did you like it?"

"Well...yeah." Her face turned pink.

"Then why not?"

"Well..."

"I like the way you taste, baby. Like sweet cream mixed with honey." He watched her a moment longer. "Lay back and enjoy, okay?"

"A-Alright." She did as he asked but didn't entirely relax.

"Tell me if I hurt you, but try to focus on how it feels, okay?" Steve knew that despite what she'd been through, in many ways she was still a virgin. He knew he needed to be patient, but it wasn't easy. He adjusted himself inside his jeans then leaned back down. "I'll tell you what, give me your hands."

She gave them without argument.

He put her hands on his shoulders. "Keep your hands on me, my shoulders, my head, even tangled in my hair. That way, if you don't like anything I do, you can pull me away, all right?"

"All right." She repeated, more confident.

He lowered his mouth to her once more and ran his tongue around the edge of her opening tasting the sweet cream before pushing it as far as he could reach inside.

Jade's fingers curled in his hair, not pulling him away but holding on. He licked and kissed her core, dragging out as much of the sweet moisture as he could. He moved upward, running the tip of his tongue around the hard bundle of nerves that sat exposed. He slid one finger carefully around her opening, moistening the tip as he flicked his tongue over her clit.

The fingers in his hair tightened. They pulled him closer, as if she was unwilling to let him stop.

He sucked hard on the small nub as he slowly pressed one finger into her, easing out and back in, letting the slick fluid flowing from her ease the way.

"Steve?" Her voice was threaded with fear but her grip didn't relax, she still pulled him into her, not away.

It's okay, baby, I know it's a little scary the first time. Trust me. Let it come. He sucked harder on her clit, flicking his tongue back and forth over the tip while working his finger in and out of her.

Her hands in his hair tightened until he thought she might pull his hair out.

Without realizing what he was doing, he purred. A deep rumble that started in his chest and echoed up his throat and mouth, vibrating through her. She screamed his name and her cunt clamped around his finger as she came. He lapped at her center, drinking the sweet honey leaking from her as she relaxed her grip on his hair and went limp against the bed.

"What was that?" she asked once she could speak again.

"That, sweetheart, was an orgasm." He moved up and lay beside her.

She gave him a lazy smile. "I like that."

"I thought you might." He grinned back.

"I didn't know you could do that." She rolled onto her side and curled against him.

"Do what? Make you feel like that?" He wrapped his arm around her and held her close.

"That too, but I mean what you did with your mouth."

"Sweetheart, that's just the tip of the iceberg. We could go on for months, pleasing each other in different ways and finding our favorites."

Her expression turned sad. "But we still have to get past one thing first."

"What's that?" he asked.

"My first time, I mean, except for…" she trailed off.

He rolled to his side and gave her a soft kiss on the lips. "Baby, I thought you did great for a first time, especially with everything you've been through."

"But that wasn't sex." Her face turned red. "It was great, but-"

Steve chuckled. "It's called oral sex for a reason."

"You know what I mean." Her embarrassment faded as she argued.

"I do, baby, but we don't have to do more if you don't want to."

"I want to. I want to be able to put it behind me." She pushed against his chest and he rolled to his back, giving her the space she wanted. "I

154

just…don't know if I can handle it, that feeling of…of being trapped."

"You mean on your back?"

"Yeah." She lost her relaxed manner. "Like then."

"Sweetheart, that's one position. We can go a lifetime and never do that, if it bothers you."

"We can?" She sounded unconvinced.

"Come here." He tugged on her arm until she sat beside his reclined body. "You sure you want to do this?"

"Certain." She gave him a decisive nod.

"You want to help me with my jeans or do you want me to take them off?"

"Can you do it?" She bit her lower lip. "But leave your shorts on, please?"

"No problem." He quickly shed his jeans and lay on the bed where he'd started. He folded his hands behind his head and looked up at her, "What do you want now?"

"Can I touch you? Like you touched me?"

"You mean when I put my mouth on you?"

She looked at him, hesitated then nodded.

"Normally, I'd love to have you use your pretty little mouth on me, but right now I'm not sure of my control. If you put your mouth on my cock right now, I'd come so fast I'd shame myself."

She turned bright red.

"But if you'll hold off on that, I'll do my best to make you come again, when the time comes." He pulled one hand from behind his head to run the backs of his fingers down her cheek and along her jaw.

She slid one tentative hand across his chest, stopping to flick her thumb over one nipple.

He groaned and arched his back, lifting his body into her hand.

"You like that?" she asked.

"Did you?" He countered. "If you liked it, chances are, I will too."

The idea seemed to boost her confidence. She lowered her mouth to his chest taking one small nipple into her mouth. She sucked on it a moment before teasing it with her tongue.

"Bite it, not hard, just a little nip," he encouraged. He drew a sharp breath when she did it, and whimpered. "Just like that. That feels good, Jade."

More sure of herself, she slid her hands down his chest to his hips and

155

fiddled with the waistband of his shorts for a moment before sliding past it. She ran her hands over the soft cotton of his briefs, finding his thick erection. She wrapped her hand around his cock and squeezed through the fabric.

He groaned and fought the urge to pump his hips against her. He pulled her hand away. "I'm too close, baby. Another time."

"How do we do this?" she asked, the uncertainty back in her voice.

"Are you ready?" He looked at her.

She met his eye. "I think so. I'm all hot and tingly all over."

"Hang on a sec." He rolled until he could reach the drawer of his nightstand and pulled out a condom. "Here." He handed her the foil packet then rolled back and slid his shorts off, kicking them aside.

She looked at the condom in her hand. "I didn't even think about this."

"It's okay, Jade, I did." He took the small square from her and ripped it open, unrolling the condom over himself. "Come here." He curled his finger. "One leg on either side, like earlier." He helped her into position, lining himself up with her opening. "Now, it's up to you. You can go as fast or as slow as you like."

"I'm not sure I know how to do this." She looked at him, a worried frown on her pretty face.

"Of course you do, follow your instincts." He slid his hands up her sides until he was cupping her breasts. Flicking his thumbs over the tips he teased them until they drew into tight beads. He squeezed the globes, kneading the soft flesh while he leaned up and flicked his tongue over the tight tips in turn.

Jade groaned at the sensations and her legs relaxed under her, letting her body slide down onto his. Her eyes widened and she froze.

"See, you're hot and wet and you slide easily on my cock. I wish you'd go a little farther though."

She relaxed a little and sank lower onto his manhood.

"God, you feel good." He dropped his head back and groaned at the tight heat surrounding him.

"I don't know how." Her voice shook and he knew she was scared.

He moved his hands to her hip. "Sure you do, lift up a little," he guided her as she rose on her knees, "then relax. Let your weight do the work for you." He groaned as she did exactly as he said and sank all the way onto his cock, her pelvis resting against his. He was completely buried inside her.

He didn't have to urge her to do it again. She slid up then settled back over him, setting a slow, torturing pace.

He moved his hands back up to cup her breasts, flicking the tips before lightly squeezing. He knew it would inflame her senses and make her desperate for more.

She began to move faster, up and down, and her breath came in short gasps. "Steve," she cried. "Help me!"

"Hang on, stop moving for a second." He waited until she came to a stop, her pelvis against his. Her cunt started to clench around him, she was close, but not quite there. "Try this." He shifted her legs, so she had her feet on either side of him, her knees in the air. "Now try."

She moved, her eyes widened at the change in sensation from the different angle and in just a few strokes, Steve felt her tightening around him again. He slipped one hand between them and used his thumb to press against her clit. She screamed and her body seized, tightening around him until he couldn't hold on to his control any longer either. He came with a shout. He caught her as she collapsed against him, his penis still buried inside her.

When they both could breathe normally again, he rolled them both to one side. He went into the bathroom to dispose of the condom and clean up. Taking a wet cloth back to the bed, he cleaned her up before tucking her into bed.

He was tugging on his sweatpants when she stopped him.

"What are you doing?" Her voice thick with satisfaction.

"Putting on my pants."

"Why?"

"Because I always wear them when you're in bed with me."

"Do you sleep in them when I'm not here?"

"No." He frowned.

"Then why bother? It seems silly now that uh we've… you know."

"You sure?" he asked.

"I'm sure. Now come here."

He tossed the pants aside and climbed between the sheets, sliding over to pull her against him.

Chapter 40

The next morning, JV slipped out of bed before Steve woke. She pulled one of his shirts over her head and headed for the kitchen. She was making coffee when strong arms snaked around her waist.

She jumped.

"I didn't mean to startle you," he said against her neck. "I just wanted to see what you're up to."

"Making coffee." She continued what she was doing despite the flip her stomach made as his breath feathered across her skin.

He pressed against her from behind and she felt his erection hard against her ass. "I can see that." He slid one hand under the loose tee shirt and moved it upward along her belly to cup one bare breast. "You sore this morning?" he asked, his mouth barely leaving her neck.

"No."

"In that case, I thought I might see how you felt about morning sex."

His day's growth of beard rubbing against her neck sent shivers through her body. She set the coffee pot aside and twisted her neck to rub her cheek against his. "Sounds like it could be fun."

His fingers found her nipple and teased it to a sensitive peak as his teeth scraped along the bend where her neck met her shoulder.

Heat pooled in her belly and she whimpered, pushing her hips back against his. Her hands fell to her sides, then she reached back and grabbed the sweats on either side of his hips, pulling him against her as she ground against him.

"Here or the bedroom?" he asked against her skin.

Her knees went weak. "I don't know if I can wait."

Chapter 41

"Then here it is." He spun her around and with his hands on her hips, lifted and set her on the counter top. In one easy move, he pulled the loose shirt off over her head and dropped his mouth to hers.

At first, he let his hands rest on the counter on either side of her hips. As things progressed, he moved them up her body. His hands settled on her breasts, covering them while he teased the sensitized tips.

Her tongue dueled with his. Her hands rested loose on his hips for a moment then moved around and under the loose waistband of his sweats to grip his ass. He stood between her parted knees and she pulled him closer, pressing her hips against the hard length of his cock.

Heat from her body poured through the thick cloth. Unable to stop himself he rolled his hips, rubbing his length along her core.

She purred.

The sound only served to make him hotter. He moved his mouth down her neck, trailing soft bites and kisses as he moved to her shoulder. His hands fell to her hips and he lifted her slightly to scoot her closer to the edge of the counter. He almost lost control when she slid her hand down the front of his pants and wrapped it around him. He tried to take her hand, to gently move it away, but she growled and shoved the loose pants off his hips.

Her mouth found one nipple on his bare chest and he dropped his head back as he fought to keep from plunging into her and taking her hard and rough.

Still teasing the tight, sensitive button she used one hand to guide him to her center. He felt her slick heat against the tip and groaned. She grabbed his ass again and yanked him against her, impaling herself on his staff as she bit down hard enough to make him groan.

The sharp sting snapped the final thread of his control. He took her hips in his hands and pulled almost all the way out before slamming into her again, burying himself as far as he would go. He repeated the move, over and over. He felt her nails curl into his back as he kept going.

She gasped. Her breath came hard and heavy. "Yes, yes, more, yes!" He continued until he felt her clench around him and knew she was coming. He kept going, increasing his speed. He tilted her hips just a little and felt as the tip of his cock started rubbing that spot deep inside. After just a few strokes Jade threw her head back, screamed, and curled her fingers into his arms as she exploded around him again. This time he let himself go as well. He held her hips hard against his as he emptied himself inside her.

She wilted against him, exhausted. He gave himself a moment to catch his breath then pulled out, mentally cursing himself when he realized he'd forgotten a condom. Gently, he picked her up and carried her back to their bed.

***

After cleaning them both and making sure she hadn't broken the skin when she'd bitten him, he lay down beside her. "I'm sorry." He laid one hand along the side of her face.

"About what?" She looked confused.

"I followed you intending to bring you back to bed. Things got out of hand and I lost control." He paused a moment, looking a way for a second before meeting her eyes again. "I forgot a condom."

"I know, I don't know why that's a problem though." She seemed genuinely confused.

"Baby, it's my job to protect you. I failed."

"You haven't failed me. You've done everything you could to help me."

"Getting you pregnant won't help you."

Comprehension dawned across her face. She brought her hand up to his face, mirroring the way he held her. "I'm not worried about getting pregnant. The only thing that makes me happier than being here with you now, is the idea of a tiny version of you."

His heart skipped a beat. She wanted to have his baby. He'd thought he'd never have a child and he'd quit even thinking about the possibility a long time ago. His heart sped with the idea. He leaned close and kissed her gently on the forehead. "We'll see."

Chapter 42

JV considered wearing a dress, but looked out the window at the snow that was almost knee deep and decided against it. Instead, she settled on a snug, low cut sweater and her nicest pair of jeans. Steve had informed her he was taking her out tonight and to dress up. Given the weather, she decided these were her best option.

Making herself at home in his cabin, she'd taken a long bath, soaking in the warmth of the hot water before shaving her legs. Afterward, she'd taken the time to work lotion into her skin, hoping he would like the soft scent from the Shae butter.

She dressed carefully, her sexiest silk panties, an indulgence she'd gotten on a whim and had never worn. Instead of a bra, she chose a snug camisole with a neckline even lower than the sweater. She pulled on a pair of warm wool socks Rebecca had given her, then her jeans and sweater. She liked that her jeans were snug without being too tight. She ran one hand up her leg and over her ass, enjoying the way they hugged her butt and thighs before flaring out over her boots.

Her makeup took longer than it should have, but she wanted it perfect and since she didn't wear it often, she was out of practice. She dried and fluffed her hair, leaving it down for a change. Finished dressing, she pulled on her jacket and headed up to the main house to wait for Steve. He'd gathered his clothing while she was in the tub and gone to the other bathroom to shower and dress.

At the back door of the big house, she knocked the snow from her boots. She didn't want to have to take them off only to carry them through the house then put them back on in a few minutes.

"Wow, look at you." Rebecca said as soon as she got a look at her.

"Thanks." JV turned in a slow circle. "You think he'll like it?"

161

"Honey, you could wear a burlap sack and he'd love it," her friend said.

The idea made JV grin. She tugged off her coat to let the other woman see the whole outfit. Dropping it on the table she spun again. "What do you think?"

"I think he'll be drooling though dinner and have a hard time keeping his hands off you later."

She gave her friend a bright smile "What's he got planned? Do you know?"

"I can't say. I've been sworn to secrecy." Rebecca drew a cross over her heart with one finger.

JV sighed. "I guess I'll find out when we get there."

The sound of boots on the back porch made them turn toward the mud room, both of them expecting the same person. A cold blast of wind rushed into the room as the outside door opened, then closed, and Steve appeared in the door.

He stood a moment, speechless as he looked at Jade standing in front of him, ready for the date he was taking her on.

He went to her and pulled her into his arms. "You look amazing." He lowered his head and covered her mouth in a brief, hard kiss.

"Good evening." He turned his attention to Rebecca. "How are you this evening?"

"Good." She grinned at them. "It seems like I only get sick if I go too long without eating."

"All the more reason for that old man of yours to keep you well fed." He glanced around the room. "Speaking of, where is he?"

"In his office, he said he had some paperwork to get done." She watched them as Steve stood with one arm around JV.

"Where's Bobby?" Ever the protector, he was making sure his clan leader and wife would be safe while he was gone.

"Bobby's in the living room. We'll be fine while you're out. I promise." She seemed to read his mind. "You two go on, have fun." She moved around behind them and herded them toward the front door, to where Steve's truck parked in front of the house.

***

Steve took her to a nice family restaurant in Springerville. They sat in an out-of-the-way corner, quietly talking and eating. A woman, JV guessed to

162

be in her early thirties, appeared beside their table. She was a little heavy to be fashionably beautiful, but what caught JV's attention first were her overlarge-breasts. They threatened to fall out of her too-tight shirt. In the next instant, she caught the woman's scent and knew she was Kitsune, part of the local Chanat.

"How dare you!" The woman screeched, glaring at Steve. Heads all over the dining room turned toward them.

JV blinked, wondering what the hell the woman was talking about.

"Tiffany-" Steve started, but the woman turned on JV and cut him off.

"You! What makes you think you can show up here and steal him from me?"

JV looked at Steve, who instantly stood. "This isn't the place, Tiffany." He glanced around the half-full room, taking in who was witnessing the scene.

"He's mine. You better back off or I'll make you sorry."

"Tiffany, that's enough." Steve took her arm and spun her around to look at him. "Go home. This is not the time or the place."

"To hell with the time or place." She jerked her arm from his grip and turned back to JV. "I'll just make you pay now." She grabbed JV by the hair and yanked her out of her chair.

JV landed on her knees and tried to stand, to fight back, but she found she couldn't move. She couldn't speak or move at all. *I can't move!* She sent the telepathic message to Steve in a panic.

"Tiffany, behave yourself." He took her by the arm again.

Whatever kept JV from moving faded and she was able to push herself to her feet. She doubled her fist and hit the woman in front of her in the stomach, hard.

The blow knocked the wind from Tiffany. She loosened her grip on JV's hair. She stood, stunned, while JV straightened to her full height of 5'2", still several inches shorter than Tiffany, and spoke in a low voice. "I don't know who you are, or what kind of relationship you had with Steve, but let me make this clear. You ever lay a hand on me again, and I'll take you down. You get in my face again, and I'll slap you so hard you won't wake up until your fake boobs and overly made-up look is back in style." JV looked past the woman to Steve, who was still holding the other woman's arm. She didn't know what she expected, but it wasn't the grin on his face.

"Tiffany, I want you to meet JV." He lowered his voice so he wouldn't be overheard. "I've known JV for a long time and she won't be going

163

anywhere. She's my mate."

The shock on Tiffany's face made JV want to laugh, but she refrained.

Steve tugged the woman's arm until she faced him. He kept his voice quiet. "You lay a hand on her again and I won't wait for the Khan. I'll deal with your punishment myself. I suggest you mind your manners and leave before I lose my temper and deal with you now." He turned her toward the door and let her go with a small shove. It wasn't enough to propel her away from them, but enough for her to know he meant it. "I'm sorry." He moved to JV. "Are you all right?" He tilted her face up so he could look at it.

"I'm fine. Unless you never broke things off with her, you've got nothing to be sorry for." She pulled away and took her seat.

"Breaking it off would imply that we were actually seeing each other to begin with." He took his own seat and watched as she resumed eating.

"You weren't dating?"

He shook his head. "She's been following me around for months, asked me to a couple different functions. I've found one excuse or another not to go, but she's been persistent."

"Looks like she thought you were together."

"What is it they're saying these days?" He took a drink while he thought. "She's a special kind of crazy?"

JV laughed. From what she'd witnessed, she believed him.

Chapter 43

Steve thought about taking Jade home after the confrontation with Tiffany, but decided against it. She didn't seem bothered by the incident and if she wasn't, then he wouldn't let it ruin the evening either. He was enjoying spending time with her, doing something a little different. Other than bringing her into town to see Karen, he hadn't been off the ranch recently and he was glad to get out.

Since there wasn't a whole lot to do in town, he took her to see a movie. The only theater in town only had a single screen, but they often played two movies, a family-friendly film for the early show and a more mature one for the late show. He'd checked what was showing and planned on the later showing, knowing Jade liked action flicks as much as he did. They arrived in time to get their tickets, popcorn, and drinks, then find their seats with a few minutes to spare.

"Where do you want to sit?" he asked as they looked up at the rows of seats.

"Back row," she said. "In the center." They made their way up to the seats she wanted with no trouble, there was no one seated anywhere near them, at least not yet. "I haven't been to a theater in years," she said settling into her seat. "After I shifted, it was always too loud and gave me a headache."

He looked at her and grinned. "The manager's one of us, he doesn't let them turn it that loud. It's loud, but not too loud." He leaned over and kissed her nose. "Trust me."

"You know I do." She smiled at him as the lights dimmed. She turned toward the screen. When Steve draped one arm around the back of her seat, she turned and leaned against him, resting her head against his shoulder. He liked the feel of her against him.

After the movie, they waited for the crowd to leave before gathering their trash and heading out. "What did you think?" he asked, helping Jade into her coat before they went outside.

"I liked it," she said. "The big crash scene was neat, even if impossible, but the best part was where he fought the three guys." She shivered as a gust of wind blasted her in the face. "There were a few moves there I'd like to try."

He opened the truck door and waited for her to climb in and slide over before getting in himself.

Snow began to fall as they headed out of town. Steve drove in silence while Jade watched the large flakes fly, enthralled. He stole glances at her, enjoying her amazement at something so simple.

"It's almost like we're flying through space." Her voice was soft and tinged with awe.

He tilted his head to one side and tried to see what she did. "I guess it kinda does."

"It's like a scene in Star Wars, with stars flying toward the screen."

He stole a quick look at her and caught the open-mouthed amazement on her face. His stomach flipped and he was glad they'd stayed for the movie instead of going home after the trouble with Tiffany.

"She can freeze us, can't she?" Jade asked, as if reading his mind.

He knew she was referring to an uncommon talent among the Kitsune, one that allowed a shifter to keep another from moving, basically, freezing them in place. "She can."

"That's why I couldn't fight back when she dragged me out of my chair." She went quiet a moment. "What I'm not sure of, is how I was able to move again. Did I break her hold on me or what? How was I able to hit her?"

"I stopped her."

She looked away from the flying snow long enough to shoot him a confused frown.

"I can stop a person from using their talent, the down side is, it doesn't

166

last long and it only works if I'm touching them."

Her frown deepened. "I've never heard of that."

"It's not a common talent and not really talked about by those of us who have it. The idea that someone can take your talent, even temporarily, scares people."

"I can see how it would." Her voice changed and she sounded haunted. She went quiet again, watching the snow fly.

***

Later, as they lay in bed, Jade on her side with Steve curled around her. "You all right, baby?" he asked.

"Yeah." She twisted around to look at his face in the dim light. "I'm fine, why?"

"You sounded a little off earlier. You've been quiet since we got home." He tightened his arm around her, pulling her snug against him.

"I've been thinking, that's all."

"You sure?"

She stretched up and laid a soft kiss on his cheek. "I'm sure."

Chapter 44

The next morning JV was in the main house making breakfast for Rebecca and herself.

"Are you going with us tonight?" Rebecca asked.

JV frowned. "Going where?"

"The river walk."

"What's that?"

"It's a trail along the Little Colorado. This time of year they string it with lights and open it up at night. It's beautiful."

"I don't know. Steve hasn't said anything about it." JV was uncertain.

"Ask him. We go as a group, it's a lot of fun."

"Who all goes?"

"Nick and I, Steve usually goes with us, and we meet the Roberts. We walk through as a group, sipping hot cocoa and visiting with whoever we run into."

JV was glad to see her friend so animated. She'd been so tired lately, or sick, that JV had worried about her. She hoped Steve would agree to go tonight. It would be great to go out with everyone and a chance to meet more of the clan.

Can you hear me? She wasn't sure he'd be able to hear her from so far away. Not that she knew exactly where he was, just that he was helping feed cattle.

Of course I can. Is something wrong? His mental voice was strong as it whispered through her mind.

No, nothing's wrong, I just- She had second thoughts about asking, maybe he hadn't invited her for a reason. *Never mind.*

Jade? He sounded worried.

Rebecca asked if we can go with them to something called the river walk tonight.

Do you want to go?

168

It sounds like it could be fun, she sent, hesitantly.

If you want to, of course we can go.

Rebecca said you usually go, but you hadn't said anything, she sent.

I've had other things on my mind, baby. I didn't realize it was tonight or I would have. I do normally go, but if you wanna go. I'll have Bobby to go with them and we can go too.

Why does Bobby need to go?

Someone has to serve as bodyguard. I'll be busy enjoying the night with you.

She smiled even though he couldn't see her. *That sounds wonderful.*

"You'll need to dress warm. We'll be out in the cold a lot longer than just to and from the truck tonight.

Will do. I can't wait. She knew he sensed her excitement when he sent back a mental laugh. "He says we can go." she said to Rebecca.

Rebecca squealed. "This is great. We're gonna have to find you something warm to wear."

"Steve said dress warm. I figured I'd wear yoga pants under my jeans and a heavy sweater."

"Keep the heavy sweater, but I've got something better than yoga pants." Rebecca looked JV over from top to bottom, as if estimating her size. "You're a little shorter than I am, but I think that'll be to your advantage."

JV didn't say anything, just looked at her friend for a moment then flipped the pancakes on the griddle and checked on the bacon that was nearly done in the oven.

***

After breakfast, Rebecca dragged JV into her bedroom and started digging through drawers. "I know they're here somewhere." She moved from the dresser to the large closet and started looking through the small boxes stacked over the rack. "I just don't remember where I put them last spring."

"Is there anything I can do to help?" JV was uncomfortable standing in the middle of the bedroom watching her go through things.

"They should be – Ah ha!" she interrupted herself. "I knew they were here." She pulled a blue and white flowered box, about the size of a shoebox, from the shelf and went to the bed. "Here," she tossed the lid in the middle of the bed, "put these on under your jeans and sweater." She

169

pulled a thin pink shirt and pants from the box and handed them to JV. "They'll keep you a lot warmer than yoga pants or even two sweaters."

JV held the almost weightless outfit in her hand, rubbing it between her fingers and thumb. "What is it?"

"Thermal underwear, it's silk." Rebecca pulled a second set, black this time, from the box and tossed them on the bed.

"Silk?"

"Yep. Do you have clean wool socks?"

"No, but I was planning to steal some of Steve's, he's got several pair."

"That works."

"I can't take these." JV held up the thermal underwear. "How will you stay warm?"

"I've got another set I'll wear tonight, but I won't be going out as much this winter. I won't be able to wear them much longer anyway. I'll feel better knowing you have them. Take them."

She looked down at the things in her hand, then back up at Rebecca. "Are you sure?"

The other woman smiled. "Positive."

"All right. What else do we need to do? Are we going to take anything with us?"

"The chairs and blankets are already in the truck and they'll have cocoa and a fire there, we just show up."

"Nice."

"It is. It will be better if I can find a pair of pants that fits."

"Yeah, right. You're not even showing yet."

"I may not be showing, but my pants don't fit either." She lifted the tail of the long t-shirt she was wearing to reveal that her pants were unbuttoned and only half-zipped.

"Wow, that didn't take long."

JV sat on the bed and watched while Rebecca tried on several pair of pants before finding a pair she could zip, but they still wouldn't button.

"Do you have any rubber bands?" JV asked, suddenly remembering something

"Yeah," Rebecca frowned. "Of course,"

"Where are they? I want to try something."

"On the counter, in a dish." She motioned to the attached bathroom.

JV retrieved a rubber band and went to her friend. "Let's try this." She threaded the hair tie through the buttonhole on one side of the jeans then looped it through itself. "Now, slip this end over the button."

Rebecca easily slipped the elastic over the button, closing her jeans without cutting off her ability to breathe.

"You're a genius," she said, grinning. "You just kept me from having to wear sweats tonight."

JV returned the smile, happy she'd remembered the trick Matt's late wife, Claire, had shown her. She hadn't known her sister-in-law well, but she knew Matt still hurt from her death, as well as the loss of the baby she'd carried.

***

That afternoon Nick, Rebecca, and Bobby took Nick's truck, while Steve and JV followed in Steve's.

"There's not enough room in that one for all of us," Steve said when JV had asked why they didn't all go together. "Especially not with the blankets and chairs."

"Rebecca mentioned blankets and chairs, but if this is a walk, why will we need blankets and chairs?" JV'd asked, confused.

"For the parade. Didn't she tell you?"

"She didn't say anything about a parade, just the walk."

"The parade is before the walk. We'll find a good spot, wait for it to get dark and watch the parade. Then we'll all ride one of the buses to the river walk."

"Dark?" JV was even more confused now. "They wait until after dark to start the parade?"

Steve chuckled. "It's a light parade, babe."

"Oh." She didn't know what to say. She'd heard of light parades but had never seen one. She fell quiet as they reached the highway and turned toward town.

***

They parked in the vacant lot beside Sonic and found an empty spot along the sidewalk, where their backs would be to the open field to set up their chairs. Bobby stayed with JV and Rebecca while Steve and Nick went to find hot drinks for them while they waited for the parade to start. People passed by on their way to find their own spots, many stopping to chat for a

171

while,

"Hello, ma'am. How're you tonight?" Tiffany asked Rebecca as she made her way past the group, totally ignoring JV.

"I'm good," Rebecca shook her hand. "Have you met my friend JV?"

"We met last night." JV smiled, trying to be friendly despite the previous confrontation.

Tiffany shot her a disgusted look and turned back to Rebecca. "I hear congratulations are in order."

"Thank you." Rebecca was gracious, but she didn't try to extend the conversation.

Tiffany took the hint and continued down the sidewalk to find her own spot to watch the parade.

As soon as she was gone, Rebecca turned to JV. "What happened last night?"

"She made a scene in the restaurant, accused me of trying to steal her man." JV scoffed. "If he were really hers, I couldn't steal him. Anyway, she dragged me out of my chair and I knocked the wind out of her. Steve talked to her a minute and she left." She dismissed the incident with ease.

"What did Steve say to her?" Rebecca looked in the direction the woman had gone, but she was out of sight.

"I don't recall, but it looks like she's gonna try to ignore me now. Works for me."

"Seriously, though, it might be a good idea to watch your back," Rebecca said.

"I will, but as things stand right now, what opportunity does she have to cause trouble? I spend most of my time with you or Steve. I don't think she's gonna pull anything in front of either of you."

"You're probably right, but be careful."

"I will, but I'm not gonna let some vindictive bitch ruin my night."

Steve came beside her. "What vindictive bitch?" he asked, handing her a cup of hot cocoa.

Nick handed Rebecca a paper cup of her own.

"Tiffany."

He scowled. "What did she do now?"

"Nothing." She sipped her cocoa and closed her eyes enjoying the warmth filling her.

"She stopped on her way to find someone to watch with," Rebecca put in. "I tried to introduce her to JV, but JV said they'd met. Tiff ignored her, acted like I didn't even mention her."

Steve rolled his eyes. "She knows what'll happen if she screws with Jade."

Rebecca waited, as if hoping he would explain, but he didn't.

"You all right?" he asked JV instead.

"Yeah, I'm good." She took another sip of the cocoa and looked up at him, "What's in this? It's good, but it's different."

"I added some Bailey's to it. It makes it better."

"That it does." She took another sip.

Steve went to stand beside Bobby and Nick. The three of them spoke in low voices as the Roberts arrived. Karen and Izzy set up chairs and joined the girls while Julio moved toward the men.

"No Ricky tonight?" Rebecca asked, as Karen settled her blanket over her lap.

"No. He's watching with some friends. We don't need a bunch of rowdy teenagers here with us, so I didn't encourage them to join us."

"Thank you for that," JV said.

Karen smiled in return. "We may see him later. He's taking his girlfriend to the river walk. We may run into them, but I wouldn't count on it."

"Hey, hon. I see you found him," an older woman said as she approached.

It took JV a second to remember her name. "Hello, Liz. I did. Thanks again for giving me directions. I've been meaning to come in and say hi, but the one day I had time, you weren't there."

"Must have been my day off." She looked past the women and focused on the group of men still talking behind them. "Steve?"

"Yes, ma'am?"

"Stop hiding your girl on that ranch and bring her to see me once in a while, ya hear?"

"Yes, ma'am."

JV heard the respect in his tone, not the same respect he had for Steve or Julio, as his clan leaders, but the same respect she'd been taught to show her parents friends and grandparents. It made her re-evaluate Liz's age.

"There, now you'll come see me." She grinned at JV and moved on, stopping a moment to talk to Karen before continuing.

Rebecca leaned close. "When did you meet Liz?"

"When I got to town, she's the one who told me how to find him."

"Huh?" Rebecca's confusion written on her face.

173

"I knew he lived in the area, but not exactly where. She gave me directions to the ranch."

Rebecca shook her head. "I can't believe you drove for two days not knowing where you were going."

Says the woman who lived wild, as a cougar, for six months. Steve's voice whispered through her mind.

She looked back at him, wondering how much attention he was paying to them.

"Oh, look! It's starting." Izzy pointed down the street to where the first floats were coming into view.

Everyone turned and watched as the floats started trailing past. A strong burst of wind blew icy fingers down JV's collar, sending a shiver through her.

You cold? Steve's voice whispered through her mind.

A little.

Come here, bring your blanket. He took her thick fleece from her and wrapped it around his own back. *Now stand in front of me, facing out.*

She moved to stand as he'd instructed and he wrapped his arms around her, folding them both into the blanket. She realized he was sharing his body heat with her.

Better?

Much. She snuggled back against him, enjoying the secure feeling of him surrounding her as she continued to watch the cars and trailers strung with hundreds of tiny lights trail past.

Chapter 45

Once the last float had passed and the parade was over, Steve let Jade go. He folded the blanket while she collapsed her chair, then he took that from her as well. He knew Nick and Julio were doing the same. They headed back to where they'd parked the trucks, moving as quickly as the people clogging the sidewalk would allow.

While she'd been occupied with meeting and talking to people before the parade, he'd watched her. She'd seemed at home, comfortable with everyone, even Tiffany, who Steve knew wasn't all that pleasant to be around. He was glad. He wanted her to fit in and make friends. Rebecca was a great start, but he wanted her to have the ties to the clan and the community that she hadn't had in Austin.

She hadn't said it, but he suspected before she'd left, she'd missed the ties she'd shied away from when she'd first gotten there. But after so long, she probably felt like she couldn't change things. He wasn't sure he would have known how either.

Back at the truck, they loaded up and headed to where the busses would pick them up to take them to the walkway along the river. "Did you have fun?"

She looked at him, her face open and happy. "Yeah, that was great."

"You still cold?"

"No." She sent him a smile. "I wasn't really then. The wind had blown down my collar, that's what made me shiver."

"Why didn't you say so?" He shot her a quick frown.

"Because I enjoyed how you kept me warm."

He was quiet for a moment, watching the vehicles around them as he pulled into a space in the large lot. "You don't feel like you're wearing enough to be warm out there." He tugged at the waistband on her jeans half playful, half curious. "What've you got under there?"

She laughed and pulled away slightly. "Rebecca gave me some special underwear," she said as his hand fell away.

"Special underwear?" He gave her a knowing grin. "I bet it's not as good as the ones you had on last night."

Her smile changed from happy to something more carnal. "Oh, I might have some of those on too, but they aren't from Rebecca. The ones she gave me are really thin but warm." She rolled back one sleeve and showed him the pink material. "See?"

Curious, he rubbed the soft material between his thumb and forefinger and smiled. "Silk. No wonder you're not cold, silk is better than wool by a long shot."

"I'll still let you keep me warm, if you want." She flipped her sweater back over her arm and sent him a half-lidded look, her eyes filled with heat.

Steve was tempted to take her home now and take her to bed. She wanted to see the lights though, so he leaned over and gave her a quick, hard kiss instead. "I bet you will. Come on." He opened his door. "If we don't go now, we'll end up staying here."

He pulled her close, wrapping one arm around her as they headed toward a line of parked school buses. He kept an eye out for Nick or Julio so they could all get on the same bus. Spotting Nick, he steered them in that direction.

"There you are," Karen greeted them. "Julio had to take a call, but he'll be right here."

"No problem," Steve said. He looked at Bobby with one lifted brow. The look asked without words how things were.

Bobby nodded once, letting Steve know all was fine, but remained silent and a moment later Julio appeared.

"Are we ready?" He glanced around the group.

"We were just waiting for you, dear," Karen told him.

Together, they headed for the nearest bus. Steve knew they'd gathered near this one because most of the occupants would be Kitsune. It wasn't that they couldn't or wouldn't ride a bus with normal humans, but a bus full of them tended to get louder than was comfortable for most shifters. One with a large number of Kitsune would be quieter.

***

They were about a quarter mile down the trail, admiring the lights strung along the river and displays set up by local businesses. Jade seemed entranced by every one of them, as if it had been a very long time since she'd enjoyed something as simple as Christmas lights. Steve walked beside her, one arm draped around her waist as they went. He kept his thumb looped through the belt loop at her back, it wasn't much but the small contact soothed his nerves. He was uneasy in the crowd, hyper-aware of every man around them and every time one came close to touching Jade. He tugged her closer so he could protect her better.

Since they'd gotten off the bus, she'd been approached several times. Not just by people she'd met or clan members who wanted to meet the newcomer, but by several men. The nerve of some of these men. Who approached a woman who was obviously with someone? Jade had been polite but firm, refusing all offers and invitations. Even then, it had been all he could do not to growl at every man who looked at her. Holding on to her helped, it also kept all but the most aggressive of them at a distance.

"Oh look!" The wonder in Jade's voice pulled him from his thoughts.

"Hmm?" He looked down at her to find her focused, not on another display, but looking skyward. He looked up and found it had started snowing. A light fall of large flakes that floated easily to the ground. "It does that sometimes."

She looked at him. "It's beautiful." Looking around again, she kept going. "Just look at the way it picks up the colors from the lights."

He smiled, not captivated by the snow and lights like she was, but instead by the joy on her face. The rest of the group was only a few paces ahead of them, but it was as if they were alone as they strolled along the path. He pulled her closer, dropped a gentle kiss on top of her head and wrapped his arm around her shoulders. When they reached the end of the path, he took her to get a cup of hot chocolate before they went to stand near one of several small fires.

***

They'd left the rest of the group around the fires and were on the bus back to the truck when his phone rang. He frowned when he saw the caller's name on the screen.

"Romero," he said into the device, wondering why one of the hands would call this late.

177

"Sir, you gotta come quick. It's Frank." Jess's voice was frantic.

"What's wrong?"

"We were in the barn checking on the horses and he just collapsed." The other man's distress was clear in his voice

"Is he breathing?"

"Yeah, but I can't wake him."

"Is it just the two of you or are you all there?" He needed to know if the human hands knew what was going on, but he couldn't ask out right, not on a bus full of people.

"Just us. We've been taking turns. A different pair makes the check each night."

"All right, hold tight. We're in town but I'll be there as soon as I can."

"Okay."

"Call me if anything changes,"

"Will do." Jess said.

Steve hung up and shoved the phone back in his pocket.

"What's wrong?" Jade asked.

"Frank's hurt, we need to get to the barn."

She seemed to sense that he didn't want to say more, at least not here. "Okay."

Chapter 46

JV stayed quiet, even after they'd gotten in the truck and headed for the ranch. Steve drove faster than normal and she hoped there weren't any cops between them and the ranch. When he turned off the highway before the turn off to the houses, she still didn't say anything. She braced her feet against the floorboard and put one hand on the dash to keep from bouncing around too much as he drove as fast as he could without sliding off the road or smashing them into a tree.

"Jess said they were checking on the horses and Frank collapsed," Steve said, finally speaking. "He said he was breathing, but he couldn't wake him." He related what he knew. "I'd like if you'd take a look at him." He glanced at her before turning back to the road.

"Sure." She winced as the truck hit a deep hole and she bounced off the seat and barely missed hitting her head on the roof. "What if I can't do anything?" she asked, suddenly nervous.

"Then I'll push energy at him and hope he heals on his own but he's given me strict orders. No doctors." He didn't look or sound happy at the thought.

"I'll do everything I can," she said, wishing she could touch him in some way, but the truck was moving so violently she needed both hands to hold on.

The truck skidded to a stop in front of the barn and they got out on different sides of the vehicle. JV wasn't willing to wait for Steve to get out first. Together they rushed inside.

"Jess?" Steve called once they were inside.

"Back here," the other man called.

JV ran in the direction of the voice and found the older man stretched out on an old blanket covering the fresh hay in a stall. She saw Jess to one side, but her focus was Frank. She fell to her knees beside him, laid her hand on his cheek and closed her eyes.

Steve growled, low and deep.

"Knock it off," she said without opening her eyes. "You're distracting me." He fell silent and she concentrated, trying to find the cause of his blackout.

She searched his system for several long moments before she found the small blood clot. She focused her energy and pushed it into him. First to break up the already disintegrating blockage, then to repair the damage it had caused.

She didn't know how long she worked, but she knew it had been a while when she felt her energy flag. She dropped to her butt and slumped, but kept her hand pressed to his face, pouring everything she had into him.

She was vaguely aware of movement at her back then she felt a surge of energy. She no longer struggled to find the strength to keep going. She used the extra energy to finish repairing what she could, then she pulled back.

Returning to herself, she became aware of Steve crouched behind her. His upper body supporting her.

"There." She sighed. "It was a stroke. I've done everything I can. We need to try to wake him up."

"Jess, do that." Steve's tone was rough.

She tilted her head back to see what was wrong, but he picked her up instead and carried her out of the stall. Setting her on a bench in the wide aisle he bent down in front of her and looked into her face, his eyes filled with concern.

"Are you all right?" he asked.

She looked at him a moment before answering. "I'm tired, but fine."

"You'd be a lot more then tired if I hadn't given you energy to work." He paused and pulled her into his arms and held her tight. "You would have given him everything you had."

She didn't argue. She couldn't without lying.

"You can't do that, baby. You scared me."

"I'm sorry I scared you, but-"

"But what?"

"Can we go see if it worked?"

"It better have worked," he growled as he loosened his hold on her and let her stand.

She went back to the stall and found Jess, a twenty-something blonde shifter who worked as a ranch hand, helping Frank to sit up.

The old man looked up at her and blinked several times. "I hear I have you to thank that I'm not a vegetable, girl."

"I don't know that you would have been a vegetable-" she started.

He grunted and tried to push himself to his feet.

She tried to go to his side but Steve stopped her with a hand on her arm. She gave him an unhappy look then turned back to Frank. "Not so quick, Frank. Rest for a few minutes. I spent the last-" She stopped and looked at Steve.

"Hour and a half."

Her eyes widened in surprise and she turned back to Frank. "I just spent the last hour and a half putting you back together. Take a few minutes and let your body finish what I started."

He gave her a disgruntled look but stopped trying to get up. "At least you didn't haul me to the hospital and put me in one of those damned beds."

"You told me no doctors," Steve said. "I told you I'd do my best to comply. I didn't let Jess call anyone or take you to the hospital. I just brought you one of our healers. That's wasn't against your orders."

"You've got me there, son." He looked around, unhappy at looking up at everyone. "Can I get up yet?"

"Go ahead, but take it easy for a couple of days. Don't make me have to do that again too soon." She held out one hand and helped the old man to his feet.

Once standing he pulled her against him and gave her a quick hug. "Thanks, girl. I owe you one."

Steve growled.

"Knock it off." She didn't even bother to look at him.

"Frank," Steve's voice was strained. "Will you please let her go, you're hurting her."

The old man backed away and let go of her hand. "I'm sorry, I didn't mean to hurt you."

"It's nothing-" she tried to say, but Steve interrupted her.

"It's not you. It's that you're not me." His voice calmer now.

She spun around and glared at him, hands on her hips. *How dare you!* She sent at him stomping her foot for emphasis.

She was barely aware of Jess helping Frank around them and out of the barn.

181

"I told you I'd do everything I could to protect you. If that means protecting you from yourself, so be it." He took a deep breath and let it out slowly. "I understood when you said I was distracting you. I backed off, but not the second time. Not when there was no need for you to go through it." He looked her in the eyes. "I can sense your pain. It makes me crazy, sweetheart."

She saw the pain in his eyes, the conflict that he had asked her to do something that had hurt her. She also saw the anger that she hadn't let him protect her. "You can't always protect me, Steve. Sometimes I have to stand on my own two feet. Sometimes I have to endure the pain to do what's right. But that's not why I stopped you the second time." She looked away a minute, trying to figure exactly how to put it. "It was different, yeah, touching him was uncomfortable, but it didn't burn. Not like it used to."

Something flashed through his eyes, but it was gone before she could identify it. "Really?" he asked. "You're not just telling me that so I'll back off?"

"I don't lie to you, Steve," She said it harsher than she'd intended but she couldn't back down. It pissed her off that he thought she would lie to him, and about something like this. "I may not give you every detail, but I don't lie."

His face softened. "I know you don't, baby. But I had to ask. I'd know if you were lying to me and I've never sensed that from you." He tried to pull her into his arms but she stepped back, out of his grasp.

She narrowed her eyes at him. "Is it just me or can you tell with everyone?"

He blinked and stepped back, giving her the space she wanted as he looked at her a moment. "Everyone."

She relaxed a little, not sure if the relief that washed through her was a good thing or not. The idea that it was something he could do with just her had scared her but at the same time thrilled her. In theory, she looked forward to the deeper connection she could have with a mate, once the relationship was sealed, but as she was faced with the reality, it was terrifying. She took a deep breath. "All right." She didn't really know what else to say. She knew she couldn't tell him that the idea of his ability being focused just on her scared the shit out of her. She was afraid he would take it the wrong way. She had no doubts about him, but her own issues were jumping to the forefront again. She stood for a few seconds, doing nothing more than breathing and trying to calm her speeding heart. After several moments, she looked at him again. "Are we done here?"

He looked around and shrugged. "No reason to stay."

"Let's get out of here." A chill ran through her as she headed for the door.

He fell into step beside her, slinging one arm around her shoulders he pulled her against him. "Come here. You've worn yourself out and now you're chilled."

Chapter 47

After getting Jade into the house and bundled up so she wouldn't lose any more warmth, Steve built a fire and heated some soup.

"You've got to be careful," he said, putting the bowl on the small table in the kitchen where she sat. "You used so much energy healing him that, even after the extra I gave you, you didn't have enough left to maintain your own body temperature. You have to be careful not to give up more than you can safely spare." He sat across from her and made sure she ate every bite. She'd burned a lot of calories rebuilding what she'd used.

"I've never done anything that big before." She spoke between spoonfuls, "I wasn't thinking about energy or not using too much. All I thought about was the next step and how to fix it. It was wonderful."

"It was scary as hell." Steve shook his head, knowing she hadn't seen herself wilt to the floor with exhaustion. He'd seen the strain in her face, but he hadn't realized how much energy she was using until she'd fallen.

Through it all she'd kept her hand against Frank's cheek and her eyes closed as she'd worked. He'd stood and watched as she'd slowly gone pale, then nearly collapsed and he'd done the only thing he could do short of pulling her away from the old man. He'd backed her up. He gave her the energy she'd needed to finish the job. But he'd be damned if he'd watch her do that to herself again, not if he could help it.

She looked up from her empty bowl and grinned. Her eyes glowed with accomplishment and joy. He knew he was lost. He wouldn't stop her from doing the same thing again, she loved it. He only hoped that as her skill and talent grew, so did her ability to manage it. Until he was sure, he'd do his best to keep her from over-doing it again.

Chapter 48

The next morning, JV woke alone. Surprised to find the other side of the bed empty, she looked at the clock and blinked in disbelief. 12:38pm. She'd slept more than twelve hours. Stretching, she found her body stiff and slightly sore. She pushed herself out of bed and shivered as she pulled on her pajamas and headed for the kitchen.

She must have slept hard. She didn't even remember Steve leaving this morning. She shuffled to the stove and picked up the coffee pot. Cold. Growling, she set the nearly full pot back on the burner and turned it on. She didn't want to have to wait, but she couldn't drink it cold either, not in this chill.

While she waited for the coffee to heat she added wood to the coals in the stove and stoked it back to life. It wouldn't be long before the room was warm. She was on her way back to the kitchen to check on the coffee when the front door opened and Steve was blown inside by a gust of cold air. Snow flurried around him as he pushed the door closed. He shook his head and more snow fell.

"It's cold out there." He said, spotting her. "Looks like you haven't been up long."

She blinked at him a moment, trying to put the words together to answer him. "Maybe ten minutes. I'm waiting for the coffee."

"I left almost a full pot." He said with a frown.

"It was cold. I'm warming it up." She scowled. Not because she was mad or upset, but because she couldn't think. Her mind was foggy and slow, as if she hadn't slept in days.

He finished shedding his outerwear and moved closer. "Did you put wood in the stove? It's cool in here."

She frowned deeper. "Yeah."

He stopped in front of her and looked down at her a moment, then lowered his mouth to hers. His arms went around her as he placed a soft kiss against her lips.

She sighed as his warmth surrounded her and opened her mouth against his. Leaning into the kiss she quickly forgot about the coffee, the chill in the house or the dull ache of her muscles. Lost in his kiss, she wrapped one arm around his neck and let her fingers play through the short curls at the nape of his neck.

He cupped her cheek and plundered her mouth and she let him. A small sound escaped her throat as she melted against him. He pulled away. "How do you feel this morning?" His voice had gone deep and husky.

JV was quiet a moment. She put her forehead against his shoulder as she tried to gather her scattered thoughts. "Stiff, achy. Not nearly as rested as I should be after almost twelve hours sleep." Her stomach rumbled loudly, interrupting her.

"And hungry?"

"Yeah. Starving."

"Come on," he walked her toward the kitchen. "The coffee should be hot. I'll make you something to eat." He started pulling out pans and food while she poured herself coffee and sat at the table to drink it and watch him.

While he cooked, she asked about his morning.

"Nothing special." He spread a full pound of bacon out on a cookie sheet and put it in the oven. "We fed the cattle and broke the ice on the water trough, just like every morning."

"How was Frank?"

He shrugged. "Fine. If I didn't know about last night, I never would have guessed something had happened."

"That's good." She looked away. She was glad Frank was fine, even if she felt hung over this morning. Knowing that what she'd done the night before had been worth it, helped. She'd hate to feel like this for nothing.

***

After eating more food in one sitting than she'd eaten in more than a day, JV didn't want to do anything but lay on the couch and try to sleep but she didn't want to be alone.

"What are your plans for today?" She asked him.

"Nothing."

186

"No guard duty?"

He shook his head once. "Nick's at the house with Rebecca, if they have any trouble he'll call, but there's no need for me to hang around over there."

"Good, I don't feel like being social today."

"What do you want to do then?" He pulled her to her feet and into his arms.

"Honestly?" She looked up at him a moment before continuing, "Nothing. It's cold and nasty out there and all I wanna do is bundle up and sit tight."

"Wanna go find a couple of movies?" He held her close and spoke softly, "I'll get us a blanket and make some popcorn."

"Sounds great." She stretched up and gave him a quick kiss on the cheek, then went to find something for them to watch.

***

They sat together on the sofa, half reclined and covered with a quilt. They'd finished the first movie and were an hour into the second when she felt Steve stiffen behind her. She frowned. A moment later he paused the movie.

"Nick asked if we can go up to the house for a little bit, he wants to talk to us."

JV scowled. "Did he say why?"

"No, just that he'd like to speak to you."

She took a deep breath and let it out slowly. "Do I have time to get dressed?" She was still in the sweats she wore as pajamas, they were warm and she hadn't seen a reason to change just to watch movies.

"Go ahead. He didn't say anything about it being urgent. When you're ready, we'll head up."

Chapter 49

JV stood in Nick's office, wondering what was so important that he wanted to talk to her alone.

"Have a seat." He led her to a seating area away from his desk and sat.

She sat and waited for him to tell her what he wanted.

He sat watching her for a moment before saying anything. His silent contemplation made her want to squirm but she managed to sit still.

"Frank came to see me this afternoon." he said after a while.

So that's what this was about. She hoped he wouldn't be too upset. She knew Frank had insisted on no doctors and she'd done more than a doctor could have. "Oh?"

"He told me what happened last night, at least his side of it. Would you care to tell me your take?"

He had one of the best poker faces she'd ever seen. She had no clue what he was thinking, or if Frank had been upset by what she'd done. She recounted the events of the night before, telling him that she'd done what she could to help the old man. "He was up and moving around just fine, but I kinda got mad at Steve, Jess and Frank left before I could take another look at him. I hope he's still doing all right."

"He's doing great. In fact, he says he feels better than he has in ages."

"That's good to hear." She let out a breath she hadn't been aware she'd been holding and a huge amount of tension went with it. She'd been more worried about Frank than she'd been willing to admit.

"What you did for Frank last night, and by extension the rest of the clan, is why I wanted to talk to you." He sat back in his chair, making himself comfortable.

Her heart raced. "Oh?" She tried to keep the worry from her voice.

"I'm sure that you know by now that we have no healer."

"Yeah," she frowned. "Steve told me that some time ago."

Nick took a deep breath. "That was probably about the same time he told me you can heal. He said you weren't very strong though."

"I'm not."

"What you did for Frank last night was no small bit of healing. It was big, huge."

"But-" She started.

Nick held up one hand. "I didn't ask you here to argue about it. I wanted to invite you to join the clan and offer you the position of clan healer."

JV sat staring at him, her mouth agape. She didn't know what to say. After blinking several times she could finally form a response. "A-are you sure?"

He laughed, good-natured. "I wouldn't have said anything if I wasn't sure, JV. I respect you and Steve both too much to screw with you like that."

"I'm flattered."

"I'm not offering you the position to flatter you. I'm offering it because I think you'd be a benefit to the clan. I think you'll do your best by the clan."

"But what if things don't work out between Steve and I?" she asked, hesitant to make the commitment.

"This has nothing to do with your relationship with him. You are welcome to stay, to be a part of my clan whether you're mated to him or not, whether you take this position or not."

She closed her eyes a moment as emotion overwhelmed her. "I'll do it. I'd love to take the position."

"Then welcome to the clan." He extended his hand to her.

She took his hand and shook it. Her breath hung in her chest, heat flashed through her entire body and suddenly she heard of a multitude of heartbeats in her head. The sudden sensations overwhelmed her and everything went black.

***

JV opened her eyes to find Steve staring down at her, his deep brown eyes filled with concern.

"Are you all right?" he asked, then looked away, to someone else. "What happened?"

"I'm not sure," Nick's voice answered. "We were talking, everything was fine. Then I shook her hand, her eyes rolled back in her head and she passed out."

A deep rumble started deep in his throat as he looked at the other man. "You hurt her." He ground out.

JV lifted her hand to his cheek to get his attention. "He didn't hurt me," she said softly.

Steve looked back down at her, the anger falling from his face. "Then what was it?"

"I'm not sure, but it wasn't him. Not directly."

"Not directly?" Steve's eyes narrowed.

"Let me up and I'll try to explain." She pushed herself into a sitting position and realized she was lying on the sofa. Someone had moved her after she passed out. Steve backed up only far enough to let her sit up. He stayed close and took one hand in his while he waited for her to explain.

She looked at her new clan leader, then back to Steve. "He asked me to join the clan."

"And that made you pass out?"

"No, it was later, after I agreed to be the clan healer. I shook his hand and suddenly I felt the clan, the whole clan. Heartbeats echoed in my head. It seemed like hundreds of drums thundering through me. It was too much. My mind simply shut down. I'm fine now. It's not gone, but it's not overwhelming anymore. It's more of a distant awareness." She looked at Nick. "Have you ever heard of something like this?"

He looked at her a moment. "The heartbeats and passing out, no, but the distant awareness part, that's how the clan feels to me."

She frowned. "How strange." She put her hands on Steve's waist and moved him to one side and stood. Steve immediately wrapped one arm around her waist, as if worried she would fall.

Nick watched them a moment longer, as if uncertain what to say or do. He looked as if he wanted to say something but he wasn't sure about how Steve would react.

Rebecca appeared in the office door. "Is everything all right in here?"

JV turned and smiled at her friend. "I think so. I had a bit of trouble a few minutes ago, but I'm fine now."

Rebecca frowned, her concern obvious. "What happened?"

JV told her friend what had happened then took a deep breath and laid her head back against Steve's chest, where he stood right behind her. A wave of fatigue washed over her and she wished it was bedtime.

Rebecca scowled, looked around the room, then shrugged, her face clearing. "Looks like everything's all right now. Who's hungry?"

JV's stomach growled, loudly, and heat rushed to her face. "I guess I am," she admitted.

"Come on, let's go eat." Nick led them all from the room.

Steve kept his arm around her as they went to the kitchen.

Chapter 50

Steve watched as Jade ate, wanting to make sure she got enough to help restore some of the energy she'd spent the night before. He was worried about what had happened in Nick's office, but only because it was odd. He'd never heard of anything like it, but then he'd never heard of anyone going from being a loner to a clan healer, either. He suspected her hearing the clan like she had, was because of the position she'd accepted.

When Jade filled her plate for the third time, he quit worrying about her eating enough. She'd already out eaten him, though she was so caught up in conversation, she didn't seem to notice.

"So, now that you're officially our healer, I have a couple people I'd like you to meet. To see if there's anything you can do for them." Rebecca said.

"I'd be happy to." Jade started.

"Just as soon as she's recovered from last night." Steve interrupted. "She used a lot of energy, more than she could spare. She needs to regain her strength before she does anything else."

Jade started to protest but took one look at his stern expression and stopped.

"I agree," Rebecca said. "It doesn't need to be right away, no one is in any danger, but when you're ready. You might be able to help them."

"I'd like that." Jade replied.

The girls started talking about Christmas plans, shopping and meal plans. After a while Nick stood, picking up Rebecca's empty plate as he went. She started to get up to help him. "No, you two talk, I can take care of this." He stopped her.

Steve looked at the two women and saw no reason he needed to sit with them. He picked up his own plate and took it to the sink. He looked back at Jade, she was still slowly eating a mountain of mashed potatoes on her plate, so he left it there as he started clearing the rest of the food from the table.

He was glad to see her so happy and animated, though she still had dark circles of exhaustion under her eyes. After as much sleep as she'd gotten last night and what she'd eaten today, to still have marks that dark, she'd used more energy than he'd realized.

He bit the inside of his cheek to keep from growling. Hell, curbing his desire to take care of her and protect her from the world wasn't going to be easy. He'd known that. What he hadn't counted on was how difficult it was gonna be to protect her from herself. But he wouldn't change her if he could. He loved her just the way she was. He *loved* her.

A glass slipped from his hand and crashed to the floor. Shattering, it sent shards of sharp glass skittering in all directions.

"Shit. Sorry." He said going for the broom.

Rebecca started to stand, to help clean up the mess.

"Don't move, kitten," Nick stopped her. "You're barefoot. Just give us a few minutes, we'll get it cleaned up, no problem."

She nodded once. "You all right, Steve?" she asked, her voice filled with concern.

"I'm fine. It just slipped out of my hand. I'm sorry about the glass." He gave his Karhyn an apologetic look.

"I'm not worried about the glass. Are you cut?" Rebecca asked.

"Nope." He quickly picked up the large pieces and swept up the remaining glass. After cleaning the mess, he put away the broom and, seeing that Nick had already loaded the dishes, he stopped behind Jade's chair. "You through yet?" He kissed the top of her head.

"Yeah, I'm done." She pushed the plate away and started to stand.

"I've got it." He took care of her plate and headed back to the table. He was about to resume his seat when Jade had to stop mid-sentence for a large yawn. He took a closer look. Her eyes were surrounded with dark circles and they looked sunken. He shot a concerned look at Rebecca then turned back to Jade. "You about done for the night?"

"I'm done in." She yawned again. "Suddenly I can't keep my eyes open."

"We were out late last night. We can call it an early night." He said good night to their clan leaders and helped her bundle up for the walk home.

***

Steve woke the next morning and lay still a moment. Looking down at her sleeping face where it rested on his shoulder he was relieved to find the dark marks surrounding her eyes were gone. He had worried about how long it would take to recover her strength. Confident she would be all right, he slipped gently from the bed, dressed, and headed for work.

At the barn, he found the hands already working. Everyone knew what needed to be done on a daily basis and, unless there was something extra or some change, they didn't need much direction.

The horses had been turned out into the corrals to move around. The stalls already cleaned. Steve was helping Frank stock the stalls with food and water, when Jess appeared in his path.

"We have a problem, sir."

Steve scowled at the sir. He didn't like it but he didn't discourage it either, especially among the clan. It helped to remind them of his position and the respect due it. "What?"

"One of the heifers. She's breathing hard and moving slow. If I didn't know it was way too early, I'd say she's in labor."

"Shit." Steve took a deep breath and pushed it out in a rush. "Are you sure she's not? Is there any way she could have bred early?"

"I guess it's possible," Jess looked confused, "but I don't see how."

"Where is she?"

"Out here." Jesse led him out of the barn and toward one of the corrals where a lone cow stood.

Steve watched her for a moment. Her swollen sides heaved as she seemed to pant in short breaths. "Where'd you find her?"

"Near the tree line. She'd separated herself from the heard."

"Son of a bitch," Steve said under his breath. "Put her in one of the extra stalls and keep an eye on her. It looks like she's still in the early stages and it could be days yet before she delivers." He clapped one hand on the other man's back. "Good catch." He went back to finish helping with the feed, but found the job done. He hung around long enough to make sure everything was taken care of and that someone would check on the heifer and let him know if her condition changed, then he went up to the main house.

Chapter 51

JV woke alone. She was used to it, but now it was different. After waking in Steve's arms for a while, she missed the warm comfort of him there beside her.

Sitting up, she stretched and looked at the clock. It was already after 8:00am. She hurried with her shower and dressed to go into town. She and Rebecca were going to get groceries today and possibly a few last minute gifts while they were out.

***

At the main house, she let herself in the back door and found Nick seated at the dining room table. He sipped a mug of coffee as he watched his wife move around the kitchen.

"Good morning, sir." JV said automatically.

He turned and scowled at her. "What did I tell you about sirring me?"

She grinned. "Not to. Sorry, but it's habit and you're my clan leader now."

He shook his head and looked back to his wife.

JV turned toward Rebecca. "What's the plan and what can I do to help?"

"Have a seat, breakfast's almost ready," Rebecca said, pulling pancakes off the griddle and ladling more batter on. "After we eat, we'll take one more look at our list, then head into town."

JV pulled herself a plate from the cabinet and took it to the table, then poured herself a cup of coffee. "Who's going with us today?" She looked first to Rebecca then to Nick for an answer.

"I'm not sure yet," Nick said. "I'd like to check with Steve and see what he has in mind before we decide."

JV shrugged and took a deep pull of the strong coffee. She'd been in a hurry and hadn't bothered with coffee before leaving the cabin. The caffeine hit her system and she closed her eyes, enjoying the jolt the chemical sent through her.

***

They'd just finished eating when the buzz of a snowmobile let them know someone was on their way up from the barn. JV helped Rebecca clean up while Steve came in. She met him with a cup of hot coffee and he took a seat at the table with Nick.

As she and Rebecca went through the pantry and over the menu for the holiday meals, the two men discussed ranch business. JV followed Rebecca with a pad of paper, writing down whatever was needed, occasionally turning the page over and adding things to a list of her own, for the cabin.

After they finished, Rebecca went to change and JV poured herself another cup of coffee. She turned her back to the counter and leaned against it as she sipped from the mug. The sparkle of sunlight glinting off the snow caught her attention and she stood looking out the window over the sink. Other than the snowmobile tracks heading toward the barn and the footpath through the woods to the cabin the snow was pristine.

JV frowned. It seemed odd that nothing had disturbed the ice and snow. No animals or people playing in the snow.

"Jade?"

She blinked and turned toward the table. "Yeah?"

"You about ready to go?" Steve asked.

"Yeah." She frowned. "Rebecca just went to get dressed, then we can go."

"Good." He pushed himself out of the chair and took his mug to the counter to refill his cup. "How long do you think?" he asked pouring more coffee. "Fifteen, twenty minutes?"

"Probably about that, why?"

"Just wanted to know if I have time to change."

"You're going with us?" Her brows lifted with surprise.

"Is there some reason for me not to?"

"No, I was just surprised. Bobby usually takes us shopping."

"Bobby's gonna stay here with Nick. They've got a heifer they're gonna keep an eye on. He's better delivering calves than I am."

"Sweet." She grinned. "Go change. You'll probably be ready before she is."

She watched him go, coffee cup still in his hand.

"How do you feel today?" Nick asked, drawing her attention away from Steve.

"Good," she said.

"Not still tired from healing Frank?"

"Nope." She shook her head. "I woke up this morning feeling great. Full of energy and ready to go."

"That's good." He nodded once and lifted his mug. "Very good." He turned and looked out the window beside him.

Not sure what else to say, JV turned back to her own coffee and waited for the others.

***

"I've got to get out. I need to shift." JV said to Steve.

Even though they'd gone to town earlier in the day it had been weeks since she'd shifted. She was getting desperate. She felt desperate. Her skin was tight and itchy and she felt like she had to get out of it.

"That's fine. Let me go with you."

She shook her head. "No need. I won't go far, and I won't be out long, but I need to spend some time with my cat, alone."

He hesitated, but finally agreed. "I'll wait for you here, let you in when you're done so you don't have to shift out in that cold."

She stretched up and gave him a soft kiss on the cheek. "Thank you." She stripped, shifted, then padded to the front door and waited for him to let her out.

Outside she shuddered at the cold, then hopped over the porch railing and took off at a run into the trees. She stayed close to the cabin, but ran through the trees. Darting under branches and weaving in and out of the scattered pines, she circled to keep from going too far from the cabin. The movement warmed muscles she hadn't been able to stretch in what felt like ages and helped to drain some of the pent up anxieties from her system. When she'd run off the worst of her tension she leapt into a tree, and hopping from branch to branch climbed as high as she dared.

Looking around she could see the barn and the glint of the fading evening light reflecting off the headlights of one of the snowmobiles. In the other direction was the bright light of a car on the highway. She watched a moment, waiting to see if they would turn into the driveway. When they continued past without slowing, she took one last look around and started to make her way down from the tree. She moved carefully from limb to limb, and as she approached the ground, she spotted a clear spot maybe ten feet away from the trunk. She was still several feet in the air when she leapt. Her front paws hit the ground first, absorbing most of the impact and a screaming pain shot through her left paw and arm. She clenched her teeth to keep from crying out.

Licking her paw to sooth the pain, she tasted blood. She flipped her tail around and brushed the snow away from where she'd landed and found a tree stump and the tree that had fallen from it lying on the ground several long sharp splinters protruding from the end.

Feeling stupid for making such a stupid mistake, she huffed out a burst of air and headed for the cabin, making slow progress on three legs, putting off admitting what she'd done for at least a few minutes.

Can you open the door for me? she sent at Steve as she approached the front door to the cabin. She went the long way around, up the steps and across the snow-dusted porch instead of over the railing.

Seconds later the door opened. His eyes found her, then flickered to the bloody trail she'd left.

"What happened?" he asked as she slipped past him.

She shifted while he closed the door. Once human again she cradled her left hand. "I jumped out of a tree and hit a broken stump hidden under the snow." She shivered in the warm room.

He picked up a fleece throw from the back of the sofa, and wrapped around her. "Let's get you warm and take a look at it." He led her through the bedroom they shared and into the bathroom. "Can you wash it out while I grab the first aid kit?"

She nodded and went to the sink while he disappeared back into the bedroom for several seconds. When he returned he was carrying a large plastic toolbox. She lifted one brow, but he never looked at her. He closed the commode, set the box on the lid and opened it.

Turning back to her he held out one hand. "Here, let me see."

She shut off the water and gave him her hand, closing her eyes. She didn't want to see how bad it was, it would only make it hurt worse.

"You've got a couple of good sized splinters in here that need to come out."

She opened her eyes to look, she needed to see how big they were. They weren't long, but one was nearly as big around as a pencil. No wonder it hurt so bad. She whimpered and her knees gave out.

Steve caught her before she hit the floor and eased her down to sit on the edge of the tub.

She'd been right, the sight of her hand made it throb even harder. She whimpered, her eyes still glued to the sticks jutting out of her hand.

Steve sighed, drawing her attention back to him. "They're gonna have to come out, baby. Sooner rather than later." He glanced down at her hand again. "You're already starting to heal, if we wait too long you'll heal around them and it will just take that much longer."

She nodded. She knew this was gonna hurt.

The front door opened. "Steve?" Nick's voice called.

"In here." Steve called back. "I can't do this alone. I called for some help," he said to her.

Rebecca appeared in the bathroom doorway. "What's up? Nick said JV's hurt?"

Steve moved so she could see the hand he still held by the wrist.

"Oh, my." Rebecca looked around. "It's too small in here for all of us, can we move to the kitchen table?"

JV looked back and forth between the two of them, uncertain.

"Let's do that," Steve said. "Can you grab the first aid kit? I'll get her in there." He waited for Rebecca to leave before taking a clean towel off the shelf, loosely wrapping JV's hand in it and resting her hand against her chest. "Can you hold that there?" He met her eyes.

She nodded still lost in a haze of throbbing pain.

Steve picked her up and cradled her against his chest as he carried her into the kitchen.

In the kitchen, Steve settled into one of the dining chairs and sat JV sideways on his lap. He gently pulled her hand from where he'd propped it against her chest and extended it over the table toward Rebecca. "Don't look at it, baby. Just look at me." he said, trying to distract her.

JV felt Rebecca unwrap the towel and move her hand and arm around several ways, trying to get a good look at the wound.

There was a sharp hiss as someone gasped through their teeth.

"Steve," Rebecca said, her voice strained.

JV kept her eyes focused on his face as he looked past hers at her hand. He grimaced. Now she had to look. Slowly, not really wanting to see, but she had to know, she turned. It didn't make sense at first. She blinked and slowly her mind made sense of what she was seeing. There were not two but four sticks coming out of the back of her hand. The world spun and started to go dark.

"It'll be okay. We'll take care of it," Steve murmured in her ear.

She looked back at his face, happy for the opportunity to look away from the mess of her hand.

His eyes were filled with concern. She met his look. "I trust you, do whatever needs to be done." She closed her eyes and laid her head against his shoulder. He would take care of her, she had no doubt.

Chapter 52

Steve closed his eyes and prayed for strength.

"Grab the whiskey from the cabinet." He looked at his Khan. They had no way to keep from her from hurting and he knew it was gonna hurt like hell when they pulled those pieces of wood from her hand.

"You think this is a good idea?" Nick asked, setting the bottle and a tall drinking glass on the table in front of him.

"Not really, but it's all we've got." He poured about four fingers of the amber liquid into the glass and picked it up. "Jade, baby, I need you to drink this." He put the glass in her uninjured hand. "It's gonna burn, but drink it as fast as you can."

She looked at him once then tipped the glass back and drained it in a few quick gulps. Coughing she set the glass on the table with a thunk. "What was that?"

"Whiskey." He poured another two fingers. "We don't have anything quick enough to help with the pain." He nodded at the glass. "Again."

She threw the contents down her throat with a move that spoke of someone used to doing shots. "One more." She held the glass out.

He poured until she told him to stop and watched as she quickly drained it once more. She set the tumbler on the table with exaggerated care. "Okay. Do it." She closed her eyes again and put her head back on his shoulder.

Steve picked up the bottle, took a long drink, then nodded to Rebecca. "Do it."

Nick went to the sink and washed his hands while Rebecca uncapped the bottle of alcohol from the first aid kit and poured it over the wounds on both sides of Jade's hand.

She inhaled sharply against his neck but didn't move. He did the only thing he could. He held her close and did his best to hold her arm still.

201

Steve watched helpless, as Nick and Rebecca each took a pair of forceps and, at the same time, pulled different pieces of wood out the back of Jades hand.

Jade whimpered and pressed her face into his neck.

"It's okay baby, we're half way there."

"But there were four, that was only one," she said.

"They're working together, so it's faster and hurts less."

She pushed her face tight against his neck and he nodded at his Karhyn.

Together, the clan leaders pulled the last two pieces from her hand. Blood flowed freely onto the towel beneath it.

"Hard part's done now, baby." Steve whispered.

Rebecca poured alcohol over the wound again, flushing away some of the blood. "How did this happen?"

"I'm not sure," Steve said. "She shifted and went out for a little bit, she wanted to be alone. Maybe forty-five minutes later she came back like this."

"I can't tell how much damage there is here," Rebecca said. "JV, can you move your fingers for me."

Jade picked up her head and, her eyes still closed, flexed each finger in turn. "There's some damage there but nothing's severed as far as I can tell. It'll take some time and I'll have a weak hand for a while, but I'll heal."

"All right then, I'll make sure there are no more bits of debris in here and close you up."

"No stitches," Jade warned. "Even as bad as this is, you'd have to pull them in just a few hours. Just close it up and bandage it tight."

Rebecca used the tweezers to pull small bits of debris from the wound on Jade's palm then carefully pulled the skin as closed as she could. She used several gauze pads and a lot of tape as she bandaged both sides of the hand. "Can you tell us how you did this?"

Jade told them what she'd done, stopping several times to breathe through the pain. By the time she'd finished, so had Rebecca. Jade curled her bandaged hand against her chest, near her shoulder to keep it above her heart, while her friend worked on cleaning up the mess.

"Leave it," Steve said, still holding Jade in his lap. "I'll get it."

"I've got it." Rebecca ignored him. "You've got your hands full."

Steve shook his head, knowing he had no way to stop her.

"She's gonna need to eat so she'll have the energy to heal that." Rebecca dumped the trash from the bandages into the can at the end of the counter.

"Not now, please." Jade stirred in his arms.

"You need fuel." Steve protested.

"Not now. I won't be able to keep it down."

"Are you sure?" He knew he was frowning.

"Yeah. Give me a little while for the throbbing to fade and the alcohol to wear off."

"I didn't realize you'd had that much."

"I didn't, but I hurt bad enough, I'm lucky I'm keeping even that down."

"I'm sorry, baby." He pulled her tighter against him and wished he could do something.

Rebecca put the things she'd used back into the first aid kit and closed the case, but left it on the table. "Let us know if there's anything we can do."

"Will do." Steve said, lifting Jade in his arms as he stood. "Thanks for the help." He followed the clan leaders into the living room, still carrying her and held her as he said goodbye, then he took her into the bedroom and laid her on the bed. "Hold on, baby, I'll be right back."

He dug through the first aid kit until he found the bottle he was looking for, then took it and a glass of water back into the bedroom.

Sitting on the bed beside Jade he dumped several pills into his hand. "I need you to take these, Jade." He helped her sit up.

"What is it?"

"Tranquilizers. They'll help you sleep for a little while so your hand can stop throbbing enough that you can eat."

She took the pills without another word, swallowing them down with a small sip of water. He wanted her to drink more, but understood that she didn't want to put too much in an already upset stomach. He laid her down and started to go in the other room.

"Wait."

He turned back to look at her.

"Stay with me, just for a while."

A small smile formed on his lips. "No problem." He rejoined her on the bed. He lay on his back and she curled against his side, resting her injured hand on his chest.

He wrapped one arm around her, holding her against him and wishing he could have done more. He knew it would likely be an hour or more before he could get her to eat anything, so he pushed energy into her body to help her heal faster. He hated seeing her in this much pain. He felt helpless. He hated feeling helpless.

He waited until her breathing slowed and he was sure she was asleep, then eased out of bed and headed for the kitchen. He wanted to have something ready when she woke.

Chapter 53

JV woke slowly, the ache in her left hand reminding her why she was in bed. The pain had faded some, but she was afraid to move fearing any movement might make her hand throb again.

She lay on her back, her hand resting on her chest as she stared blankly up at the ceiling. Her stomach rumbled, making her realize how hungry she was. Starving.

Where was Steve? She frowned. She knew he'd stayed with her until she'd fallen asleep, but she couldn't hear him moving.

Where are you?

Don't worry, I'm right here. His voice slid smoothly through her mind. Seconds later, he appeared in the open doorway. "How you feeling, baby?"

"Better."

"Think you could eat?"

"Oh, yeah." She glanced at her injured hand. "But I don't want to move and make it hurt more."

"Here." He sat on the edge of the bed and picked up a pill bottle from the nightstand. "Take this." He gave her a single pill and held the glass of water, waiting while she popped the pill in her mouth.

"I hope that doesn't knock me out like the stuff earlier did."

"It's the same stuff, but it shouldn't. I didn't give you as much, plus, alcohol amplifies the effects, that should be gone by now."

"How long did I sleep?" She looked toward the clock, but he sat between her and it, blocking her view.

"About two hours."

She blinked, surprised. "Are you sure it's not too soon to give me more meds?"

"Yeah. Under normal circumstances it takes us about an hour to metabolize a normal dose of that stuff. You're trying to heal, so yours is moving faster than normal."

"Then why did I sleep so long?"

"Because I gave you a lot of it. I wanted it to knock you out for a while."

"What is it?"

"Animal tranqs"

She frowned. "Animal tranqs?"

"It's used on humans too, but it's easier for us to get a hold of them through the vet."

She lifted her brows, "Especially with the number of animals kept around here."

"Exactly. The vet is clan, but he still has to be able to give an accounting for where it goes."

"You use a lot of it?"

"Not a lot, but I keep it on hand, just in case."

"I for one, am glad you do."

"You ready to try getting up?"

She wanted to, but her hand had just quit hurting. She didn't want to go through that pain again, much less so soon. She looked at him, reluctant.

"Come on," he said. "I'll help." He moved around to her side of the bed. "Keep this arm curled against you. Rest your hand above your heart if you can." He helped her position her hand just so. "Now give me your other hand."

She put her good hand in his and let him pull her to her feet. The room spun for a moment and she leaned against him and closed her eyes.

"You all right?" He sounded concerned.

"Just a little dizzy." She opened her eyes again and found the spinning had stopped. "It's better now. Let's go." She started for the kitchen.

He held on to her. "Are you sure?"

She frowned. "Of course I'm sure."

"Be careful. Dizziness and impaired judgment are side effects of the meds."

"Then walk with me. But let's get moving, I'm ready to eat."

He chuckled. "All right, let's go feed you."

***

206

JV gritted her teeth and balled her left hand into a fist. It had been three days since she'd hurt herself. The new skin was shiny and pink but it was whole. She'd burned a lot of energy, in short bursts, to heal the broken bones, the damaged ligaments and muscles. There was still a ways to go, but she was able to leave the bandage off. Steve had made sure she didn't exhaust herself again, and that she ate enough to replace what she was burning. He'd taken good care of her. She felt guilty that Nick and the rest of the hands had had to work harder to get everything done so he could be with her.

Today was the first time since her injury he'd left her alone, as in gone farther than the next room, for more than ten minutes. Even when he'd taken her to see Karen the day before, he'd never been more than a few minutes away. She was starting to feel a little smothered but she hadn't said anything. He was only trying to take care of her and she appreciated it too much to say anything to hurt his feelings. Still, she was glad to be alone, even for a few minutes. She flexed her hand several more times, despite the pain, then got dressed and followed Steve up to the main house. She had too much to do to let a stupid accident stop her for long.

***

When JV reached the main house, she found Rebecca already working on the baking. They knew there would be a lot of people in and out and there was a lot to be done. She was glad they had agreed to start earlier. She moved past Steve and Nick without a word, washed her hands and stopped beside Rebecca.

"What do you need me to do first?"

"You sure you're up to it?" Her friend looked at her hand instead of her face.

"It's fine. A little tender but I'm not letting it stop me."

"All right," Rebecca said, her face uncertain. "I've got the first batch of dough in the refrigerator chilling, can you get out the cookie sheets and start scooping it?"

"No problem." JV said and went to work.

They worked until lunch time. During that time Nick and Steve had gone out to the barn, come back, and disappeared into Nick's office.

Taking a break, the girls headed for the office. They stood in the doorway, side by side, watching their men.

Nick was seated at his desk while Steve stood beside him. They focused on something on the computer screen. JV couldn't tell what they were looking at but it held their attention.

Rebecca cleared her throat and Nick quickly clicked the mouse as both men looked up, guilty looks on their faces.

"Should I ask?" Rebecca asked, turning and going to one of the arm chairs in the seating area on the opposite side of the room.

"It would be better if you didn't, but if you ask I won't lie." Nick replied.

Rebecca lifted one brow and looked at him, silent for a moment. "I'll take the season into consideration and refrain, for now." She laughed.

Steve looked relieved and JV wondered if the clan leader had been showing him what he'd gotten Rebecca for Christmas.

"You done for the day?" Nick pushed himself to his feet and went to Rebecca. He pulled her out of the chair, then sat in her place and settled her in his lap, one hand resting low on her belly.

"Not yet, but we're taking a break while the next round of dough chills."

"And you wanted to see what we were up to, right?" he asked.

A small smile formed on her lips. "Maybe."

JV had been watching her friend and hadn't noticed Steve moving from behind the desk until he pulled her into his arms.

"Mmm. You smell good," he said.

"I smell like cookies." Her stomach flip-flopped and her heart skipped a beat.

"Like I said, you smell good." He buried his nose in the crook of her neck and took a deep breath. Then he took a gentle bite, making her giggle. "Have you eaten anything?" he asked, pulling away.

"Not since breakfast." She looked up at him a moment, amazed by what just being close to him did to her.

He frowned. "How's your hand?" He lifted her arm and ran gentle fingers over the still pink skin.

"Sore, but not bad."

He glanced back at the other couple, then spun her around and nudged her toward the kitchen. "Come on, I'll fix us something to eat."

"You don't have to do that."

"No, but you've been cooking for hours and you'll be at it for days yet. I wouldn't feel right asking you to feed me and you need to eat."

She had no argument, he was right.

Nick gathered everyone's empty paper plates after the meal, he'd just dropped them in the burn box, when everyone heard a pair of vehicles pull into the yard. He frowned. "Expecting anyone?"

"I'm not." Rebecca said.

JV shrugged. She had no clue.

"I'll see who it is." Steve stood, and headed for the door.

JV heard the front door open before anyone knocked, then Steve's voice.

"Um, Jade, can you come in here?" his voice sounded funny and it made her wonder what was going on.

Frowning, she went to see what he needed.

She stood beside him in the doorway, speechless. Matt standing in the doorway surprised her, but she was shocked at who he'd brought with him. She should have expected he would tell their parents and they would visit, but she hadn't. Still, her parents weren't the ones that shocked her. There was another couple standing beside them at the base of the steps.

She didn't know exactly how long it had been, but she was sure it had been more than a couple years since Steve had seen his parents. She'd seen them the last time she'd gone home, a few months before she'd come to Arizona.

"Well," Matt broke the silence. "You gonna invite us in, or are you gonna leave us standing out here in the cold?"

"It's not my house." Steve grumbled. "Hang on." He turned and looked at the clan leaders, who'd followed them.

"Invite them in." Nick said, his eyes glinting with humor.

Steve's eyes narrowed. "You knew they were coming?"

"You think your folks would show up in someone else's territory without permission?" Nick grinned, obviously enjoying the surprise.

Steve shook his head, turning back to their families.

"Come on in. Apparently, I was the only one who didn't know you were coming."

"Not the only one." Jade leaned against him and wrapped her arm around his waist.

He guided them both out of the doorway to let people in. Her family came first, Matt shook his hand, then hugged JV. Then came her parents. She hugged them each and Rebecca invited everyone into the living room.

Steve's mom stopped to give him a hug. "I've missed you. I'm so happy to see you again. You look good."

"You look good too, Mom." he said.

She hugged JV on her way by. "It's good to see you, too. You look better than you have in a long time."

"I feel better than I have in a long time, thanks Mrs. Romero." JV hugged her back, then let her go.

Mike Romero was the last in the door. He looked at his son for a long moment and JV wondered what he was thinking.

"About time you came to your senses." Mike clapped one hand on Steve's shoulder then turned to JV. "I knew you were the one years ago, but I wasn't sure you'd have what it took to convince him." He leaned down to give her a hug.

Steve started to growl, but JV stepped on his foot, silencing him. When his father had released her and followed the others into the living room he turned to her. "What was that for?"

"You were gonna stop him from touching me and I didn't want you to."

"It hurts you." he protested.

"Not that much, not anymore." She lifted her still healing hand. "This hurts more and it's just a dull ache right now."

He frowned but let the topic drop as they followed everyone into the living room.

Chapter 54

Living room seating was somewhat limited, they didn't often have so many people in the house at the same time. There was only one seat left so Steve led Jade over, sat and pulled her onto his lap. Matt frowned at him, but he was the only one to react.

"So you've surprised us, now what?" he asked, not particularly pleased at having been ambushed.

"Now we get to spend the holidays together." his mother said with a happy smile.

"I really wish you'd called first." he said, his voice almost a growl.

"If I'd called you, you would have said no." She was right, he would have.

Steve looked at Matt. He was still frowning, though not at him anymore. "This is your doing, isn't it?"

"Who?" His frown turned to a guilty grin. "Me?"

"Yes, you. Who else would have had the balls to spring this on me?"

"I knew you wouldn't tell them, so I did." Matt seemed to be enjoying his discomfort.

Steve took Jade's injured hand in his and gently worked his fingers over the new skin. He focused a little and pushed a trickle of energy into her hand so it would heal a little faster. He'd been doing it since she'd gotten hurt. "I hope you had a good trip." he said, not talking to any one pair in particular, but hoping someone else would say something.

"It was good," Jade's mother said.

"Since neither of your vehicles have Texas plates, I assume you flew?"

"We did," his mom said. "We came together. It made for a nice trip."

"Where are my manners?" Jade seemed to shake off her shock. "Mom, Dad, Mr and Mrs Romero, I'd like you to meet Nick and Rebecca Hastings,

211

our clan leaders and friends. Nick, Rebecca, these are our parents: Kim and Alex Walker," she motioned to where her parents sat, "and Tina and Mike Romero. You've already met the trouble maker." She shot her brother a dirty look and gave Steve's hand a quick squeeze.

"Nice to meet you all," Rebecca said.

"Welcome," Nick put in.

"Thank you for allowing us to invade your home and holiday." Tina said. "I realize adding five more to your holiday is a big imposition, but Steve hasn't been home in so long. He didn't seem to want us to visit for some reason."

Steve frowned, he hadn't kept his parents from visiting and he didn't know why his mom thought he hadn't wanted them to. From the corner of his eye he saw Jade and Rebecca look at each other and try to contain their laughter.

"We always have a big meal, Mrs. Romero. A few more is no big deal." Rebecca said.

"Please, call me Tina," his mother said.

"Very well, I prefer Rebecca."

"JV, did I hear you say 'our' clan leaders earlier?" Kim asked.

Jade smiled wide. "You did. Last week Nick invited me to join their clan, he also asked me to be their healer. I accepted."

"That's wonderful, dear," her mother replied, clearly pleased. "I didn't realize your talent had developed that far."

"I hadn't either until recently."

"She saved the life of one of my men," Nick said.

"And scared the shit out of me in the process." Steve frowned at her a moment. "It took her two days to recover, but now she even heals herself faster." He picked up her newly healed hand and held it for them to see the new skin on her palm. "72 hours ago she drove four pieces of wood as big around as a finger all the way through this hand. It looked like hamburger and this is all that's left. I'd say by Christmas morning there'll be no sign left." He knew he sounded proud of her. He was. Gently kissing her hand, he laid it back in her lap.

Tina and Kim had cringed as he'd explained the injury.

Alex frowned. "How did you do that?" He looked at his daughter.

"I jumped out of a tree and landed on the stump of a fallen tree."

"Why?" He looked mystified as to why she'd done it.

"I didn't do it on purpose, Dad." She rolled her eyes. "It was buried in the snow. I thought it was a clear spot."

"Obviously not." Matt put in.

"What were you doing in a tree in the snow?" The entire idea seemed to confuse her father.

"I'd been restless, so I went out for a run. I wasn't very far from the cabin but I wanted something more. Running in snow isn't particularly easy so I climbed a tree. It was great, a good release. I felt much better on my way down, until I jumped from the tree and hit that stump."

"Ouch."

"To say the least." she said.

"Did they take you to the hospital?" Kim asked.

Jade shook her head once. "I limped back to the cabin and shifted. It hurt like the devil but I wouldn't look at it. I knew if I saw it, it would only hurt more. Steve had me wash the worst of the debris out of it while he got the first aid kit and called Rebecca." She looked at her dad. "He has the biggest first aid kit I've seen outside of an ambulance. Anyway, they sat me down, dosed me with some whiskey and pulled the splinters out, then she bandaged me up."

"I know some grown men who couldn't have handled it as well as she did." Nick put in. "Hell, I probably would have screamed when we pulled the sticks out. One of them was this big around." He held up his index finger so everyone could see. "That she didn't make a sound, amazed me."

"She didn't make a sound?" Matt asked, awed.

"I did too," Jade said.

"She whimpered and hid her face. That's all." Rebecca said. "I've treated lesser wounds on men who whined about it a lot more than she did."

Jade turned red. "So, where are you staying?"

Steve knew she was trying to get out of the spotlight, to give them something else to talk about.

"We have rooms in town," Tina said. "We knew there wouldn't be room for all of us. We've already checked in and freshened up."

"How long are you staying?" Steve asked, grunting softly when Jade elbowed him in the stomach

What was that for?

You're being rude.

I was curious.

She frowned at him.

"A few days," His mother said, a small smile on her face. Obviously she'd seen the exchange and was amused by it.

"Well," Nick pushed himself to his feet. "I have a new calf I need to check on. Anyone care to join me?"

"I'd like to see your operation." Mike said, standing.

"I'll go," Matt said.

Jade's dad hesitated, Steve thought he looked like he wanted to go but something was holding him back.

"Go ahead, Mr. Walker. I'll stay here with the ladies." Steve said.

Alex looked at him a moment. "All right, but all things considered, call me Alex." His eyes flicked to where Jade still sat on Steve's leg then back to his face.

"I'll try, sir, but I can't say I won't slip up now and then."

"Understandable. You've been calling me Mr. Walker for a long time, son." He followed the others out, leaving Steve alone with four women.

Hearing Jade's dad call him son warmed something inside him. He couldn't speak for a moment. Jade squeezed his hand as if to say I-told-you-so. He looked at her and found her smiling at him. He smiled back. He shook his head, wondering what he'd gotten himself into.

"You hungry?" Rebecca asked the visitors, "I can fix you some of the sandwiches we had for lunch."

"No, thank you." Tina said. "We ate before making the trip from town."

"Don't let us interrupt whatever you've got going. I'm sure you still have a lot to do to get ready for the holiday." Kim put in.

"We've been working on cookies." Jade said. "We took a break for lunch but we need to get back to work."

"I'd love to help if you'll let me," Kim offered. "It'll make me feel better about crashing your Christmas."

"We've got enough to do over the next few days that I'll take you up on that." Rebecca pushed herself out of the chair. "We better get started or we'll never get done."

Steve let Jade up while their moms stood and followed the Karhyn. He stood and stopped her from joining the others right away.

Bending down, he kissed her with gentle lips.

Are you okay with this?

You mean our parents?

Yeah. He pulled her into his arms and opened his mouth against hers.

It's not how I expected to tell 'em, but it's all right. I told you my dad wouldn't freak like you thought. She slipped one hand up his neck and into his hair, curling

214

her fingers into the short length as her tongue rubbed against his.

I'm not in the mood to think about your dad right now.

Rebecca's mental voice interrupted them. *Unless you want your moms to catch you at whatever you're doing, you should knock it off and get your butts in here. They're about to go looking for you.*

Reluctant to let it end so quickly, Steve pulled away. "Guess you have some cooking to do."

She smiled up at him. "Yep, come on." She pulled him toward the kitchen, as if he wasn't gonna go with her anyway. She let him go once they got there and went to the counter to see what she could do.

Steve stood in the entryway and took everything in. Jade's mom was arranging cooled cookies into containers for gifts, while his mom scooped dough onto cookie sheets. He went to the coffee pot and filled the mug he'd left on the table. While there, he pulled a spoon out of the drawer, and before his mom had a chance to realize what he was doing, he reached over and stole some dough from the bowl in front of her.

"Damn it, Steve." She swatted at him as he danced out of her reach, a grin on his face.

Jade took one of the already done cookies and gave it to him. "Just wait until they're cooked first." She stretched up and gave him a quick kiss on the cheek.

Kim didn't say a word, but he knew she wasn't missing a thing.

He grinned at Jade and bit the cookie she'd given him. Then he took his coffee and cookie to the table and picked up his book.

Chapter 55

JV took a deep breath and tried to calm herself. She'd finally gotten past the shock that Matt had brought both their parents and Steve's with him. She'd been hoping she could keep from telling their parents until after she and Steve had sealed their mating. Not because she wanted it to be too late for them to put a stop to it, but because she wanted to deal with things on her own. Still, she was glad to see them.

It had been years since Tina and Mike had seen their only son and she knew they'd missed him. Their happiness at seeing him again made her happy. She'd been worried how his parents would react to them being together but after what his father had said, she felt much better. She wasn't as certain about how Tina felt, though so far, things had gone well.

She looked around the kitchen, taking note of everything that was going on. Her mom was running the oven, while Tina managed the shaping of the cookies and putting them onto pans. Rebecca was mixing up the next batch to go in the fridge.

One counter was lined with cooling racks half covered with still warm cookies and the tubs for gifts were lined up on the back of the counter, waiting for the next additions to cool. Not seeing anything she could add to the process, she started gathering ingredients that wouldn't be used again and putting them away. Then she picked up the dirty dishes and loaded them into the dishwasher. Looking around again, she didn't see anything that needed to be done right away.

"Mom, Mrs. Romero, what can I get you to drink?" she asked.

"I don't know," Kim said. "What is there?"

"Call me Tina, JV. Mrs. Romero makes me look for my mother–in–law and you're not a little girl anymore."

"All right, Tina it is. We've got soda, milk, tea, eggnog, hot chocolate, beer and several hard liquors."

"Do you have Pepsi?" Kim asked.

"How about a Dr. Pepper, if you have it." Tina said.

"We have them both. Coming right up." She fixed the drinks, adding iced tea for herself and the hot cocoa she knew Rebecca was likely craving, and set them on the counter next to each person. Her mom and Steve's thanked her.

"You're a life saver." Rebecca leaned over and gave her a flour dusted hug. "Thanks." She picked up the mug, took a sip and closed her eyes with pleasure.

JV took her own glass and sat at the table next to Steve. She took a deep breath and her head fell to the table.

He laid his book down, picked up her sore hand and started gently massaging the healing muscles. "Tired?"

"Uh huh." She said without picking her head up. She didn't want to think about how much more there was to do over the next two days. Her hand was on fire and her entire body ached. Healing had taken more out of her than she'd realized.

Steve's fingers working over the new skin felt heavenly. She suspected he'd been feeding her energy, if she didn't feel so bad she might have argued about it. All she could think about right now was how much worse would she feel if he hadn't. How much more healing had his energy enabled? She didn't know what kind of shape her hand would be in if he hadn't been feeding it to her.

"This is the last batch for tonight." Rebecca put her mixing bowl in the refrigerator.

"What's the plan for tomorrow?" Tina asked.

"Pies." JV answered, her head still on the table. The only thing keeping her hair from falling into her face was the ponytail that she'd pulled into so it wouldn't get in the food.

"How many?" Kim asked.

"A little over a dozen." Rebecca said.

"A dozen?" Tina looked surprised.

"You're gonna bake more than a dozen pies in one day, in one oven?" Kim asked.

"I think the count is actually fourteen." JV picked up her head and reached for the list lying on the other side of the table. "But we have two ovens." She nodded at the stove. "We've just found with cookies it's too much. Things move too fast for the two of us to manage. With pies it's easier. "

"What do you do for crust?" Kim asked.

"I make it," Rebecca said.

"Do you refrigerate it before you roll it out?" Tina wanted to know.

"Yeah." Rebecca frowned, not sure where they were leading.

"Have you thought about making your crusts tonight? Then tomorrow all you have to do is roll it out as you need it." Tina asked.

Rebecca's brows shot up as she thought about it. "It would save a lot of work tomorrow."

"I'll get stuff out." JV pushed herself up and headed for the pantry.

It took them another hour and a half to get all the piecrusts made and clean up their mess, but it would be worth it. By the time they were done, Nick had come back with the rest of the men.

When they'd finished, Rebecca pulled out a dining room chair and fell into the seat. "My feet are killing me." She rubbed both hands down her face. "Give me a few minutes and I'll make dinner."

"No, you won't." Nick said.

"I won't?" She twisted around to look at him.

"Nope." He leaned back against the counter top, his thumbs tucked in the front pockets of his jeans, one leg crossed over the other. "You're gonna rest for a few minutes then go change clothes. We're goin' into town for dinner."

"We can't do that, not with guests." she protested.

"Sure we can." He stopped her. "You've been cooking all day and you'll be doing it again tomorrow. No one's gonna mind goin' to the diner for dinner tonight." He looked around, almost as if he dared anyone to argue with him.

"He's right," Steve seconded. "You don't need to worry about cooking dinner. It's obvious how tired both of you are." He pinned JV with a look. "There's no point in arguing. You can change clothes if you want, or not. Either way we're going out."

The fight draining out of Rebecca was visible. She slumped for just a moment, then perked back up again. "Okay, you convinced me. But I've got to change." She headed for the bedroom at the back of the house.

"She's not the only one." JV looked down at her flour-dusted clothes. "Besides, I didn't bring up a coat suitable to wear to town." She looked at her parents a second. "Mom, you wanna come with me to the cabin while I change?"

"Sure, sweetheart."

"Be careful on the path, it warmed up enough to melt some of the snow today, there may be ice." Steve kissed the top of her head as he pulled her to her feet.

"I will. We won't be long."

Her mother came back, JV put on her jacket and they headed out.

***

"It's just a couple minutes' walk, Mom. " She led her mother down the steps and away from the house.

"It's awfully cold here." Kim said, shivering.

"It's different than we're used to, but I like it." JV turned to check on her mom, making sure she wasn't having trouble on the trail. "I love being able to shift and run anytime I want. I missed that while I was in Austin."

"You were always welcome to come home."

"I know, but it wasn't the same."

They made their way through the narrow strip of woods separating the two houses.

"Oh, wow." Kim said when she caught sight of the house. "When you said cabin I pictured something small and rustic."

"No, it's a full house, but it's smaller than the big house. I've gotten in the habit of calling Nick and Rebecca's place the house or the main house and ours the cabin." She led the way up the stairs and opened the door for her mother. "Go ahead. It's probably a little chilly inside, though." She followed her inside and closed the door. "If we weren't headed into town I'd build up the fire and warm it up in here, but there's no point." She headed for the bedroom. "Come on in with me."

Her mom looked around, taking everything in as she followed JV through the house. "Are you sure this is what you want, dear? It's so far from everything."

"I love it out here, Mom. I'd probably stay even if Steve weren't here."

"About that, are you sure about Steve?" She hesitated. "I mean, he's so much older than you."

JV was quiet for a moment as she dug through the closet looking for the sweater she wanted and trying to find the right words. "I've known for a long time that Steve and I are potential mates, Mom. I fought it for a long time, so did he. But there's more to it than you know." She held up one hand, stopping her mom from asking. "I'll tell you about it later, now's not the time. For now, let me just say, I'm sure. Steve is the one for me. We haven't sealed it yet, and I have no idea when we will, but I am sure we will, when we're both ready." She pulled her shirt off and slipped on a thin cotton tee shirt, then the sweater she'd finally found.

"You're sure?" her mom asked one more time.

"Positive." JV stripped out of the yoga pants she'd worn to cook in and pulled on the silk long-johns then her jeans.

"What are those?" Her mom asked, pointing at the pale pink pants she'd pulled on.

"Silk thermals, I love them."

"I assume they keep you warm?"

"Toasty."

Kim was quiet a moment. "All right then. As long as you're certain that he's the right one for you, I'll support you. What about your business? How will you manage that out here?"

"I can work from pretty much anywhere, Mom. As long as I've got internet access, I'm good."

"If you say so," her mother gave in.

JV smiled and looked at her mom. "Even if I had to close my business, I'm okay with that, Mom. I'll still be healing when I'm needed. I genuinely like Rebecca and Nick and I feel like I belong here." She sat down and tugged on a pair of wool socks. "I'm happier here than I've been in years, Mom."

"I can see that." Kim watched her. "You're more relaxed, more at home here with Steve, than I've seen you in years. Since before you left school."

JV pushed her feet down into her boots, laced and tied them. "I am. Come on, I'm ready."

Together they went back up to the house.

Chapter 56

The next morning, JV got up when Steve did. He was headed to help take care of the cattle and she was going up to the house to do more baking. She'd pulled on her yoga pants but was still only in her bra when she smelled the coffee. Not bothering to put her shirt on, she headed for the kitchen.

She poured a cup and stood with one hip against the counter, watching the snow dance in the early morning light as she sipped the dark ambrosia.

"Hmmm. Look at what I found." Steve said, moving up behind her. He wrapped his arms around her waist, lowered his mouth to her neck and gently bit her.

"Hey, babe." She smiled for a moment before the glittering snowflakes caught her attention again. "I'm glad we're not gonna be on the roads in this, but our parents will. They're not gonna sit in the motel room in town when they could be here with us."

"They'll be all right. Nick warned them about the snow last night and Matt's used to it. He'll probably drive them all out. Besides, they've got phones and our numbers if they need anything."

She turned away from the window to face him, her arms automatically going around his waist as she met his look. "Thank you."

"For what?" A small crease formed between his eyes.

"For being you. For taking care of me. For being there for me when I needed someone stronger than I was. For giving me extra energy so I healed faster." She curled her fingers into his back. "For loving me."

"Baby, there's no one stronger than you. You lived for years with a secret that few could have kept, much less dealt with on their own."

"I didn't deal with it, you did."

"No, I just held on to you while you faced it, head on. Dealing with your demons and beating them to the ground was all you, baby."

She laid her head against his chest and wished he hadn't put a shirt on yet. She wanted to feel his skin against her face. Instead, she took a deep breath and pulled his scent around her like a cloak. He held her against him, until she pulled away. "I've got to get up to the house before Rebecca starts without me."

"Get dressed and go ahead. I'll be there when we get the animals taken care of. We're not doing anything extra, so I shouldn't be too long. Nick'll stay with you two until I get back."

"Good, I'll see you then." She finished her coffee, finished dressing and slipped out of the cabin before Steve had gone.

***

She made it to the kitchen before Rebecca, but not before Nick. He was sitting in the corner next to the window, sipping coffee in the dark, when she came in. She turned on the lights and got started.

"How are you this morning?" she asked the clan leader.

"Good. I knew you'd be here early so I got the coffee going."

"Thank you. Is Rebecca all right?"

"She's fine, just a little slow getting started this morning."

"How's her stomach?"

"It was a little upset when I headed in here, but she was working on her second cracker. She said it was getting better."

"That's good."

JV had the first pair of pies in the oven before Rebecca appeared. She shuffled in from the bedroom, not exactly dressed but not in pajamas either. She was wearing loose knit pants, what looked like one of Nick's button down shirts and a pair of fleece lined slippers.

"Coffee." she said, heading straight for the pot.

"What sounds good for breakfast?" JV asked.

"You don't have to cook." Nick said.

Rebecca ignored him. "Bacon, eggs, biscuits and gravy."

JV headed for the pantry to get what she needed.

"I mean it," Nick said again when she came back out, her arms full. "You aren't here to cook for us."

"I know that." She smiled at him. "I offered. Besides, Rebecca has cooked for me enough, and one meal isn't gonna hurt anyone."

She got to work making a large batch of biscuits and gravy, there would be a lot of people around and it would be something to feed them as they came and went.

***

The bacon and gravy were already done when JV pulled the biscuits out of the oven. She set the pan on the counter and had started cracking eggs into a bowl when a knock sounded on the front door. It startled her into dropping a whole egg into the bowl.

"I'll get it," Nick said, stepping past her.

She went back to what she was doing, fishing the egg from the goo and cracking it into the bowl. She wondered who was at the door but was too busy to go look. If she waited too long the bacon would be cold before the eggs were ready. She was pouring the eggs into the skillet as Matt came into the kitchen.

"Look, Mom, she does know how to cook." Matt said.

"Knock it off, Matt," their father, Alex, said from behind him.

JV kept stirring the eggs as she looked over and saw that everyone was there. "You hungry?" she asked. "It's no trouble to make more eggs if you'd like."

"I'd like some," her mom said.

"Please," Mike said.

"If you don't mind." Tina put in.

"No problem." JV answered. "Just let me finish these and I'll get you some in no time."

"No hurry," her dad said.

She finished the eggs in the skillet, serving them onto three plates. She gave one to Nick and one to Rebecca, who tried to say she'd wait, but JV insisted, saying that she is the Karhyn and the baby needed to eat. That put an end to her protests.

"One of you take this one," she said cracking more eggs into the bowl. "It was gonna be mine, but I'll take mine from the next batch."

Mike took the plate, adding a couple of biscuits from the pan before joining Nick and Rebecca at the table.

"Help yourself to coffee, milk, juice, whatever you want. Matt can show you where to find what you need." JV told the others.

When everyone finished eating they put their plates in the sink and the men headed for Nick's office. They said they didn't want to be in the way and JV was happy they wouldn't be under foot all day.

The four women quickly established a system for putting together the pies. One rolled the crusts, while another made the filling, a third made them pretty and the last manned the oven. They got the second round in the oven and everything ready to do the next batch when it was time, then sat at the table to wait.

JV knew the time had come to share what she'd been hiding for so long. Her stomach was in knots. But her mom and even Steve's, needed to know. She could tell them but she couldn't tell her dad. She knew her mom would tell him, which was all right. She just couldn't be there when he found out. She couldn't look him in the face and tell him. She considered waiting until later, putting it off for a few hours. She knew it had to be done but she didn't know how to bring it up.

"You look good, JV," Tina said. "Real good. Steve's happier than he's been in years." She looked down at her mug. "I may not have seen him in a while, but we talk some. I've heard him laugh more in the last day than in the last ten years." She shook her head and met JV's look. "That bit yesterday with the cookie dough? That's something Steve would have done as a teenager. He changed while he was in the Marines. I noticed it after his first stint overseas. He didn't laugh much after that. And I've seen him smile maybe a half dozen times over the years." She reached over and laid one hand over JV's. "You're good for him. He smiles when he watches you and he's laughing and playing again. Thank you for that."

"He's not the only one who changed," Kim said. "You have too." She looked at JV. "You're more relaxed, more at ease than you've been in a long time. I don't know what caused the old wariness in you, but I'm glad to see it gone."

JV looked at the table a moment, she knew it was time to come clean. "About that, Mom." She took a deep breath. "There's something I should've told you a long time ago." She fell silent for several minutes as she searched for the words. "I don't know what happened to Steve, what he saw or did that changed him, but I'll tell you happened to me." JV proceeded to tell her story, stronger than she had before.

"Why didn't you tell us?" Kim asked, shock and concern plain on her face.

"I made it home and hid until I healed, then I did my best to put it behind me. It wasn't until recently that I realized it was affecting me a lot more than I'd been willing to admit. Steve's helped me come to terms with it. He got to me to talk to a counselor and we're working through it. It hasn't been easy and it won't be fast, but we're working through it"

"Sweetheart, we never had any idea." Her mother said. "Was he caught?"

JV looked up. "Yeah, they caught him. He was convicted and sentenced to death. His execution was about six months ago, he won't be hurting anyone else."

"That's a relief." Tina said.

"Are you really okay?" her mom asked.

"Honestly, Mom, I spent a while just surviving. Getting through one day at a time. For the first time in a really long time, I'm doing all right. I'm not past it yet, but we're working through it."

"That's good." Kim said. "I'm glad you're getting the help you need. Though, I wish you'd felt like you could share it with us when it happened though.

"It wasn't you guys, Mom, it was me." She looked back down at the table. "I was just starting out, I felt like I needed to do it alone. I couldn't go home and admit that I'd been beaten and raped. I was afraid you guys would close in around me and I'd never get out again. I couldn't have handled that, not then, probably not even now."

Kim looked away and nodded slowly. "I don't know how we would have handled it, but you were and are an adult, though I admit, it's sometimes hard to treat you like one. I'm glad you told me now."

A timer beeped, reminding them to start the next batch of pies.

"I guess it's time to get back to work." Rebecca said, speaking for the first time in a while. She grabbed one of JV's hands and squeezed it, letting her know she was there for her.

They finished the rest of the pies and after dinner their families went back to the motel with plans to be back early the next morning to help with the cooking and chores.

Mike said something about a football game they could watch if there was time.

Chapter 57

"Come on, baby." Steve steered Jade into the bedroom that evening. "I know just what you need."

"As long as I don't have to stand, you can do anything you want to me." She shuffled into the bedroom, so tired she was shuffling her feet.

"If you can stand for just a few more minutes, you can relax for the rest of the night. I promise."

"I'll try. But I can't guarantee my legs will last another five minutes."

He left her standing in the bedroom while he slipped into the bathroom and started water running in the large tub, then went back to her. "Let's get you out of these clothes." He unbuttoned the shirt she wore, it was one of his and way too big for her, but he loved seeing her in it. After tugging the shirt off her arms he eased her yoga pants, underwear and all, off her hips, stopping when he got to her knees.

"You just can't wait to get in my pants, can you, cowboy?" Her voice was light and he looked up to find her grinning.

"Cowboy?"

She giggled, "As in save a horse, ride a cowboy."

He shook his head and gave her a light kiss on the mouth. "Sit down for a minute, baby. Let me take care of you." He eased her down to sit on the bed so he could take off her boots and pants.

Leaving her on the bed, he checked the water in the tub and adjusted the temperature, then picked her up and carried her into the bathroom.

"I can walk."

"I know you can, but I'm taking care of you tonight, remember."

"I remember." A smile curved her lips.

"So stop worrying and let me take care of you." He lowered her into the steaming water, then stripped and climbed in. He stretched out his back to the opposite end of the tub and his legs along the outside of hers. "Give me your foot."

She put one foot in his hand and slipped lower in the water as he started kneading the pad of her foot with his thumbs.

Jade groaned. "You're a god."

"That's usually a reaction to sex, not a foot massage," he chuckled.

"But you're so good at both, cowboy."

"You're really enjoying the cowboy bit, aren't you?"

"Wouldn't you?"

"Probably." He laid the foot in his hand down and picked up the other, giving it the same attention.

She moaned and let her head fall back against the edge of the tub. He worked her foot for a few minutes then let it fall to the bottom of the tub.

"Turn around here and let me wash your hair."

"I'm not sure I have the energy to wash my hair."

"Just spin around, I'll take care of the rest."

He waited while she did as asked, carefully washing and rinsing her hair, then he pulled the plug. He lifted her from the tub and set her on her feet on the floor. He blotted the water from her skin then quickly dried himself before taking her back to the bedroom.

He tucked Jade into bed, turned out the lights and climbed in beside her. He lay on his back, one arm wrapped around her as she curled against him, her head resting on his shoulder. Her breathing was low and even and he thought she'd fallen asleep until she spoke. "I told Mom today." Her voice was soft, barely over a whisper. "Yours too."

He tensed, then relaxed again and started moving his hand up and down her back. "How did it go?"

She fell quiet a moment. "If it had gone badly, you would've heard about it at the time."

"True." He was quiet a moment, waiting for her to say more. "How are you handling telling her?" he asked when she stayed quiet.

"I'm okay. I think." Her voice was stronger.

"You think?"

She took a deep breath and let it out slowly. "It wasn't easy, but it wasn't as hard as I expected either." Her fingers played across his chest as she spoke. "I'm sure she'll tell Dad."

"How do you feel about that?"

"I'd prefer it." Her hand fisted on his chest. "It would be a lot harder for me to tell Dad than Mom."

"I can see how that would be harder." He took her fisted hand in his and held it tight. "I could always talk to my dad more easily than to my mom. I think it has something to do with not letting them down, but hell, I don't know."

"Me either."

He held her hand and kept rubbing her back as her breathing changed and she fell asleep. He lay there a long time, waiting for sleep to come.

Chapter 58

JV woke to gentle caresses. Steve's fingertips ran down the side of her face and along her jaw line. She smiled before opening her eyes. She loved waking up with him. Finding him already gone was always disappointing. She opened her eyes and found him watching her, his head on the other side of her pillow.

"Merry Christmas, baby," he murmured, then laid a soft kiss against her mouth.

"Merry Christmas to you, too." Her smile grew. The memory of how carefully he'd cared for her the night before warmed her and she stretched up and kissed him again. "Thanks for the bath, cowboy." She moved over him. "Now it's my turn to take care of you." She leaned down and kissed him.

"As much as I would appreciate that, I have something I wanted to ask you?"

She sat up, her hips resting on his thighs. "What?"

"Come over here a second." He tugged at her hand until she slid off him and once more lay beside him on the pillow.

"What?" she asked again.

He rolled to his side so he lay face to face with her. "I know we've been moving fast and I'll wait until you're ready." He slid one hand under the pillow and pulled something out. "Spending the last few weeks with you has been a revelation. I'd forgotten what it was like to laugh, to enjoy life. You've brought a joy for living back into my life. You've brought light back to my dark world." He ran a light finger down the side of her cheek and along the line of her jaw. "I don't want to go back to living like that."

She frowned, not understanding what he was getting at.

"Jade, will you be my wife, my light, my reason for living?"

Her heart skipped a beat and she blinked, stunned. It took her a moment to process what he'd said. "You… um." She blinked again.

He lifted his hand and showed her what he'd pulled from under the pillow. He held a gold ring with a piece of jade cut like the a cat's eye lying along the band.

She looked down at the ring for a second, maybe two, then her eyes flew back to his face. "Really?"

He grinned. "Really, Jade."

"Yes. Of course, yes." Her eyes filled with happy tears and she felt them start to fall as he slid the ring onto her finger.

She stared at it a moment, not really seeing it, then looked back at him. "I don't know what to say."

"You said everything you needed to when you said yes."

Her stomach flipped and she stared at him for a moment, stunned. "I love you." She spoke plainly, but from the heart. Leaning in, she wrapped her arm around his neck and kissed him. Sliding her body against his, she lifted one leg and wrapped it around his hip, pulling him closer. "Come here and let me show you how much".

***

After getting the smokers going and the turkeys prepped and put inside them, JV and Rebecca went in the living room to sit down. Knowing they would have a busy day, they took the opportunity to rest while they could. A light knock sounded before the front door opened and Kim and Tina came in, closing the door behind them.

"Where are the guys?" Rebecca asked.

"Matt said he was taking them to the barn to help with the chores." As Kim spoke, they heard a pair of snowmobiles start behind the house. "He said it was all arranged." She shrugged.

JV said. "Have a seat. We have a while before we have to get to work."

The newcomers had just taken their seats when Nick came in from his office. "Was that Matt on the snowmobiles, JV?" he asked before spotting Kim and Tina. "I guess it was. Hello ladies.

"Hello."

"Hi."

"How are you this morning?" Nick asked.

"Frozen solid," Tina said.

"Why didn't you say something? We have coffee and cocoa to help warm you up." JV said.

Tina looked at JV a second. "I didn't mean in here. I meant all the snow. It's a little cooler in the house than I'm used to, but not bad."

"It is a little cool in here, but before long it'll be too hot and we'll want to open a window," Rebecca laughed.

"I'm sure."

"We'll likely have people in and out all day. That's how holidays are around here." Rebecca said.

"Then we'd better get busy." Kim stood and headed for the kitchen.

JV stood and offered Rebecca a hand. JV pulled her to her feet and together they went into the other room.

***

Hours later, the men had come back and most had retreated to the office where they were watching a football game, except Steve. JV had tried to convince him to join the others, but he'd refused. He'd parked himself at the kitchen table and done what he could to help, lifting things he thought the women shouldn't and keeping himself busy like he had at Thanksgiving.

So far there had only been a few visitors, but JV knew there would be more later in the day when there was more likely to be food available.

It was about noon when they heard several snowmobiles pull up behind the house. It wasn't long before Frank, Jess and a couple other hands came in the back door.

"Good afternoon, ladies," Jess said, leading the group into the kitchen.

It was apparent they'd taken the time to change after chores. Jess was wearing new-looking black jeans, a designer western shirt and cowboy boots. There were two men behind him dressed similarly. They looked barely out of their teens.

"JV, have you met Nathan and Vincent yet?" Jesse asked.

"I don't think so."

"They're local hands, just came up to pay their respects before heading out to spend the holiday with their families." He turned back to the men. "This is JV, she's the foreman's girl."

JV blushed. She knew by the way he'd called her the foreman's girl and talked about their families that these men were human, that's why he hadn't said mate. Still, being called the foreman's girl made her feel funny,

231

especially with the ring on her finger.

"It's nice to meet you both." She held her hands up. "I'd shake, but I'd get you all dirty. You look too nice for that." Turning, she motioned first to her mom, then toward Tina. "This is my mom, Kim Walker, and Steve's mom, Tina Romero."

"Nice to meet you, ma'am, ma'am," Vincent said

Nathan just nodded at each one.

"The rest of the guys are in the office," Rebecca said. "You're welcome to go on in and join them."

"Come on guys," Jesse said. "Let's go see the boss. Later, ladies." He led the way and the two younger men followed.

Frank held back and JV looked at him a moment. He was cleaned up as well, but not in the same way as the younger men. He wore a pair of dark blue jeans with creases down the front of both legs and a light colored checked shirt with pearl snaps.

He waited until the humans were gone before speaking. "It's nice to meet you." He dipped his head to both Kim and Tina, then turned to JV. "I haven't had a chance to talk to you since you helped me out last week." He looked down at the pale gray felt cowboy hat he held in one hand. "It means a lot that you'd exhaust yourself like that to help an old man." He looked back up, meeting her gaze. "The boss said you've agreed to be our healer, I just wanted to say welcome to the clan. I owe you. If there's anything I can do for you, anything, you just have to ask."

She picked up a towel and wiped the extra flour from her hands. "Thank you, Frank. I'm happy I could help you and I'm thrilled to join the White Mountain Chanat." She stepped close and pulled him into a quick hug. "I'm glad you're feeling better." She pulled away and went back to kneading the dough on the counter.

"Ease up, young 'un." Frank responded to Steve, totally disregarding the unhappy stare the Shaku was giving him. "I can smell your scent all over 'er and I see the ring on her finger. I'm not after your girl." He gave a dry laugh. "As if an old man like me could compete." He shook his head. "I'll go check in with the boss, if you don't mind, ma'am." He dipped his head at Rebecca."

"Go ahead, I'll see you later," Rebecca said.

Frank had been gone for nearly a minute when JV realized all work had stopped and everyone was looking at her. "What?" she asked, wondering if she'd managed to smudge flour across her face.

"Ring?" her mother asked. "Does this mean you're engaged?"

JV's face flamed. She hadn't even thought about telling her mother, she'd had other things on her mind. She looked at Steve. He looked relaxed and amused as he watched her in return. "Yes, Mom. We're engaged."

Kim squealed, a high-pitched sound that hurt JV's ears. "Why didn't you tell me?"

"He asked me this morning," she said. "I've been busy and it seemed so natural that it didn't occur to me."

"Can I see?" Tina moved close.

JV wiped off her hand on the towel again, then held her hand, ring and all, for everyone to see. She looked back to Steve and found him grinning.

"Everything all right in here?" Alex asked, stepping into the room.

"We're fine, Dad. Mom just got a little excited." JV said.

"What's up?" he asked.

"She's engaged!" Kim's excitement made her voice high and loud. Her whole body vibrated with barely contained excitement.

JV saw her father's eyes flick to Steve and darken for a moment before going back to her. "Are you happy here?" he asked.

"I am."

"Is this jade?" Tina asked, oblivious to the tension in the room.

"It is." Steve answered his mother.

"I like that," she said. "Jade for your Jade." She looked at Steve. "It fits."

"It's sweet." Kim said.

Alex watched them in silence for a moment, then met JV's eyes and nodded once. He looked at Steve. "Can I speak with you for a moment?"

Chapter 59

Steve saw panic flash across Jade's face. "Sure." He stood, stopped a moment to drop a soft kiss on Jade's head. "It'll be fine, baby," he said against her hair, then followed her father into the living room.

"Are you sure you aren't moving too fast?" Alex asked, his voice low so the women in the next room wouldn't overhear them. "Kim told me what happened."

"I figured she would, so did Jade." Steve's hands fisted at his sides. "If I could go back and keep it from happening, I'd do it in a heartbeat. But I can't." He paused a moment. "Yeah. We're moving a little fast, but I'm being very careful to let *her* set the pace." Steve looked away a moment, then met her father's gaze again. "I've walked away from her twice. I knew she was too young, too innocent, for someone like me. That didn't do her any good, all it did was hurt her and my family. I stayed away as much as I could, to give her a chance at finding someone better." He shook his head, not sure what to say. He'd known her father wouldn't approve.

"It's not that I have a problem with you. You're her choice, but this just started a few weeks ago and she's just starting to deal with her trauma. Now you're engaged." Alex was frowning again. "I'm concerned you're going faster than is wise."

Steve tipped his head back and looked at the ceiling a moment, trying to figure out how to talk to the man who would be his father-in-law without being crass or giving more detail than either wanted. "I'm not unaware of how quickly we've moved. I want to assure you that I'm not pushing her into anything. I've been very careful to let her make every first move since I found out about her attack, and even before then." He dropped his head and looked at his feet, finding it hard to look Alex in the face. "I talked her into seeing a therapist and she's doing really well."

234

"I'd say. It has to have been less than a month or Matt would have known. She's already moved in with you, and now you're getting married."

"I don't know when we'll get married. I do know it'll wait until she's ready. I didn't ask her to push her into something she's not ready for. I asked so she would know I'm serious about her, about us."

Alex's eyes narrowed as he watched Steve. It felt like he was trying to gauge the truth in his words.

"I'm not sure how much Matt told you or what you already know, but her attack caused some long term damage." Steve turned and looked out the picture window toward the driveway. "For years the touch of any man not related to her, has burned." His voice had turned rough.

"She'd been here for more than a week before I found out about it." He shook his head. "She says it's fading, but Julio, our Kadri, said it probably wouldn't go away completely until she felt entirely safe and secure about her position in a clan and her future." He turned back and looked at the other man. "I'm trying to give her that."

Her father stared at him, his face gave no clue to what he was thinking. "All right then," Alex said after several minutes. "She's still my little girl, I just want to be sure you're not pushing her into something she's not ready for. You seem to be doing your best to keep from pushing her into anything. I expect you'll take good care of her."

"I will, sir."

Chapter 60

There were more people around after dinner than for the actual meal. There was never a big crowd, rather there was a pretty steady flow in and out. JV, Kim and Tina insisted that Rebecca rest and spend time with her guests while they put the food away.

"Why don't you go check on Rebecca, see if she needs anything?" Kim said once the food was put away.

"We can take care of the dishes," Tina put in, "Go, spend some time with your new clan."

"You sure?"

"Of course we are," Tina said, spinning JV toward the living room and giving her a light shove. "Now, go."

In the living room, JV looked around. She'd been busy and hadn't paid attention to who was there. She found several faces she didn't recognize and a couple she did.

First, she went to Rebecca. "How are you doing? Can I get you anything?"

"I'm good." She scooted to one side on the sofa. "Here, sit with me."

JV took a seat, sighing with relief at getting off her feet.

"That's how I felt an hour ago." Rebecca said with a small smile.

"Merry Christmas."

A woman's voice drew their attention. JV looked up to find a girl that looked barely out of her teens standing in front of them.

"Merry Christmas to you too, Amanda." Rebecca said, her smile broadening. "How has school been?"

"It's keeping me busy. I'm almost through. One more semester."

"That's great." Rebecca turned to JV. "Amanda is almost through with her AA in Business Administration." She looked back at Amanda.

"Amanda, this is JV, she's our new clan healer."

"How wonderful!" Amanda sounded excited. "We usually lose clan members, not gain them. I'm happy to meet you."

"It's good to meet you, too."

"Where are you living?" Amanda asked. She seemed to want to get to know JV better.

"I live on the ranch." JV replied.

Amanda tilted her head to one side, intrigued. "You're staying with the Khan?"

"No, I live with Steve."

She frowned. "Steve?"

"The Shaku," Rebecca put in.

Amanda's mouth fell open and she took a surprised breath. "Oh. Someone's finally captured him, huh?" She slid onto the sofa beside JV. "There's gonna be a lot of jealous girls around here." She grinned again. "My older sister used to sigh over him and make plans about how she would be the one to get him to settle down." She laughed, her nose wrinkling. "I mean sure, he's good looking, but he's a little old for me. She's mated and living in Tulsa now, but you should watch your back. There are some around here who think he's theirs and they won't hesitate to fight you over him."

JV looked across the room to Steve. She had to agree with Amanda, he was good looking, but that wasn't what drew her to him. Well, other than biology and magic, it was the way he treated her. The way he took care of her as if she was fragile but at the same time, trusted her as if she were made of steel. She knew she wore a distracted smile when she looked back to Amanda. "Thanks for the warning. I'll keep my guard up."

"Have a good evening and congratulations on the baby, ma'am. I'm so happy for you." Amanda said the last to Rebecca before turning and moving toward Jess. JV watched as the girl talked to him, her fingers playing with her hair as she laughed. The girl was definitely flirting with the hand. The scene in front of her warmed her, they made a cute couple.

"Merry Christmas, ma'am." Another woman said in front of them, this time JV recognized the voice. She wasn't surprised to see Tiffany standing in front of Rebecca when she turned back, but she was surprised by Tiffany's clothes, or more accurately, her lack of them.

Tiffany wore a tiny red and green dress and glossy green stilettos with heals at least five inches tall. JV blinked, not really believing what she was

237

seeing. The outfit might have been appropriate in a dance hall or strip club, but not at a clan gathering, at least not one where families were welcome, even expected.

"Merry Christmas," Rebecca said. "You've met our newest clan member, haven't you?" She turned, including JV in the conversation.

"How are you and the baby doing?" Tiffany asked, ignoring JV and the question about her.

JV started to stand. She was just gonna walk away, there was no reason to put up with Tiffany's attitude. Something was off. Her muscles were sluggish, not moving as quickly or as easily as they should. Remembering Tiffany's talent, her eyes flew to the older woman.

There it was. In her eyes, JV saw a glint of triumph. She thought she was winning. Drawing on the same energy that had made her hear the clan's heartbeat about a week earlier, JV used it to fight the resistance. She felt the energy trying to hold her stretch, then snap, under the pressure of the compounded and superior strength.

JV stood, but instead of walking away like she'd planned to do, she stepped closer to Tiffany. "Listen here, bitch." She kept her voice quiet but hard. She wasn't trying to keep people from hearing her, she was trying to keep from screaming her rage. "The last time you tried that trick, I was a loner. I had no clan to support me. That's not true anymore. I guess I just proved who outranks whom." She started to walk away.

"You're just temporary. He'll get tired of you and come back to me." Tiffany didn't bother to keep her voice down, she yelled it for everyone to hear.

JV turned around, but didn't bother to close the distance between them. "Really?" She lifted her left hand. "Looks like I'm the one with the ring, not you."

Tiffany's face turned red, she spun on one heel and marched out the door, slamming it on her way out.

"Guess she wasn't as happy about the news as the rest of us, huh?" Matt said with a grin.

"Guess not." JV said.

Now that she'd made their engagement public knowledge, people she'd never met came up to her and offered congratulations. Most seemed genuinely happy for them, but there were a few women she could tell were jealous. They were nice enough when they spoke with her, but she caught the nasty looks they shot at her from afar.

After what seemed like hours of shaking hands and accepting well wishes she slipped into the spare bedroom. The one she'd once called hers. She needed to get away from all the people for a while.

***

JV had been sitting in the dark room for several minutes when a soft knock sounded on the door.

"Jade, you in here?" Steve's voice was muffled by the door.

"I'm here."

He stepped inside and closed the door behind him. "You all right?"

"I'm fine. I just needed to get away for a few minutes."

"I'm sorry about Tiffany." He sat on his heels in front of her and watched her face.

"It was only partly her. It was more me. I've been around people since early this morning. I was overwhelmed and needed a few minutes to decompress."

"Come here." He stood, pulling her to her feet and into his arms. "We can slip out of here, go back to the cabin if you'd like."

"No." She looked up at him. "I'll be okay. I just need a little while."

"You sure?"

"I'm sure. It's just one of my quirks." She gave him a soft kiss on the cheek. "Go, keep an eye out for trouble. I'll be out in a few minutes."

He looked at her a long moment, as if uncertain. "All right, but if you're not out soon, I'll be back."

She laughed and kissed his cheek. "I'll be there."

After he left, she sat down in the chair again and rubbed some of the soreness out of her newly healed hand as she looked around. It occurred to her how different her life was now than it had been the first time she'd seen this room.

She'd been alone then, or at least she'd felt like she was. Now, less than two months later, she had a clan, good friends, and a mate. Her mating wasn't sealed yet, but she had no doubts it would be. All it would take is her making the first move.

Was she ready for a commitment that big? Could she tie her life to Steve's for the rest of their lives? She knew that once their mating was sealed, there was no going back, no way to undo it. The idea should have scared her but it didn't. Instead, it made her feel better. The knowledge that he would always be there wasn't terrifying, it was comforting. Could she actually be ready? Was it too soon?

Rebecca, is Karen near you? She sent to her friend.

Yeah, she's right here. Are you all right?

I'm fine, but I'd like to talk to her if she doesn't mind.

There was no response for a minute, then Karen's voice sounded in her head. *Of course I don't mind. Where are you?*

I'm in the guest room. Would you mind coming in here for a few minutes?

I'll be right there.

Moments later, the clan's Emine slipped quietly into the room, closing the door behind her with a soft click.

"Is something wrong?" Karen asked, sitting on the side of the bed facing JV.

"No. I'm fine. I just wanted to talk for a minute."

"Does this have anything to do with your announcement a few minutes ago?"

"Some."

Karen watched her a moment, waiting for her to elaborate.

"Is it too soon for Steve and me to seal our mating? Am I crazy for wanting it?"

She looked at JV for a long minute. "Do *you* think it's too soon?"

JV took a deep breath and let it out in a rush. "I should have known you wouldn't give me an easy answer."

"Would you have trusted it if I had?" Karen said with a sympathetic smile.

"Probably not."

"So talk it through." She paused a moment. "Do you think it's too soon?"

"I don't know." JV shook her head. "I just don't know."

"Let's try it from a different perspective. What makes you think it might be too quick?"

"We've been moving kind of slowly. He's been very careful not to push me into anything. He waits for me to make the first move."

"And you're thinking about making this next step?"

"It occurred to me, but I'm not sure."

"What aren't you sure about? That he's not the right one?"

"No. Not that. He's the one. I have no doubt."

"That you'll change your mind?"

240

JV shook her head. "No. I'm sure I won't."

"You think he will?"

"No," She focused on the window across the room. "Since he stopped fighting the attraction, he's been great. I have no doubt about how he feels.

"Is it the sex involved?"

She looked down at her lap and smiled a genuine smile. "No, it's not the sex I'm worried about."

"What other people will think? Is that what's holding you back?"

JV was silent for a moment, wondering if worry about what others would think was what gave her pause. "Maybe." She'd learned that she couldn't move forward unless she was honest, both with Karen and herself. "I don't know." She sighed in frustration.

"Well, if it's not that you're unsure of yourself, or him, and you're not afraid of the sex, what else does that leave?" She fell silent a moment, letting JV think. "Maybe it's not others in general, maybe it's a specific someone or someone's you're worried about."

"What do you mean?"

"Perhaps you're concerned with how your parents will take the news, or his, or maybe even the some of the clan."

JV thought about that for several minutes. "That may be it. I'm not worried about my parents, and I love his too. We get along great, always have, so I don't think they're the ones giving me reservations."

"Maybe the clan?"

JV sighed. "I don't know. I haven't met much of the clan yet. I don't want anyone to think I'm marrying him for his rank."

"Honey, you're the clan healer. You have rank all of your own. Then there's the way you put Tiffany in her place this evening. I know she tried to freeze you. She always does with anyone she thinks she can best."

"She did it to me a few weeks ago," JV said, her head hanging. "It worked then, Steve got her to release me."

"She thought it would be the perfect way to publicly put you in your place. We all saw how well that worked for her. With a clan to draw from, you're more powerful than you were as a loner. You're more powerful than she is. The only reason she managed it then, was because you didn't have a clan to back you up."

JV was quiet. She didn't know how to respond to that. She'd spent too long as a loner. She was out of practice in the art of clan politics. "You're right."

Karen's eyes narrowed and she watched JV for another minute. "You still undecided on what you're going to do?"

"No, I know what I'm gonna do. I just have to figure out the right moment. I'm sure it will be soon, though."

"Good." Karen stood. "Come on, there are some cookies in there I want to try. Don't make me feel guilty by making me eat alone."

JV laughed and went with her.

Chapter 61

Steve was relieved when Jade came out of the bedroom with Karen. He'd seen the Emine go through the door. He'd wondered if he should check on Jade again but he'd waited, watching. Jade's appearance in the doorway, smiling and happy as she headed for the kitchen, was a relief. She smiled at something Karen said and some of the worry lifted.

He caught her as she passed him, heading toward the kitchen. "Hey, baby, you alright?"

She looked up at him and smiled. The light in her eyes thrilled him. "Yeah," she said. "I'm good."

He kissed the end of her nose. "Good thing. I might have to hurt someone if you weren't."

"That's sweet, but not necessary. I can take care of myself."

"I know you can, but I want you to know you don't have to. I wanna take care of you."

"Thank you." She placed a brief kiss on his lips then pulled away and continued into the kitchen.

He watched as she considered all the deserts arranged on the kitchen table and chose a couple of cookies.

"You've been good for her." His best friend's voice came from beside him.

Steve turned and looked at Matt for a moment then back toward Jade. "You think so?"

"You're not the only one who's laughing again. She's laughing, happy, like the girl I remember."

"I love to see her like this." Steve said, his eyes never leaving Jade. She was leaning against a countertop, talking to several clan women. She was relaxed, at ease, very much in her element.

243

"Me too, but I haven't seen it in years. I have you to thank for this."

Steve turned and looked Matt again. "Does this mean you don't mind that I asked her to marry me?"

Matt grinned. "The look on that woman's face when JV told her that she had your ring, and JV's as she said it, that's something I won't forget for a while."

Steve grinned and looked back to Jade. "Me either. She was magnificent."

"Have you set a date yet?"

"Not yet, that's gonna be up to her."

"Soon?"

Steve shrugged. "That's up to her. I'm not pushing."

Matt was quiet a moment. "It's obvious you've found out and dealt with it, you wanna tell me what happened to change her?"

Steve wasn't sure how to answer. He was surprised that Matt hadn't heard yet, but he wasn't sure it was his place to tell him.

Baby, he sent to her across the room.

She turned and looked at him. *Yeah?*

It looks like your mom didn't share with Matt. You mind if I tell him?

Go ahead. She looked around. *But not in the middle of this crowd. Take him in the office or, better yet, out to the cabin. He's not gonna react well and that'll give him some space to vent.*

Good idea. He turned to Matt. "Let's go outside for a bit."

Matt frowned, but agreed.

***

"What's so bad that we had to get out of the house so you could tell me?" Matt asked once they got to the cabin.

Steve looked away. Time didn't make it any easier for him to say and he knew it had to be worse for Jade. "You should know, I asked her if I could tell you. She's the one who suggested we come out here."

"Just spit it out, man, the stalling is only making it worse."

"Matt, man." He paused. "She was raped."

The color drained from his friend's face. "What? When?"

Steve fell back into the recliner as if his knees had given out beneath him. "While she was still in college."

Matt sat on the edge of the sofa and buried his face in his hands. "Why

244

didn't she tell us?"

"She didn't tell anyone, not until I got it out of her."

Matt stared at the floor for several minutes. Steve waited while his best friend processed the heartbreaking news. He pretended not to notice the way his shoulders shook or the tears that fell from his lowered face. He stood and walked across the room, only to turn around and retrace his steps.

"I'll kill the son of a bitch." Matt said after a while.

"You'd have to stand in line, but we're both too late." He watched her brother pace, stalking back and forth across the room as he filled him in about the chain of attacks and killings and how the man responsible had been caught and sentenced to death.

Chapter 62

JV got ready for bed carefully. She'd decided tonight she would make her move and she wanted things to be right. She'd spent the last couple of days thinking about what Karen had said, and had come to the conclusion that people would think whatever they wanted to think, it didn't matter what the truth was. With that in mind, she knew it was time.

She'd told her mother her plans before their parents had left earlier that day. Her mom had been hesitant at first, but when she'd realized JV was ready, she'd become nothing but supportive.

JV pulled the blankets back and slipped between the sheets while she waited for Steve to finish brushing his teeth.

She was lying back, looking up at the ceiling, absently twisting the new ring on her left hand when he came in.

"I hope that look is because you're thinking of me."

She jumped as her eyes flew to him. "Guilty." A slow smile spread across her face.

"I know that look," he said, suddenly wary. "It means you're up to something."

She let her eyes follow him as he moved around the room and her smile grew wider. "Maybe, maybe not."

"Definitely." He looked sure of it now.

"The real question isn't whether or not I'm up to something."

"What is it then?"

"Is it gonna be worth it?" She arched her back, stretched and the sheet fell off her breasts to pool around her waist.

He grinned, pushed his jeans off his hips, and climbed in beside her. "I have no doubt it'll be worth it." He pulled her close.

JV rolled toward him, stopping when she lay face to face against him.

He leaned forward to kiss her lips. She kissed him back, hands roaming his body for several minutes. She drew away and trailed her mouth down the side of his neck, raking her teeth along his skin as she went, then set her teeth into the large muscle along his shoulder and bit down hard.

"Careful," he said. "You don't want to break the skin."

She pulled away for just a moment. "I wouldn't mind if I did."

He pulled farther away. "Are you saying you're ready?"

She looked up at him through her lashes. "I am."

"You sure?"

"I'm sure." She bent and bit him just above the tattoo on the left side of his chest then soothed the sting with a kiss. Meeting his gaze, she found his eyes had darkened until they were almost black.

"You amaze me," he said, lifting her chin to drop a kiss on her lips. "You're a gift I'm not sure I deserve and I'm thankful for the light you've brought back to my life." He paused. "But I don't want you to feel rushed or pressured, I'd wait until the end of time if that's how long it takes for you to want this."

"I know you're not rushing me. I love you for that." She looked away, down at the tattoo on his chest, outlining the cat there with one finger, then met his gaze again. "I've thought about this since before you proposed, you're not pressuring me into anything. I want this. I'm ready for it."

His eyes went soft and he ran the back of one finger down the side of her face. "Like I said, amazing."

She gave him a flirty smile. "I bet I can still amaze you." she lifted and dropped her eyebrows making the simple phrase sexually suggestive.

"I'll bet you can."

She moved over him. He took her hips and helped her settle astride his legs. "Tell me how you wanna do this."

"I'm gonna take my time," she leaned low over him. "And make you beg."

She lowered her mouth to tease his nipple. She licked and bit first one nipple then the other for a long minute. Then, stretched up his body and kissed him before trailing kisses along his jaw. Tracing her tongue along the rim of his ear, pausing only to whisper, "I can't wait to feel you deep inside me but I'm gonna make you beg first." She gently bit his earlobe before sliding her body along his until she was once more face to chest with him.

Raking her nails down his sides, she swirled her tongue over the tattoo high on the left side of his chest.

He shivered.

"You like that?"

A sound rumbled out of his chest.

"Did you just purr?" she lifted one brow.

He let the deep sound roll through him again.

She laughed. "That feels cool."

"It'll feel better later." he growled

"But it's my show now." she lowered her mouth to his skin once more.

Running her fingertips over his legs while she worked her mouth down his body, she tormented him, never actually touching the one place he wanted her to touch the most.

His body moved, restless beneath her.

Looking up at him through lowered lashes she touched and tormented him until he couldn't take it any longer.

"Please, baby. I'm not sure how much longer I can keep from taking over."

"What if that's what I'm waiting for?"

Steve closed his eyes a moment, composing himself. "I don't want to scare you Jade, not now."

"Nothing you have done has scared me. Sometimes I frighten myself but not you, you make me feel safe."

"You sure?"

She didn't respond, instead she gave him a wicked grin and lowered her mouth to lick his straining erection like a lollypop.

Unable to keep himself from moving he lifted her up his body, laid her on the bed beside him while he reached past her for the condom on the night stand.

She grinned as he ripped the foil packet open with his teeth. He couldn't resist the temptation to kiss her while he covered himself. Condom in place, he moved over her, mouths still locked together. Holding himself over her, his hands on either side of her head he broke away. "You still okay?" he asked on a breath.

"Uh huh," she ran her hands up his sides and over his back to grip his shoulders.

Watching her face to make sure she didn't slip into a flashback, not that she ever had before, he lined up and pushed inside her. He groaned and buried his face in her neck as her heat surrounded him.

Her nails dug into his shoulders and her legs wrapped around his hips as he established a rhythm. Her scent was driving him wild and he licked the long line of her neck until he gently nipped the large muscle in her shoulder.

Her body started to squeeze around him and he knew she was close, so was he. Her teeth against his own shoulder made the deep purr rumble through him again and he surrendered himself to instinct.

The sharp sting of her teeth in his own shoulder only pushed his climax higher. He bit deep into the muscle of Jade's shoulder as he erupted inside her. Spent, he gasped for air and licked the wound. It was deeper than he'd intended.

"You all right, baby?" he asked, looking at her face.

She opened her eyes and a thrill of satisfaction went through him at the sated expression she wore. "What?" she asked.

"You're shoulder, how does it feel"

"Hmm?" She blinked, not yet back to herself.

He licked away the blood oozing from the wound and she moaned. "Did that hurt?" he pulled away, immediately concerned.

"Not hurt, felt amazing. Do it again."

Not knowing what else to do, he did as she asked. She gasped and arched her back.

He pulled away, slipping quietly from the bed.

"Where you going?" she asked, her words breathy and slurred with pleasure.

"To clean up. I'll be right back."

"M'kay." She curled on her side.

He finished in the bathroom and slid back into bed where she curled against his side, her head resting on his shoulder. Her breathing slowed and he thought she was asleep.

"Steve?" her voice startled him, but he did his best not to let it show.

"Yeah, baby?"

"Summer wedding. Here at the ranch if we can, with the clan, my family and yours all here, how does that sound?"

"Sounds perfect."

"I love you."

"I love you, too." He knew he was laying in the dark grinning like an idiot. For the first time in a long time he looked forward to the future instead of just dealing with it as it came along. Life was good.

Dictionary of Terms

Chanat	Local group of cougar shifters under one leader.
Clan	Local group of cougar shifters under one leader.
Khan	Male clan leader, usually mated to the Karhyn.
Karhyn	Female clan leader, usually mated to the Khan.
Kadri	Second male in the clan, usually mated to the
Emine	Second female in the clan, usually mated to the Kadri.
Shaku	Head enforcer /head of clan security, often serves as the Khan's personal bodyguard.

If you liked Jade's Peace, turn the page for a look at another series about the shape-shifters of the Kitsune with,

Change

1

It was early June, and I had big plans for my weekend. Today I was going hiking over a new trail with Brandon, my best friend. We'd been friends since kindergarten and I thought of him almost like one of my brothers, only he didn't torment me like they did.

It was Friday, and the day had dawned beautiful and clear. We had planned for a full day trip, letting our families know where we were going to be. I had even packed my lunch the night before so I had one less thing to do before I could leave that morning.

At just after six, the sun and I had both been up for almost an hour, and I was nearly ready. I ran the brush through my hair, smoothing it into the ponytail I was forming in the back of my head. Winding an elastic tie around the tail of hair I had created, I turned and looked out the window, and saw a familiar car pull into a parking space in the lot below me. I picked up the brush and finished brushing out my hair as I watched the tall athletic frame climb out of the car and head around the end of the building. I was packing the last of my things into my backpack when his knock sounded on my front door.

"It's open!" I yelled.

"You always just holler at anyone who knocks on your door at six in the morning that the door's open, and why exactly is the door open while we're at it?" Brandon demanded as he walked in.

"Just the ones I'm expecting," I said, zipping my bag before looking up.

"So you were expecting me, so what? It still could have been anyone at the door," He said, still intent on the point he was trying to make.

"Could have, except that I saw you pull in as I finished my hair. And I unlocked the door a couple of minutes ago, just before grabbing my lunch. I knew it was you, Brand."

"Ok, fair enough, I'm just looking out for you, Chica," He told me, his tone much calmer now, his hands up in front of himself as if in surrender.

"I know," I told him calmly, "And I know you only push the issue because you care. Otherwise you'd be choking on your balls right now."

"Jeez, Nickie, don't bottle up your emotions like that, you'll get hurt. You need to learn to express yourself, or someday it'll all come exploding out, then where will you be?" He said, deadpan.

I didn't bother responding other than to flip him off as I turned away and went to use the restroom one more time before we headed out. When I returned I asked him, "You got everything you need?"

"Everything but you and your pack."

"Then let's get a move on, we're burnin' daylight." I said flippantly as I picked up my bag and slung it over one shoulder. I led the way out and turned to wait for him to exit the apartment before activating the lock on the door behind us. He looked confused, as if he didn't quite understand but I didn't explain the film reference and let it drop.

The drive out to the parking area where we had planned to start our hike took us about forty-five minutes, by then it was almost seven and the day was starting to warm up. It was still relatively cool but it was already hinting at the heat that the sunshine and desert floor would bathe us in. We strapped our backpacks onto our backs and I tucked my Personal Communication Device, more commonly known as a PCD, into the pocket of my jeans where I could easily reach it, and we took off.

We started out headed west, away from the cars, the ground was rough and uneven but I was used it and I moved over the loose rubble and small rocks with ease. We followed what appeared to be a wildlife trail. A path made by frequent passage of animals like deer and javelina, it was narrow and winding but had very little overhanging brush, so it was a pretty easy walk. As we walked over the still flat ground, I called out to Brandon.

"What have you been up to lately?"

"Not much, work, sleep, eat. You?"

"About the same, throw in spending time with the family and you have my life."

"I'm glad we were able to get out today, it's a beautiful day and I really needed the escape from life for a while and this is a great way to do it."

"I agree," I said continuing along the trail that was starting to turn and lead uphill. "Careful through here, it's really loose," I warned him as I placed my feet carefully to keep from losing my balance as the bits of rubble that had washed off the mountain above us rolled and shifted under me.

Several minutes later we came to a spot where water running down the hill had washed away the softer soil leaving a sharp drop off that was taller than I was. I stopped and waited for Brandon to make the last few steps up beside me. When he reached my side I could see that the obstacle wasn't quite as tall as he was, but that didn't mean that either of us could get over it alone.

"We're gonna have to work together for this one." I said.

"Yep," He replied, "How do you wanna do this, you up first or me?"

"You're gonna have to go first, I can boost you from the bottom but I don't have the strength to pull you from the top."

"Makes sense," he said, nodding, "You ready?"

"You wanna go up with your backpack or should we take them off and hand them up separately?"

"Let's try it with them first, we can always take them off later if we need to."

"Ok," I said, moving to one side of where we wanted to go up the face and bent down on one knee so that the leg that was in front was placed for Brandon to step onto.

"Will that work for you?" I asked.

"I think so, let's try it." He reached up and braced his hands on the top of the small cliff before he carefully placed one booted foot on top of my knee.

"Ready?" He checked with me. At my nod he quickly pushed up onto my knee and used his arms to pull his body up onto the ledge, like one would lift themselves out of a pool. Seconds later he was standing on top of the small cliff looking down at me.

"How are we gonna do this?" I asked, craning my neck to look at him, "There's nowhere for me to step on my way up."

"Just stand right there," He pointed to where he had gone up the cliff face, "And hold both arms above your head. I'll do the rest."

"Are you sure you can lift me?" I asked, skeptical.

"Pretty sure," He sounded confident, "But we won't know for sure until we try, will we?" He stood right at the edge he had just climbed over, "Come on, let's give this a try."

I looked up at him and he bent down until he was almost sitting on his heels and reached his arms down to take mine. I extended both my arms over my head and reached past his arms to grip his wrists as he wrapped his long fingers firmly around my wrists.

"Are you ready?" he asked, looking at my face for signs of fear. I nodded and he started to stand up, using his legs instead of his back to pull me up the rock face. He kept an eye on my face, I guess he was watching for signs of panic in case I started to struggle. I resisted the urge to try to walk my feet up the cliff face, knowing it would only push my body away and possibly over balance us both. Instead I settled for bending my knees and using them to crawl onto the ledge as soon as I was high enough. He stepped back slightly, keeping his grip on my arms as he asked, "You good?"

"Yeah," I said, releasing his arms as he let go of mine before I stood up, "I wasn't sure that would work, but I'm glad it did."

"Me too," He said, "You want to take a break here, or continue to the top of the fan first?"

"I'm ready to go if you are. You didn't pull anything lifting me like that, did you?"

"Nah, I'm fine, let's go then." He said, turning to take the lead for a while.

It was mid-afternoon when it happened. We'd already stopped for lunch and started making our way back, taking a different route. This one wasn't as clear of trail but the going was easier, which was good as I was starting to feel a bit fatigued. We had stopped a couple times on the return trip but I admit, I wasn't being as careful as I should have been. I was walking along thinking about something else, I don't even remember what anymore, but my mind wasn't on where I was going or what was around me. I tripped over a rock, stumbling for an instant before I fell to my hands and knees.

The fall jarred me back into the present, knocking the breath out of me and leaving me momentarily dazed. I heard a buzzing sound, but didn't register it for what it was. I thought it was just my ears ringing from the jarring of the fall. Crap, that's what I get for not paying attention. I heard Brandon stop on the trail ahead of me, and without even thinking about it I tried to get up. I'd already started moving, trying to push myself up with my arms so that I could get back onto my feet, when I spotted it.

By the time I realized it was a snake, it was too late. He was already in mid-strike and I didn't have time to avoid getting bitten. He'd seen my movement as a threat and was only doing as his instincts demanded, defending himself. I felt the fangs as they pierced the denim of my jeans and sank deep into the flesh of my calf, and the hot, burning sensation as the venom pumped into my body. The snake quickly disengaged his fangs from my leg and escaped across the sand, having already done his damage and hopefully slowing the threat long enough to let him get to safety.

"Oh, shit," I said, my mind spinning in panic so intense that I couldn't put more than the two words together, even in my head.

I froze, trying to slow my mind so that I could think and not just react.

"What is it?" Brandon asked, backtracking to my side to see what had happened.

"Snake. It got me." I told him, speaking in short gasps as I struggled to calm my mind enough to think.

"Rattler?"

"Yep."

"Where?"

"My right leg. On the calf." I was starting to be able to think again What are we going to do now? We're still at least a half mile from the car, and there's no way I can hike it now. It'll take hours for anyone to get out here to us, if they can even find us and do they even keep anti-venom in the area anymore? My mind was still racing but I could at least make out my own thoughts. I knew I had to keep from getting hysterical, that would only pump the venom through my body faster. Stay calm.

My skin suddenly felt too small, as though it were shrinking but the rest of my body had stayed the same size. My whole body started stinging. Wow, I didn't know that snake venom acted this fast.

Suddenly, or at least it seemed sudden to me, I felt like things were starting to move inside my body, bones and muscles moving into new places. I must be starting to hallucinate. The thought only drove my panic faster. I felt as though I had lost control of my body. Suddenly it all stopped, the burning pain of the bite, the stinging in my skin, the sensation of bones and muscle moving and grinding against each other beneath my skin.

Have I died? I wondered, confused. I'd never heard of a snake bite numbing like that, I'd always been told how painful they were and how a victim suffered the pain for years, if they survived that is. Something strange was happening to me and I had no idea what it could be.

I looked up at Brandon. He was standing next to me, and I could see the surprise on his round face, not panic, not fear, just surprise. I tried to speak to him, to ask what was going on, but all that came out was a high pitched whine. What the hell was that? It was a sound I had never heard from my own throat in my life. It was a sound more like a puppy would make than a human.

"Well, I'll be damned!" Brandon said, running one hand through his short brown hair, "I'd given up the hope it would ever happen." His voice seemed very loud, almost as though he were screaming instead of speaking. I whimpered and ducked my head, trying to pull my shoulders up around my ears.

"Whoops," Brandon said softly, his voice dropping to a whisper, "Sorry, I forgot how sensitive your ears are when you change the first time."

Change, what did he mean change? He bent down on one knee and reached one hand toward my face, I felt his hand under my chin as he lifted my face to look into my eyes. I knew something was different, but I didn't know quite what.

"Are you OK?" he asked gently, still speaking very softly. "Do you feel better now?"

I tilted my head to one side, as I thought about what he had asked me. It was gone, all of it; the pain from the bite, even the sting of my hands where I'd caught myself when I fell. What's more, thinking about it made me realize that I felt really good, like I could run back to the car and laugh the whole time. I wasn't even tired anymore, a little hungry, but not tired. I tried to say so to him but this time it came out as a short bark, which made me jump and look around me. What the hell was that? I could hear Brandon chuckling at my reaction,

"It's okay." He sounded reassuring, "Do you think you can walk back to the car now?"

I started to get up and that's when it hit me. I was no longer walking on two legs, instead I was on all fours. I twisted around and looked at myself and I was so surprised I fell on my butt, my body was no longer my own and this one didn't function in quite the same way. I was now in the body of a dog of some kind, a big brown one that looked almost red in the sunlight. I turned and looked at Brandon again and whined, scared at not knowing what was going on. I couldn't think about what was happening right now I had to just go, when it was over and I was safe I would have time to question it, and to have a breakdown if I needed to. Right now I just had to go on.

"You're all right, trust me, it's okay. Let's go back to the car. I'll explain it all, but you're gonna want to be human so that you can ask the questions I'm sure you'll have, plus you don't have any other clothes here. And trust me on this, you do NOT want to hike through this stuff naked," He said, motioning to the thorny mesquite and rough creosote brush that surrounded us. He picked up my backpack by the carry handle at the top and that's when I noticed that the arm straps were broken. He stood and started back down the path we'd been on, headed toward the car. I whined and barked at him, refusing to move from where I was standing. He turned around to look at me.

258

"What?" He asked.

I nosed the shredded remains of my clothes, smelling the acrid scent of the venom on my jeans as my nose brushed the rough cloth.

"You shredded 'em, just leave them."

I refused to give up and I sat down, indicating to him that I was staying with my clothes. After watching me for a couple of minutes he came back and stuffed the remains of the clothing into my backpack.

"Happy now?"

Satisfied he wasn't leaving my things behind, I silently stood up and padded along the path toward the car.

Once I started moving it only took me a few minutes to get used to the way my new body moved, to get the hang of walking on four legs instead of two. After that first few minutes of fumbling around and tripping over my own feet the trip seemed much faster than I thought it should be. I have to admit that I found moving on four feet through the brush and over boulders much easier than hiking on two, but I tried not to think about it. I was just going to have to wait for answers, and freaking out in the meantime would do me no good. When we reached the parking lot Brandon went around to the driver's side of the car and unlocked the doors. I followed him, not willing to let the only person who knew what had happened to me out of my sight.

"I'm glad we brought my car instead of yours," He said, opening the rear door and motioning me into the back seat, "Hop in, I'll be right back." He moved away from the still open door and toward the rear of the vehicle. If I'm in the car he won't be going anywhere without me, it's not like he's gonna walk all the way back to town. I reasoned with myself as I hopped up into the backseat, turned a small circle on my feet and then sat down to wait for his return. It was only a couple of moments later that he appeared in the doorway, slid into the car and sat down on the bench seat next to me. He was silent for several seconds, his expressive golden brown eyes focusing on the stack of folded clothes he held in his lap as if he didn't know where to start.

He cleared his throat as he turned to face me, "Okay, here are some clothes for you. Don't worry, they're clean. I need you to listen closely and try to do exactly as I tell you. All right?" He looked directly into my eyes. By now I knew better than to try to speak, so I just nodded my head once, maintaining eye contact. "You're going to need to concentrate, picture your body, not as it is now but your human body, focus on that image. You have

259

to will yourself back into that body, to want to be like that enough that your body shifts. Do you understand?" I nodded again, unsure I could do what he was asking, but really, what other choice did I have? "I'm going to leave these here for you. I'll get out and close the door, and then I'm going turn my back and wait. You'll need to knock on the window, or open the door when you're dressed and then we'll talk, Okay?"

Not seeing any other option, I nodded. He slid off the seat and out the still open door, before turning around and setting the stack of clothes on the seat where he had been sitting. He looked at me again briefly before he closed the car door and turned away. Through the window I could see him lean against the side of the car, as though he were patiently waiting for someone to walk out of the desert in front of him. He pulled his PCD from the front pocket of his jeans and it looked like he was making a call, but the enclosed car muffled his voice enough so that I couldn't hear what was being said.

I felt a little lost, Can I really be me again just by doing what he said, by thinking about and wanting to be me again?

I sat for just a moment, wondering how this could possibly work, Has Brandon ever lied to you? Would he ever do anything to hurt you? I trusted Brandon and if he said I could do this, then I could, I just had to do what he told me to do.

I took several deep breaths as I tried to relax some of the tension in my body, closed my eyes and concentrated on clearing all the outside thoughts from my mind. I pictured my body just as I had seen it this morning in the mirror. I started at the floor and worked my way up. I could see my feet standing on the tan carpet of my bedroom floor, the teal nail polish I had applied to my toe nails earlier in the week. I worked my way up, picturing the round bones on the outsides of my ankles and the muscles in my calves, and there was the small scar just below my left knee from a fall off my bike as a child. I could see my thick, muscular thighs, the rounded shape of my rear sloping up to my smaller, but not quite slender waist, and up farther past the generous curves of my breasts to my face.

I concentrated on my round face, the large green eyes that dominate my face. I pictured in my mind my full lips and auburn hair, curling gently as it had settled around my shoulders while I brushed it out before pulling it up. I thought of how badly I wanted to be back in that body. When the tingling sensation all over my skin started again it surprised me, and I almost lost the mental picture of myself, but I managed to ignore it and I continued to will myself back into my body, to concentrate on how badly I wanted to be me again. The tingling intensified until it was almost stinging, and I felt my muscles begin to stretch and my bones start to shift and grind against each other.

After what seemed to be several minutes the uncomfortable sensations started to fade, they slowed to a stop, no more bones shifting, or muscles popping, even the tingling faded until I felt normal once again.

I opened my eyes and anxiously looked down at myself, half afraid of what I would see. I was sitting naked, but human in the back seat of the car. I scrambled to quickly put on the too large clothes that Brandon had left for me, worn, soft, sweat pants and matching top, but no shoes. If he had any they probably wouldn't have fit anyway. I leaned across the car and knocked on the window to let him know I was decent. He looked relieved when he turned and popped the door.

"Climb up into the front, let me grab something and then we'll talk," He closed the door again before heading for the back of the car.

As I climbed between the front seats and settled into the passenger's seat, I heard the trunk open and close again before Brandon came back around and got into the driver's seat beside me. He handed me a couple of protein bars "Eat up."

I looked at the bars he had put into my hands and scrunched up my face in distaste.

"Those things are nasty." I said. He didn't say anything but took one back and opened the packaging, I could suddenly smell the bar inside and I realized I was starving. Before I knew it, I had them both gone. When I realized that I had just eaten both bars in under a minute I was embarrassed at having inhaled the food, and with little memory of what kind of manners I might have shown in doing so. It must have shown on my face, because Brandon chuckled.

"Don't worry about it, Nick, I know how hungry shifting can make you, especially when you're healing at the same time, that's why I went back and grabbed them. They aren't going to be enough, but they're all I have. They'll take the edge off, and hopefully hold you until we can get you something better to eat."

"So, what's going on? What do you mean you know hungry shifting can make you? I've figured out what you mean by shifting, but how? How is it possible? And how can I be healing so fast? I noticed when I got dressed that wound from the snake bite is healing, it's not possible! Am I hallucinating from the venom?"

"Been saving all your questions up, huh?" He asked me, laughing softly again, his smile showing the deep dimples in his cheeks. "No, you aren't hallucinating. You really did change shapes. The process of shifting most likely pushed the venom from your body and at the same time healed the worst of the damage that it had done."

"You've lost your mind and I'm hallucinating, or better yet, it's all just a nightmare and I'll wake up and it will be Friday morning."

"Do your dreams ever hurt like the snake bite did? Mine don't. You're not hallucinating or having a nightmare, Nickie."

"But it can't be true - I must be going crazy…"

"Nope, not crazy, just Kitsune," He told me, interrupting my ranting.

"Kitsune?" I repeated. I'd never heard the word before.

"Yep, Kitsune, we're a species of shape shifters."

"There's an entire species of people who turn into dogs?"

"Actually, we're not dogs, we're wolves. But that's not exactly what the Kitsune are. There are several different animal forms that different Kitsune can shift into, though, generally it's limited to only one animal form per person. You're a wolf, I'm a wolf, and there's an entire pack of wolves in Gila Valley."

"An entire pack of wolves around here? Now you're the one who's dreaming. I've never seen a real wolf before, at least until I was one, and I've lived here all my life."

"Not real wolves, Nickie, Kitsune wolves, there's a difference. Though, you should know, the accepted phrase is natural wolves, not real, because we're just as real as they are."

"Okay, not real wolves, natural wolves. How can there be an entire pack in the valley and nobody knows about it?"

"Actually, there are a lot of people who know about it, the pack members, but very, very few outside the pack. Our secret is well kept."

"How did I become…Kitsune? Is that what you call it? I've never been bitten by a wolf, and I'm sure it's not something I would forget."

Brandon rolled his eyes, "There's only one way to be Kitsune, you're born one. Kitsune can only be born, there is no other way to become one of us. The biting thing is pure myth, Hollywood and fantasy novels."

"News flash, Brandon, so are werewolves." I couldn't help but point out.

"Point." He conceded, "You're going to find that some movies and fantasy novels aren't as make-believe as you thought. I know it's hard to believe but

I'm not lying to you. I wouldn't do that to you, and you know it." He said calmly, and I shifted in my seat, feeling guilty that I had suspected him of doing just that.

"You're sure? I mean about the whole wolf thing." I asked, looking out the passenger window to avoid looking at him.

"Absolutely certain. Look, do you mind if we head back into town while we talk? While you were shifting back to human I called the Anikitos, our pack leader, and he's expecting us. I'd prefer not to be late and risk angering him."

"Do I have to?" I asked, apprehensive at the thought of meeting the leader of the local wolf pack. I tried to think of everything I had ever read about werewolf packs and their leaders and nothing I was coming up with was reassuring.

"Don't worry, you'll be fine. Plus he'll have a lot answers for you that I don't. I may have been raised as one of us, but I'm still pretty young, and honestly, not all that high in the pack. There's a lot that I just don't know."

"Okay, but you have to promise not to leave me alone. I don't want you to just drop me off at some stranger's house and leave me. I'm uncomfortable enough with everything that's happening to me as it is, without being told what to believe by some stranger."

"I'll promise you that I won't leave you alone with the Anikitos unless you want me to, all right? You may decide after meeting him that you don't want me around."

"I can't see why I would do that, but if you say so I'll take your word for it. You've done nothing but help me this afternoon and I thank you for it." I said. Brandon started the car and pulled out on to the highway that headed back toward town.

About the Author

Melissa was born and raised in Arizona, she's spent her entire life living across the southern half of the state. She's found that, along with her husband and three children, she prefers the small towns and rural life to feeling packed into a city.

She started reading at a very young age, and her love for series started early, as the first real books she remembers reading is the Boxcar Children series by Gertrude Chandler Warner. Through the years she's found that there's little she won't read, and her tastes vary from westerns, to romance, to sci-fi / fantasy and Horror.

You can find her online on Facebook or her website, http://melissastevens.us

Made in the USA
San Bernardino, CA
30 December 2013